Deadly Institution

Holly Copella

Holly Copella

ISBN: 0986441643
ISBN-13: 978-09864416-4-6

In loving memory of
Kenny Apgar, Sr.

ACKNOWLEDGMENTS

Copella Books – First Paperback Edition 2015
Cover Artist: Fantasyart
SelfPubBookCovers.com/Fantasyart
Printed by CreateSpace, An Amazon.com Company

PUBLISHER'S NOTE

Chapter One

11:00 P.M.

*T*he little house sat on the quiet back street in the small town of Stony Ridge. The house itself was in desperate need of paint and the lawn needed a gardener's touch. Despite the limited activity at the surrounding homes on the warm summer evening, there were several cars parked along the street before the little house. The dingy, crudely appointed basement den was filled with cigar smoke and contained old, worn furniture that had seen better days. Six men varying in age from their twenties to their sixties sat around the poker table and puffed on cigars. Bottles of beer and snacks cluttered the table. A large pot of plastic poker chips were piled in the center of the table. Three men remained in the current hand. Five of the men stared impatiently at the sixth man who held his cards and stared at his chips as he played with them. A stocky, African-American man in his early thirties, Deputy Monroe Carson, held his cards and chewed on his cigar while staring at the silent man across from him. Monroe was obviously losing patience with Konrad Asher. Asher was a distinguished looking man in his early thirties. His light brown hair was neatly trimmed, and he dressed with a fashionable business-like style. He seemed almost out of place with the other five, who dressed in jeans, flannel shirts, and were sporting a day's worth of stubble on their faces.

"Are you going to make love to those cards, or are you going to play poker?" Monroe finally bellowed out.

Monroe was large and intimidating to behold, but he wasn't nearly as imposing as he'd allow others to believe. If it weren't for the growth of stubble on his chin, his boyish baby face would give him away. Asher again glanced at his cards with a solemn expression, despite the commotion of the five other men. He then lifted his head and looked at the men in the smoke-filled den. A tiny smile crossed his face as he fanned the cards together.

"I'll raise another fifty cents," Asher announced in a gentle, monotone voice.

"Too rich for me," said the older man, Fred, who sat alongside Asher. He tossed his cards onto the table with a disgusted sigh.

Monroe removed the cigar from his mouth, chuckled lowly, and tossed in another fifty cents. "I'll call your bluff," he said firmly with a broad grin. He laid his cards on the table to reveal three queens. "Three of a kind. Beat that, sucker."

Asher fanned out his cards and stared at the full house in his hand. He closed the hand, appeared humored, and tossed the cards face down on the table.

"You called my bluff," Asher said simply.

Monroe laughed with a subtle arrogance and collected the pot of nearly five dollars. "You were just meant to lose tonight, my friend."

Asher shrugged without care. "I'm having a good time," he replied. "I suppose that's what's important."

"And it's best not to antagonize the law," Fred remarked, nodded to Monroe with a smirk, and then drank the last of his beer.

Monroe laughed while stacking his chips. "I'm not on duty. If I was, I'd have to arrest us all," he teased.

The others laughed.

"You wouldn't even know how to make an arrest," Fred remarked with a soft chuckle. "If it wasn't for our local drunk and old Mrs. Skyler speeding, you'd have nothing to do all day. Nothing ever happens in this town."

Monroe grinned in response and didn't deny the comment. Derek Falcone, a much younger man in his mid-twenties, collected the cards and shuffled them while the other five tossed their ante into the pot on the center of the cluttered table. Derek was a classically handsome man, who easily reminded some of a high school football player with his tall frame and sturdy build.

"Maria said you and Katie were planning a cruise this fall," Fred said to Asher.

"We'd hoped to, but one of the nurses quit last week," Asher remarked while casually puffing on his cigar. "Dr. Talbert may be reluctant to allow her the time off."

"A cruise, huh?" Derek remarked as he laughed lowly without looking up from the cards he was over shuffling. "Kate certainly has it good these days."

Asher stared at the small stack of chips before him with little expression. He'd obviously heard the comment, but refused to acknowledge it. The four other men glared at Derek. Derek prepared to deal the cards, saw the looks he was receiving, and smiled innocently.

"What?" Derek asked with an unnatural laugh.

"Just stop it, okay," Monroe scoffed and looked back at his healthy stack of chips.

Asher looked at Monroe and smiled lightly. "It's okay, Monroe," he informed him. "Derek has a tendency to dwell on the past when he's drinking."

Derek laughed as he violently dealt the cards. "What? You think I'm still jealous after all these years?" He snorted and grinned. "It doesn't bother me one bit."

There was an odd silence at the table. All five men watched Derek as he vigorously dealt the cards. Monroe folded his arms across his chest, chewed on his cigar, and raised a brow. All five waited for what was sure to follow.

"I mean," Derek continued as he picked up his five cards. "I only dated Kate all through high school and college."

There were several groans around the table. Asher just shook his head and frowned. They collected their cards and attempted to resume their game.

"Doesn't bother me that he's only in town for six months before stealing her away from me," Derek sulked then looked at the others and attempted a smile that resembled a sneer.

"It's been three years, man," Monroe announced with a disgusted moan. "Let it go."

Derek shrugged while staring at his cards. "Don't know what you're talking about. It doesn't bother me," he chirped. As he looked up, his smile twisted, giving him an almost psychotic look. "Girl knew I couldn't provide the kind of lifestyle she wanted."

Asher tossed his cards to the table and sat forward. He remained calm but was obviously disturbed. "Say what you wish about me, Derek. You can accuse me of seducing the only love of your life, if it makes you feel better, but don't disrespect Katie. I won't tolerate that sort of behavior."

Derek laughed aloud. "Don't act the role of her father. She's already got one of those," he muttered.

Asher looked up at the ceiling with a humored smile. "Ah, yes, I almost forgot the age thing." He looked back and Derek and tilted his head. "I know where this is leading, Derek. I don't want to fight you again. I take no pleasure in kicking your ass."

Derek's smile curled into a frown. He abruptly stood, knocking his chair to the floor. "Kate and I had it good until you came along with your expensive suit and philosophical attitude. You have no idea what it's like having the woman you love taken from you!"

All five men watched Derek dart from the den. The front door slammed just moments after. The men looked at one another with little emotion.

"I'll raise a quarter," Monroe announced simply.

✝

11:20 P.M.

*T*he Stony Ridge Institution sat away from the road on a large parcel of land surrounded by tall, chain-link fencing and stone walls. The institution encompassed more than twenty acres of land and the grounds were painstakingly maintained. The building itself was a massive marvel of stone and concrete. Castle-like in appearance, it was an eerily imposing sight. There appeared to be lights on within every room, giving it a creepy glow. Outside lights brightened half the grounds. The institution was easily mistaken for a hospital. It actually was a hospital. The sign on the stone wall near the security guard's building read, "Stony Ridge Mental Institution". The building itself had once been a college, but the isolation of the town made it undesirable to college students. The town rejoiced the end to hordes of drunken college kids, but they got the surprise of their life once it was converted into an insane asylum. It was quite the culture shock to the small, conservative community.

A nurse hurried along the elegant hallway on the first floor of the east wing. Her long, red hair was pulled back in a French twist. Kate Asher was a beautiful woman in her mid-twenties, but tonight her face expressed what appeared to be anger or rage. Her strides were long and determined as she approached the nurse's station. She entered the area cluttered with thick charts piled ten high along the massive desk. She stormed past another nurse seated at the desk behind the tall counter. The second nurse, Roseanne Pierce, looked up from her magazine and gazed after Kate with surprise. Roseanne was a youthful beauty in her own rights with long, wavy dark hair and an impressive figure that captured more than her share of male attention.

"You look pissed," Roseanne said with a curious stare. "Did Dr. Talbert deny your vacation request? I swear he doesn't want to see anyone happy."

Kate didn't respond to her comment. She removed her purse from her locker, stuffed an envelope in the front pocket, and returned the purse. She took two strides to the desk near Roseanne and snatched the phone from its cradle. Roseanne watched in silence as Kate punched a series of numbers into the phone. Kate was still a moment, though uncomfortable, and then slammed down the phone. She spun to face Roseanne and looked at her for the first time.

"I'm going to make my final rounds," Kate said firmly. "Will you page me as soon as my husband arrives?"

Roseanne slowly nodded with her mouth partially opened. "Is everything *okay?*"

"No," Kate retorted tersely. "But I intend to deal with it, believe me!"

Kate stormed out of the nurse's station just as quickly as she had entered, leaving Roseanne nearly speechless.

†

*K*ate walked more slowly now along the dimly lit corridor and looked into each room through sliding, metal windows with less thoroughness than usual. She appeared preoccupied, but at least her rage had diminished. A handsome young man in his early twenties wearing a guard's uniform approached from the opposite direction with a pleasant smile on his youthful face.

"Good evening, Mrs. Asher," Jameson Ramos said and touched his hat respectfully.

"Evening, Jameson," she said with little enthusiasm. She paused in the hallway, despite her eagerness to press onward. "Are we secure?"

"Everyone's tucked away on the second floor," he replied with a boyish smile. "I was just about to get some coffee before I patrolled your floor."

Jameson was a relatively handsome man who looked particularly good in his security guard's uniform. His outgoing personality gained plenty of female attention throughout town. Kate showed little interest in the handsome security guard despite the interest he showed in her.

"Take your time," she replied. "I have some research to do in the archives anyway."

"Don't be too long," he announced. "Nearly time for you to go home."

"Well, I may be a few minutes late," she said simply. "I'll page for you when I'm ready to leave the building."

"Certainly, Mrs. Asher."

Kate continued along the corridor and paused just outside a room with a frosted window over metal pigeon wire. Written on the window was the word, "Archives". She entered the dark room and turned on the lights. There were shelves of books, filing cabinets, and boxes of old documents. She proceeded down the first row of filing cabinets with a particular mission in mind.

✝

11:30 P.M.

*R*oseanne sat behind the cluttered counter while chewing on her nails and documented in one of the thick charts. Asher approached the nurse's station on the first floor of the east wing and stood by the counter. He appeared puzzled while looking at the young nurse.

"Good evening, Rosy," Asher said to the nurse behind the counter.

Roseanne looked up and her smile brightened. She dropped her pen and immediately sprang to her feet. "Good evening, Asher," she breathed almost romantically as her eyes swept over his distinguished features.

More than good looks, Asher was possibly the most charming man in all Stony Ridge. He was definitely not local, and the women appreciated his refined personality and undeniable charm. He pointed down the hall in the direction he had come.

"Are you aware there's no guard at the front door?" he asked while looking curious and possibly concerned.

"That would be Roy," she replied cheerfully. "He's never at his post."

"Kind of dangerous to leave the door unlocked and unattended in this sort of place," Asher remarked.

Roseanne shrugged while smiling warmly. "What could possibly happen in this hick burg?"

He leaned on the tall counter and smiled charmingly at her. "I suppose you're right. How are you?"

Roseanne blushed slightly to his charm. "I'd be better if I didn't have to work tonight. It's such a beautiful, warm evening," she announced with an almost lustful grin. "Perfect night for lovers." She seductively leaned on the counter, allowing her cleavage to be clearly displayed before him. Her smile was almost devious. "You're a little early for Kate. She just started her last rounds. She'll be another twenty minutes, I'm sure."

"I don't mind waiting," he replied simply. "The poker game wiped me out early, and I didn't see the point to making the trip home just to turn around and come back here."

Roseanne giggled inappropriately with a lustful look in her eyes. "Lost again, huh?"

He shrugged. "I'm not much of a gambler, I suppose."

Roseanne gave her dark hair a flirty toss from her shoulder. "Could I get you some coffee while you wait?"

"That's kind of you, Rosy, if it's no trouble."

"None at all." She flashed a smile. "Don't go away. I'll be right back."

"Actually, I think I'll sneak over to the second floor lounge for a quick cigarette," he announced then smiled deviously. "Katie doesn't appreciate it when I smoke in the house. She claims it kills her plants."

"Kate and her plants," Roseanne replied warmly with a shake of her head.

"Yes, our sunroom looks more like a greenhouse these days," he replied with a soft laugh. "But as long as I don't have to touch them, I suppose they can stay."

"I'll get us some coffee and bring it to you in the lounge," Roseanne offered a little too quickly. "Maybe I could bum a cigarette off you."

Asher tilted his head thoughtfully and hid his smile. "You don't smoke."

"Sure I do," she replied and shifted as if being caught in her lie. "Just not often."

"Alright," he replied pleasantly to her admission. "I'll meet you in the lounge."

Roseanne watched Asher walk away from the nurse's station. She gently bit her lower lip then smiled deviously. She hurried into the back and lifted the empty coffeepot. Roseanne groaned with frustration.

"Damn it, Jameson," she snarled and set it down.

Roseanne picked up the empty coffee can and peered into it with the disgust evident on her face. She tossed it in the garbage and approached Kate's locker. She opened Kate's locker, removed an unopened can of coffee, and then noticed the envelope Kate had placed in the front pocket of her purse. She stared at the envelope and appeared curious.

†

Kate stood before a large filing cabinet toward the back of the filing room and rummaged through several files. She slammed the drawer shut then sighed with disgust. She looked around the room while strumming her fingers on the cabinet.

"It couldn't have disappeared that quickly," she muttered softly to herself.

Kate randomly opened each file drawer and rummaged through every file. Her frustration increased with each drawer. As she slammed the last drawer, she heard an unusual thump from the front of the file room. The sound of the door closing followed. Kate looked across the filing cabinets in the direction of the door. It seemed odd anyone else would be in the filing room this time of night. It was the shift change and most of the other nurses were making rounds and documenting in charts. She walked through the aisle of storage shelves filled with boxes of old documents and toward the closed door. She stepped out of the aisle, approached the door, and turned the knob. The door wouldn't open. She appeared surprised and gave it a firm tug. It still didn't budge.

Out of the corner of her eye, she saw something move from the next aisle. Before she could turn, a hand slipped over her mouth from behind. She was forcibly pulled backward and against her assailant. Kate clutched the latex-gloved hand over her mouth and attempted to scream while thrashing with her body. She dug her fingernails into the latex glove, as her head was held immobile against her assailant. She saw the scalpel appear before her face. She again attempted to scream. The scalpel pierced her neck and slashed across her throat. The scalpel was sharp and the cut so quick, she was bleeding profusely before she even felt the pain. As the blood spilled from the gaping wound on her neck, she began to sink. Her assailant swiftly released her, allowing her to collapse to the floor.

Chapter Two

*D*r. Talbert's office was located on the second floor of the east wing in Stony Ridge Institution. It was rather lavish compared with the rest of the facility. After all, he was in charge. An elegant, carved desk was proudly displayed toward the back of the large office near the wall of glass overlooking the front grounds. Lights from the quiet town could be seen in the distance. One wall was lined with bookcases displaying every medical book imaginable, while the opposing wall proudly displayed framed degrees. It would appear Dr. Talbert was a very intelligent man. In the middle of the opposing wall was a small fireplace, which added that extra touch of elegance. Dr. Talbert, a distinguished man in his late thirties, poked at the embers in the fireplace then straightened and replaced the poker to the rack. He looked around his office with a deep sigh then glanced at his watch. He scratched his slightly gray hair then approached the large, antique desk. The desk was mostly in order except for several files lying scattered about the top. He sorted through the files, stacked them neatly, and then picked up the vacation request paper near the desk calendar. He stared at Kate Asher's name and appeared deep in thought. Talbert picked up the desk phone and dialed an in-house number. He straightened and stared at the framed degrees on the wall alongside the fireplace. Someone answered the phone on the other end. He appeared surprised by the voice.

"Hello? Roseanne? I didn't know you were in already. Is Kate there? I'd like to speak to her please." There was silence as Roseanne responded. "Oh, yes, of course." He sighed and set down the paper on his desk as the woman continued to talk. "No, don't bother paging her. Just ask her to give me a call when she returns." He then laughed softly at something she said. "Yes, Roseanne, it's about her vacation request. Just give her the message, okay?" He hung up the phone and smiled with a look of relief.

†

11:50 P.M.

*J*ameson walked along the first floor of the east wing swinging his large, baton flashlight and whistling a lively tune. He shined the light into each locked room through the small slide windows as he passed. He finally approached the file room at the end of the corridor and noted that the lights were still on. He appeared amused while smiling slyly.

"Ready when you are, Mrs. Asher," he chirped and reached for the doorknob. It didn't open. He removed his keys with a gentle shake of his head. "Of course it's locked," he muttered lowly. Jameson unlocked the door, stepped inside, and looked around. "Mrs. Asher?"

There was a long, bloody streak along the floor that led down the first aisle of shelves. A bloody scalpel lie on the floor at the opening of the nearby aisle. Jameson's eyes widened with a look of horror. He uncertainly looked around, appeared apprehensive about entering the file room, and then cautiously took several steps toward the aisle containing the blood.

"Mrs. Asher?" he gasped softly and clutched his flashlight in a deadly fashion.

He uncertainly peered down the aisle and saw a redheaded woman in a nurse's uniform lying in a bloody heap on the floor. There was blood surrounding her lifeless body and covering her white nurse's dress. A blood-soaked, white mound lie suspiciously just before her body.

"Oh, my God," he gasped then looked nervously around the narrow aisles.

He set his flashlight down on a nearby shelf and quickly drew his nightstick. He hurried for the dead woman then stopped and stared at the blood-soaked straitjacket. The fear was evident in his eyes. Jameson carefully stepped over the dead nurse to reach the phone on the wall. There was a metallic scraping sound behind him. As he spun around with a startled gasp, he was struck on the head with his baton flashlight. Jameson staggered a moment, unable to focus. His nightstick dropped to the floor as he fell against a filing cabinet with a dull, metallic crack. He leaned heavily on the filing cabinet and looked down the aisle. His attacker was gone! The file room door was heard as it slammed shut. Jameson pulled himself along the filing cabinet as blood streaked his face and fell against the wall near the mounted phone. He fumbled with the phone in his trembling hand.

f

*D*r. Talbert sat reclined in his large, leather chair with his hands folded peacefully across this abdomen. His head rested against the back of the chair and his eyes were closed. His faint snores were barely heard. The ringing phone abruptly woke him from his nap. He leaned forward with a soft groan, glanced at his watch, and picked up the ringing phone on his desk.

"Dr. Talbert here," he announced in a weary tone. There was a loud chirp from the other end. Talbert held the phone away for a second then abruptly sat up straight in his chair. "Damn it, boy, call a security alert!" Talbert launched back. "The wing must be sealed. He can't be allowed to escape!"

Dr. Talbert slammed down the phone, appeared alarmed, and ran his fingers through his thinning hair.

"This can't be happening," he said under his breath.

He looked at the phone and was about to pick it up when he heard the dull sound of bare feet running in the corridor outside his office. Dr. Talbert looked at his office door with wide eyes then opened his right hand desk drawer and removed an old revolver. Talbert stood and cautiously approached the office door and paused when he heard another door open. He cautiously opened the door and peered into the second floor hallway. The fire door to the stairway closed at the end of the hall. Dr. Talbert clutched his gun and hurried along the corridor.

"Security to the east wing first floor, stat," came Jameson's voice over the intercom system.

Dr. Talbert paused near the fire door. He was about to open it when smoke lingered into the hallway from behind him. He quickly turned and looked around the hallway. Smoke billowed from the nearby linen closet. He hurried for the closet door and threw it open. Flames engulfed the entire closet. Smoke now poured into the hallway. Dr. Talbert ran across the hall and pulled the fire alarm. Nothing happened. His eyes widened and his mouth fell open.

"God, no," he gasped then looked to the ceiling at the sprinklers. "Damn it, turn on!"

Nothing happened. Dr. Talbert attempted to close the closet door, but it was too late. The flames were already at the doorway. He shoved the gun down the back of his pants and ran along the hall.

✝

11:55 P.M.

*R*oseanne walked along the second floor hallway and headed toward the lounge while carrying two cups of coffee. She glanced at the ceiling and appeared curious by Jameson's intercom page. It was more his tone then the page itself.

"Security?" she questioned with a dreary sigh. "Wonder who flipped out this time?"

It wasn't uncommon for security to intervene with a typically docile patient. Their actions were often erratic and to be expected. Roseanne entered the lounge with the coffee and her sweet, innocent smile returned. As she looked around, she saw that the lounge was empty. On the coffee table alongside a magazine lie a pack of cigarettes.

"Asher?" she questioned and looked around with apparent confusion.

Jameson's voice once more came over the intercom, this time with the sound of panic. "Code red, east wing, first and second floor."

Roseanne suddenly looked up at the intercom in the ceiling, gasped with alarm, and threw both cups of coffee to the floor. She ran for the nearest fire extinguisher.

✝

12:05 P.M.

*A*sher ran along the corridor on the first floor as smoke filtered throughout the halls. Several guards and nurses hurried into rooms and evacuated the patients. Some wore straitjackets while others didn't require them. Several patients broke free in the chaos and ran amuck through the halls. One patient plowed into Asher and threw him against a nearby wall. Asher regained his balance and now coughed from the thick smoke.

"Katie! Katie," he called out while looking at each nurse he passed.

"Where's the fire department," one of the nurses could be heard screaming hysterically as she battled with one of the unruly patients in a straitjacket.

The patient slammed her into the wall with his shoulder, causing her head to strike the wall and knocking her to her knees. The patient ran back the way they had come, straight into the smoke. She clutched the wall for support and remained dazed a moment. Asher ran to her side and helped her to her feet. She had a freely bleeding cut on her forehead from where she'd struck the wall. Her eyes met his for a brief moment.

"Oh, my God, Asher," she suddenly gasped with panic in her eyes. "They're all going to die! Where's the fire department? The alarm never sounded. The entire wing is on fire!"

"Where's Katie?" he demanded to know while clutching her shoulders. "Have you seen her?"

She slowly shook her head while dabbing the blood. She chattered softly in near hysterics. The flames were now visible just twenty feet up the hall. The screams of patients echoed throughout the floor. Asher turned toward the frightened, babbling nurse and gave her a firm shake.

"Listen to me," he said firmly and attempted to jolt her back into reality. "Get out of the building. Direct the fire department to this area. Do you hear me?"

She uncertainly nodded. "Yes," she said more firmly. "I'll get them at once."

The nurse unsteadily ran along the corridor for the exit. Asher continued to cough. He removed a handkerchief from his pocket and placed it over his nose and mouth. He hurried deeper into the smoke-filled hallway. Dr. Talbert assisted a panic-stricken patient, who cried out profanities. His eyes met Asher's concerned gaze only briefly.

"It's gone," he cried out while shaking his head. "No more can be saved. Save yourself!"

"Where's Katie?" Asher shouted out with more determination. "Did she get out?"

Dr. Talbert stopped and stared at him with a blank expression on his face. The patient pulled away and ran down the hallway for the exit. Dr. Talbert jerked and watched the patient a moment. He looked back at Asher with the same blank expression.

"Oh, Asher," he gasped softly. "One of the patients--"

Asher suddenly grabbed Dr. Talbert by the shirt with such force and vigor; he nearly pulled him off his feet. "Where is she?"

Dr. Talbert's eyes were wide with horror. He pointed down the hall just before the fire itself. "The archives."

Asher released him and charged down the hallway. He skidded to a stop just before the door, held his handkerchief to his mouth, and bolted inside. Flames were now seizing boxes of old documents at a tremendous rate and the smoke was so thick, he could barely see. Asher looked at the floor to his left and saw the blood. His look was horrified. He quickly followed the blood and looked down the first aisle. For a moment, he stood paralyzed and stared at the blood surrounding the redheaded nurse. He dropped his handkerchief, took two slow steps toward the dead woman, and then sank to his knees alongside her. Asher began to sob uncontrollably as he slowly touched her shoulder. He gently rolled her over and stared at the familiar face void of life. The large, gaping slit across her throat glared back at him as blood saturated her white uniform. She appeared to stare back at him, but there was no life in her eyes. There was an odd symbol carved into her neck just below the deep gash. Asher sobbed as he pulled her into his arms and cradled her face to his chest. He brushed his cheek to her red hair and stared at the burning filing cabinets while gently rocking Katie in his arms. He kissed the top of her head.

"I won't leave you, my darling," he said softly while watching the flames. "Without you, I have nothing."

t

12:20 P.M.

$\mathcal{F}$ire trucks surrounded the entire east wing of the institution as smoke and flames billowed from the windows. Firemen raced around the chaotic exterior of the building as the few nurses and guards attempted to gather the roaming patients in their hospital gowns and, in some cases, straitjackets. Several townspeople began to gather on the institution grounds just beyond the small cemetery and stared at the burning building with horror. An expensive black car pulled up to the fire trucks and a man in his early forties stepped out. He paused and watched the building burn as his mouth hung open. He was rendered speechless. Howard Norad, the hospital administrator, looked toward the main door of the institution as Dr. Talbert and Roseanne emerged from the building. He ran from his car and hurried toward them. Roseanne coughed uncontrollably and sat on the grass while Dr. Talbert aided her, now kneeling alongside her.

"What happened?" Howard demanded to know as he stared down at them on the grass with the look of shock still present on his face.

Dr. Talbert looked up at the administrator and slowly shook his head. "It was one of the patients. He somehow escaped his room and set fire to the linen closets on all three floors."

"The fire alarms?" Howard demanded. "What about the sprinklers? They couldn't contain it better than this?"

Dr. Talbert was silent a moment. He inhaled deeply and slowly stood, looking Howard directly in the eyes. "They didn't work," he said, hesitated, and then spoke softly. "It's almost as if they were *disconnected.*"

"The patient?" Howard demanded.

Talbert shook his head. "I don't know. He could have done it, I suppose."

Howard looked back at the burning east wing. "The patients?" he announced, looked around the yard, and then back at the young doctor. "This can't be all of them."

"There was no warning--limited staff," Dr. Talbert replied softly with remorse. "We rescued the ones we could and suffered many staff casualties."

Howard's eyes were wide with horror. "How many didn't get out?"

"Twenty, maybe thirty," Dr. Talbert said sadly. "It's hard to say."

Howard held his head in his hands and groaned softly. The loss of the building was one thing, but the loss of lives would be devastating.

"Mick!" came a frantic female voice. "Mick!"

Howard turned to the voice and came face-to-face with a conservative looking woman in her late twenties, Jill Sutten. Jill's eyes were wide with the same look of horror.

"Where's my brother?" she demanded to know.

Howard looked at Dr. Talbert with question in his eyes. Talbert frowned and slowly shook his head. Howard shut his eyes and held his breath. Jill began to scream hysterically and called out her brother's name while running toward the burning building. One of the firemen seized her. She fought against him while reaching for the building.

"Mick!"

Jameson ran across the grounds and approached Dr. Talbert and Howard. "Mr. Norad," he gasped while out of breath. "We have a serious problem."

Howard looked at the burning institution then back at the young guard. "I know," he replied coldly. "Round up the patients before they find their way off the property."

"That's the problem," Jameson replied with a look of concern on his face.

Howard grabbed Jameson by the arm and pulled him away from Dr. Talbert and Roseanne. "What's that supposed to mean? Are you trying to tell me one of the patients may have escaped?" he demanded to know.

"Not just any patient," Jameson said softly. "It was Hal Burgess."

Howard's brows knitted as the expression drained from his face. "Are you sure he's not around or still inside the building?"

"No, he attacked Tim at the gate. Nearly broke his neck. He was wearing a green scrub suit and a lab coat." Jameson stared at Howard with a look of deep concern. "There was blood on the lab coat."

Howard rolled his eyes shut. "God help us." He looked back at Jameson. "Alert the police at once."

Chapter Three

1:00 A.M.

The McMurray farm was nestled on a large parcel of land with sprawling pastures lined with wooden fencing. A large, black and white pinto pony grazed lazily in the pasture not far from the newer, two-story barn. The farmhouse was a much older, remodeled two-story home with an elegant wraparound porch and stereotypical rocking chairs on it. The night seemed peaceful so far from the bustle of town and the frightening scene at the infamous institution. The plump pony suddenly lifted its head and watched something. It snorted and pranced around excitedly at what it saw. Twelve-year-old Jacey McMurray looked out of her second story bedroom window as her pony neighed from the fence near the barn. Something had the pony upset. Jacey jumped from her bed in her colorful pajamas and ran to her mother's bedroom next door. She entered without knocking. A man and woman jumped apart with surprise to the interruption. Her mother clutched the sheets to her naked body and forced a tiny smile while touching her flushed cheeks.

"Told you to lock the door," came a male murmur from beneath the covers.

"Jacey," her mother said while gently clearing her throat. "Were you having another nightmare?"

"No," she replied quickly. "Patches is running around the fence. There could be a wild animal out there." Her eyes were suddenly wide. "Maybe a wolf."

There was another male moan and the covers moved from the man's head as he sat up. He scratched his mussed hair.

"I've told you before, Jacey," he announced with a sigh. "There are no wolves around here."

Jacey eyed him with a scathing look that conveyed her distaste. "Daddy wouldn't like you sleeping in his bed with Mommy, Uncle Russell." She looked back at her mother. "Can we put Patches in the barn tonight?"

Her mother looked down at the sheets, appeared ashamed, and slowly nodded. She raked her trembling fingers through her hair. "Russell, would you mind?"

Russell frowned and nodded slowly while sharing the guilt. It wasn't easy on any of them being he married his deceased brother's wife. "Yeah, I'll get the pony."

Jacey ran from the room and into her own bedroom. She slipped into her shoes and crawled through the open bedroom window.

"What are you doing?" Russell's voice demanded to know from the doorway.

Jacey looked back at her Uncle Russell with surprise to his question. "Going out the back door," she said matter-of-fact. "Meet you outside."

"Jacey," he growled firmly.

Jacey scaled the porch roof, jumped into the big tree, and climbed down to the porch railing. She teetered a moment on the railing then jumped onto the porch and waited impatiently. The front lights came on, lighting the area between the house and the barn. The excited pony ran around the fence. Something moved in the woods near the barn. Jacey stared into the dark woods with great interest. The front door opened. Jacey looked at Russell with some disapproval.

"Daddy always brought the big gun," she informed him.

Russell groaned and rolled his eyes. "We don't need the big gun. Besides, there aren't any bullets."

They walked off the porch together and approached the paddock and barn where the excited pony watching them and the woods.

"They're on the closet shelf on the right behind the dirty magazines," Jacey replied simply.

He glared at her but didn't comment.

"I could show you how to load it, if you'd like," she added.

Russell groaned and rubbed his eyes. Something rustled in the woods. Patches snorted and ran along the fence while watching the woods with great interest. The pony's head was high, and he remained motionless. Jacey approached the fence and climbed on top of it.

"Here boy," she called to her pony.

The pony didn't respond but, instead, stood perfectly still with its eyes on the woods. Russell studied the dark, wooded area and appeared almost motionless. He turned his head slightly to the little girl.

"Jacey," he said faintly. "Go get the big gun."

She stood straight on the fence and stared into the woods with big eyes. The brush moved causing the pony to snort. She clutched the fence with alarm.

"Is it a wolf?" she gasped softly.

Russell didn't look at her but nodded slowly. "Yeah," he replied nervously. "Go--now.".

Jacey jumped from the fence.

"Russell!" Jacey's mother suddenly cried from the bedroom window. The sound of terror in her voice was chilling.

Russell spun and ran a couple of steps closer to the house. "What's wrong?" he called back.

Patches bolted across the fence and snorted fiercely. Jacey looked back at her pony and gasped. She grabbed the lead rope on the fence, climbed over the wooden rail, and jumped into the paddock, oblivious to the grown-up conversation. She approached the frightened pony. The pony squealed and bolted past her, nearly knocking her down. There was rustling from the woods, causing her to look with surprise. She anticipated a wolf. A creepy man in a white lab coat took a step toward the fence from the tree line. Jacey cried out with surprise. He darted behind a large tree. Jacey was grabbed around the waist from behind. She screamed as Russell plucked her from the paddock and ran while carrying her through the open gate. The pony ran from the corral and across the large field.

"Patches," she cried out. "Patches! Come back!"

She kicked and fought Russell as he ran with her to the well-lit house and into the kitchen. Her mother slammed the door behind them and bolted it. She clutched her head then sank to one knee and hugged Jacey as Russell set her down. Jacey wiggled away from her mother, who immediately straightened and looked at Russell.

"Someone saw one of them leaving the hospital grounds," her mother gasped nervously.

"Is he dangerous?" Russell asked with concern in his tone.

"You let Patches get away," Jacey cried out at her uncle.

Russell pointed to the stairs beyond the kitchen in an authoritative manner. "Jacey, go to your room!"

She glared at him with hatred in her eyes. "You aren't my Daddy!"

"Jacey, please," her mother shouted as her body trembled.

She looked at her mother with surprise. She couldn't believe her mother was acting this way. It was all Uncle Russell's fault. Her father never would've allowed this. Tears filled her eyes, and she ran from the room.

t

Saturday, 7:00 A.M.

*D*eputy Monroe, now dressed officially in his police uniform, approached the nurse's station at the county hospital. A plump nurse in her late forties looked at the stocky, sturdy man in uniform, appeared to approve, and smiled warmly.

"Can I help you, officer?" she asked politely.

"Yes, I'm looking for a man who was brought here late last night. Konrad Asher," Deputy Monroe said simply.

There was a loud metallic crash from one of the rooms at the opposite end of the hall, which startled Monroe. The nurse didn't even react and smiled bitterly.

"Yes," she replied dryly. "That would be him now. Take him with you--*please.*"

Deputy Monroe inhaled deeply and continued down the hall toward the familiar, raised male voice at the end of the hall. He entered the now silent room. Asher lie reclined on his elevated hospital bed and stared out the window without a word as the young nurse cleaned up the meal tray on the floor. Whatever happened ended in silence.

"Asher," Deputy Monroe announced as he paused in the private room doorway.

The nurse straightened and sighed with relief. "I hope you're here to take him away."

Asher turned his head to the mention of his name. He stared at Monroe with little expression. "Get this insufferable woman from my sight," he scoffed lowly.

"I was just leaving," she said and took the tray from the room.

Asher once again looked out the window. Deputy Monroe approached the bedside and stood there several minutes without being

22

acknowledged. He finally cleared his throat. Asher still didn't look at him.

"I know you've been through a lot, Asher," Monroe said gently. "But you don't need to take it out on the hospital staff."

Asher's head sharply turned toward Monroe with narrow, evil eyes. "Been through a lot?" he questioned lowly. "Katie's dead. My life ended. Don't come here and attempt to downplay what occurred last night. You haven't a fucking clue what I've been through." His head once more turned toward the window and he was again silent.

Monroe inhaled deeply then sat in the chair alongside the bed. "That's what we need to talk about," he said firmly. "One of the guards at the institution reported a patient had escaped his room just before the fire. He found Kate shortly after that. He was ambushed but never saw the man's face."

Asher slowly looked at Monroe and squinted. "This monster; it has a name?"

Monroe nodded. "Hal Burgess," he replied. "Odd part is the patient was strapped to his bed in a locked room just twenty minutes before your wife's murder."

Asher turned his head, stared at the sheets, and appeared to sink deep into thought. Something occurred to him, and he looked back at Monroe. "How do they know it was this particular patient if the guard hadn't seen his face?"

"He left his usual calling card," Monroe replied.

"Calling card?" Asher asked and appeared unusually calm for the first time.

"He carves a symbol into his victim's body," Monroe replied softly. He gently cleared his throat. "You were found with your wife in the file room by a firefighter. Did you happen to see anything? Do you remember anything unusual occurring just before you found her?"

Asher tilted his head and slowly nodded in response. "Yes, as a matter-of-fact," he replied dryly then suddenly exploded. "The entire building was on fire! The whole fucking situation was a fucking nightmare!"

Monroe inhaled deeply and attempted to remain calm despite his friend's outburst and colorful language. "Please, Asher," he said gently. "I'm trying to find Kate's killer."

All emotion drained from Asher's face as he stared at the deputy. "He got away?" he asked softly.

Monroe nodded. "Shortly after the fire trucks arrived. He attacked a guard and ran from the grounds through the woods. He was wearing a green scrub suit and a white lab coat. Russell McMurray reportedly spotted him at their place a little after one."

Asher's interest appeared to increase. "He's somewhere in Stony Ridge?"

"It's quite possible he's still there," Monroe informed him. "Let's just concentrate on your wife's attack right now. You were in the second floor lounge on the east wing at approximately eleven thirty-five."

"Yes," he replied. "I was early for Kate. She was making rounds, so I went for a cigarette."

Monroe jotted notes in a small notebook. "What time did you leave the lounge? What made you leave?"

"I heard voices in the hallway. I thought it may have been Katie, so I took a walk," he replied. "While I was walking along the hallway, I heard the fire alert."

"The guard was attacked after finding your wife's body in the archives," Monroe explained. "Roseanne reported Kate was upset just before she'd gone out for her last patient check. She was very eager to speak to you as soon as you arrived."

Asher stared at Monroe a long moment and appeared confused. "Rosy said that?" he suddenly asked. "Why didn't she tell me Kate wanted to see me?"

"I'm not sure," Monroe replied. "Had you and Kate been fighting that day?"

Asher's eyes remained fixed on Deputy Monroe. His head tilted slightly. "Why do you ask?" he asked as his eyes narrowed. "Are you getting at something?"

"Just asking the standard questions," Monroe explained and began to fidget. He avoided looking at Asher. "We're not accustomed to murders in this town."

"Are you suggesting that I possibly murdered Katie and set the institution on fire to cover it," Asher snapped hotly as his hostility rose. "I've known you for three years, Monroe. You know how much I love my wife." He was oddly silent. "I think you'd better leave before I say something you'll regret."

Monroe nervously stood. "It's my job to investigate your wife's death. It's because I know you, Asher, that I'm here and not the sheriff. He doesn't believe that it's possible for Hal to have escaped his bed and the room on his own. I don't believe you were involved."

"Get out," Asher growled and pointed toward the door.

Monroe slowly nodded and left the room. Asher stared at the blank television screen. His eyes narrowed and a strange look crossed his face.

†

*D*eputy Monroe approached the police blazer in the hospital parking lot, shook his head with disgust, and placed his cowboy hat firmly on his head. Derek appeared between the two parked vehicles and forced Monroe to stop mid-stride.

"Derek?" Monroe announced with a look of confusion. "What are you doing here?"

"Are you going to arrest him?" Derek demanded to know. His eyes were narrow and fixed on the deputy.

"Arrest who? Asher?"

"You're damned right Asher," Derek snapped. "He killed Kate last night--"

"Now wait a minute," Monroe interrupted and held up his hand. "We don't know that. We had an escaped serial killer in that building last night. I don't understand why everyone's so quick to point the finger at Asher."

"Because he did it," Derek shouted. "Kate's mother told me just last week that Kate and Asher had some sort of argument. If she would divorce him, he'd lose everything."

Monroe folded his arms across his chest and glared at Derek. "Uh, huh. What about the jealous, jilted boyfriend?" he asked simply with a raised brow. "How do I know you didn't seek revenge last night?"

Derek's eyes widened. "Revenge? After three years? If I had wanted revenge, I would've taken it when she first dumped me, and it'd have been Asher who'd be dead."

"So you say," Monroe remarked. "But you were drunk last night. There was no guard at the main door of the institution. You could've gone there to get Kate back and killed her when she laughed in your face."

Derek's lips twisted in anger. "I would never kill Kate. I loved her."

"And so did Asher," Monroe snapped. "I suggest you go home, before I start checking into your alibi."

He pushed Derek aside and climbed into the police blazer. Derek stared after him and watched the police cruiser as it drove away. He sneered and looked at the hospital.

Chapter Four

Saturday, 7:00 P.M.

Roseanne sat at the old-fashioned kitchen table across from her friend and stared into her cup of coffee with a frown. Her friend, Bonnie, a bubbling blonde woman in her mid-twenties, studied her in silence. She finally sat forward and sighed.

"Come on, Roseanne," Bonnie chirped with a tiny smile. "You don't have to work tonight. They gave you a free pass. Let's go out and do something. Get your mind off what happened last night."

Roseanne slowly shook her head and didn't look up from her coffee cup. "I don't want to do anything," she remarked sadly. "All those people dead." She finally looked up. "How can I forget that? And Kate," she almost whispered. "I can't believe what happened to her. Despite it all, I really liked her."

Bonnie tilted her head and appeared curious. "Do you think Asher killed her?"

Roseanne looked at her friend with wide, startled eyes and immediately appeared offended. "Of course he didn't kill her. He's not like that," she said defensively.

"Even after the way he treated you at the hospital this morning?" Bonnie asked with a raised brow.

Roseanne shrugged and stared back at her coffee cup. "He's been through a traumatic experience. He's going to be angry for some time." She then looked up and smiled timidly. "But I'll be there for him when he's ready."

"I'm sure you will be," Bonnie replied with a slightly evil laugh. "Kate's death came at a convenient time for you. Your boyfriend is out of the picture, and Asher's suddenly available."

Roseanne glared at Bonnie with a shocked expression. "You're horrible," she suddenly snapped. "How can you even say something like that?"

"Oh, come on," Bonnie said with annoyance in her voice. "You've wanted Asher ever since you laid eyes on him. Don't pretend you're not secretly happy Kate's gone."

Roseanne shot up from her chair. "You're sick, Bonnie," she snapped and shook her head. "I'm going home." She hurried to the kitchen door and walked onto the porch.

Bonnie followed and stood in the kitchen doorway. "You know it's true though," she called after Roseanne.

She smiled smugly then allowed the door to slam shut. Roseanne's car could be heard burning out in the driveway. Bonnie began cleaning the cups from the table. A woman in her late forties entered the kitchen and shook her head.

"You're simply amazing," Bonnie's mother scolded. "I can't believe you'd upset your best friend like that."

Bonnie frowned and waved her hand carelessly. "She'll get over it, because it's true." She then laughed softly. "I wouldn't doubt if Roseanne considered killing Kate herself once or twice."

"Oh, come now," her mother snapped with a look of disbelief and shamed her daughter. "Roseanne wouldn't think of such a thing. She's a nice girl."

"Whatever you say, Mother," Bonnie said with a mocking smile.

"I'd better get the sheets off the line before it rains," her mother said and walked toward the kitchen door.

"Did you wash my pink skirt?" Bonnie asked casually while wiping the table. "I want to go out tonight."

"It's washed," her mother replied and stood in the doorway. "But I didn't have a chance to iron it. It's in the basement."

Bonnie sulked. "I hate ironing." She then smiled sweetly. "Do you think you could iron it for me?"

Her mother nodded with a displeased look. "Sure. I'll do it just as soon as I get the sheets off the line."

"Thanks, Mom," Bonnie chirped. "I have to get ready."

She turned and ran through the living room and up the stairs to her bedroom. Bonnie's mother shook her head and walked onto the porch. The clouds were becoming darker in the distance. She walked down the steps and approached the wash line strung between two large trees. She paused before the bedsheet and stared at the long slit in the center of it. Her brows knitted. She tilted her head and touched the slit.

†

*B*onnie stood before her full-length mirror in her lacy bra and panties as she finished fixing her hair. She checked herself out in her mirror then applied some final touches to her make-up. She approached her closet, removed a white, lacy blouse, slipped into it, and buttoned it as she left her room. She trotted down the stairs and into the kitchen. She opened the basement door.

"Mom, is my skirt finished?" she called down the steps to the dimly lit basement.

The basement was dreary looking with its old wood, stone walls, and cobwebs. There was no response. Bonnie looked toward the kitchen window and saw one of the sheets still flapping in the breeze. She groaned and walked down the rickety steps to the basement. The stench of mildew was overpowering. She stopped at the bottom and saw the ironing board next to a table of clothing still waiting to be ironed. Bonnie walked past the dangling lightbulb and sorted through the clothing until she found her pink skirt. There was a dull thump from the outer basement door. She sighed, tossed the skirt on the ironing board, and walked across the basement.

"Mother--"

The interior basement door was shut, and there was no one there. Bonnie stared at the door a moment with a look of confusion. She opened the lower door. Her mother fell down the last stone step and collapsed to the basement floor with blood covering the entire front of her shirt. Bonnie jumped back and screamed while staring at her lifeless mother. There was a deep slit across her throat and a symbol was carved into the side of her neck. A floorboard creaked from upstairs. Bonnie gasped and looked at the plank wood ceiling. She then looked at the basement stairs past the ironing board that led to the kitchen. Someone was upstairs in the kitchen! Bonnie looked past her dead mother to the outer basement door at the top of the concrete steps. She jumped over her mother and ran up the steps to the closed outer door. She attempted to open it, but it wouldn't budge. It seemed impossible, since it only locked from the inside. Bonnie cried out with each thrust to the door. The wooden

28

basement steps creaked. She spun with a gasp and held her breath. She looked down the concrete steps and across the basement toward the stairs past the ironing board. She didn't see anyone. She scanned the basement and saw an old ax near the small pile of firewood in the corner. Bonnie hurried down the concrete steps, jumped over her mother's slain body, and ran for the ax.

She grabbed the ax, clutched it in a deadly fashion, and looked around the basement from her position near the ironing board. As she looked around, it was evident there was no one hiding within the basement. She clutched the ax in trembling hands and looked at the steps leading to the kitchen above. If she didn't want to be trapped in the basement, she'd have to go upstairs. There weren't any phones in the basement. She looked back at her dead mother, attempted to control her emotions, and then looked back at the stairs. She nervously walked closer to the stairs while clinging to the ax. Bonnie paused to the side of the bottom step and attempted to peer to the top. The basement door in the kitchen remained opened. Nothing moved and there were no sounds from upstairs.

She inhaled deeply and slowly crept up the creaky, old steps, carefully avoiding making any sound. As she reached the top of the stairs, she paused just before the opening to the kitchen. She clutched the ax and quickly moved into the doorway. Bonnie looked around the bright, empty kitchen. There was no one there. She sighed with relief and stepped into the kitchen. When nothing moved, she bolted for the phone on the kitchen wall, and snatched it from the cradle. She pressed speed dial for emergency services and kept herself from sobbing. As the dispatch responded on the other end, Bonnie sighed with relief and turned while speaking into the phone.

"Thank God--"

Bonnie stared at the white lab coat directly in front of her. Her eyes lifted to see the moderately scruffy, burley man with wild, dark hair staring back at her. Bonnie suddenly screamed, dropped the phone, and attempted to raise the ax. Hal Burgass grabbed the ax handle, slammed it into her chest, and forcibly plowed her backward against the counter. As he held her back, he slashed the scalpel across her throat, leaving a large, gaping wound. She cried out only briefly as blood spilled down her body from the slit in a waterfall of blood. Her scream was gurgled as blood flowed from her mouth. She clutched the ax he held against her body and sank down the counter to the floor. Her lifeless eyes stared up at Hal. His pale lips curved into a pleased grin as he lowered himself over her nearly lifeless body and carved into her neck with the scalpel.

†

Sunday, 6:50 A.M.

*T*he police cruiser was parked outside Bonnie's small farmhouse with its lights flashing. Deputy Monroe walked out of the house, removed his hat, and wiped his brow on his sleeve. Sheriff Freeman, a man in his late fifties, joined him on the porch with a slightly pale expression.

"I can't believe this," Deputy Monroe breathed softly and shook his head. "It has to be the same guy."

Sheriff Freeman sighed and looked around the farmland and tall cornfields with his hands on his plump hips. "He's out there somewhere just waiting to strike again."

"Suppose this rules Asher out as a suspect," Monroe said faintly and stared at the sheriff.

Sheriff Freeman looked sharply at Monroe. "It proves nothing of the kind."

Monroe appeared surprised. "But all the victims followed the same pattern. They had the same symbol carved into their bodies. Certainly that should prove--"

"Konrad Asher is a very intelligent man," Freeman remarked sternly. "We don't know anything about his past. He's an independently wealthy man who didn't seem to exist prior to three years ago."

"With all due respect, Sheriff," Monroe said simply. "I don't believe he killed her. No man could've loved a woman more. You could see the love between them."

"I know he's your friend, Monroe, but sometimes things go wrong even with a seemingly perfect relationship," Sheriff Freeman remarked. "I'm not finished with Asher yet."

†

*J*acey sat on the corral fence at her farm and stared sadly at the lead rope she held in her hands. It had been two days since her pony took off for parts unknown, and no one would let her go out searching for him. There was no explanation; just that she wasn't allowed to leave the house by herself. Her mother hung wash on the line near the house as the police blazer drove down their long, dirt driveway. Jacey looked up and saw Deputy Monroe get out of the blazer and approach her mother. Jacey jumped off the fence and hurried toward the deputy.

Her mother saw him approach, cleared her throat, and smiled lightly. "Jacey, Deputy Monroe is going to keep watch for Patches. I'm sure he'll be back home soon."

Jacey looked at the large, imposing deputy. "You'll find him?" she asked sadly.

Deputy Monroe forced a tiny smile and nodded. "I'll find him, I promise. Why don't you go inside and play?"

She suspiciously stared at the man in uniform then looked back at her mother. "Is something wrong?" she asked.

"No, everything's fine," she said gently. "We'll talk later. I think you'd better go inside and play in your room for now."

Jacey still wasn't convinced. She turned and approached the house. As she entered the kitchen, she looked back out the door. Her mother and Deputy Monroe spoke, but she couldn't hear what they said. Her mother began pointing toward the old mining road just near the barn. It went quite a distance and eventually came out on a road on top of the hill in the woods. Her father took her for a ride to Mr. Asher's house two years ago just before her father's death. Her mother now appeared upset. Jacey went upstairs to her room and stared out her bedroom window. The police blazer finally drove back along the long driveway and to the main road. The kitchen door slammed shut. Jacey stared across the large field past the barn. Her pony stood near the tree line and grazed in the distance. Jacey jumped to her feet, lifted the screen, and scaled out the bedroom window. She hurried across the porch roof, jumped into the old, oak tree, and climbed down to the porch. She jumped off the porch railing and ran across the farm and through the recently cut field. She slowed as she neared her pony. Patches continued to graze, though he watched the young girl.

"That's a good boy," Jacey said proudly and slowly approached the pony.

There was the rustling of underbrush from within the woods. The pony's head bolted upward with a snort. The pony stared at something in the woods. Jacey looked through the trees and tilted her head. She saw something move but wasn't sure what it was. Jacey turned to her pony, grabbed its mane, and swung onto its back with ease. The pony jumped around nervously. Jacey turned the pony toward the farm with use of her legs. They trotted down the slope toward the barn. Jacey's mother ran out of the house with her mouth hanging open and stared at her daughter.

Jacey smiled proudly. "Look, Mommy. Patches came back on his own," she announced.

"You get that horse in its stall and get in this house!" her mother shouted.

She was stunned by her mother's overreaction. Something was definitely not right, and she wondered if she did something to anger her mother. All the adults were acting crazy the last few days, and she wondered why.

Chapter Five

The small town of Stony Ridge was one of those perfect places to live and raise a family. The streets were quiet and clean, and cute, well-maintained homes lined the roads. Every house had a yard with the standard, white picket fence. The townspeople mostly got along with one another, and any disputes were easily resolved. The worst part about Stony Ridge was chronic gossiping by busybodies whose sole enjoyment was minding their neighbor's business. It was never proven, but it was speculated they had a club and met three times a week. Town Hall was a monstrous building over one hundred years old and sat at the end of Main Street. Most of what happened in Stony Ridge was conducted in Town Hall. It was one of the few buildings able to hold a majority of the town at one time. Raised voices could be heard from within Town Hall that Sunday evening. Half the town gathered for the meeting held by Mayor Bradford. Mayor Bradford sat behind a table with Sheriff Freeman and Howard. Mayor Bradford didn't look the part of a politician. He was actually the town pharmacist. There wasn't room for a full-time mayor in their small town, so he volunteered for the job. The wooden gavel repeatedly slammed down on the desk. Everyone jumped and looked to the front table at the mayor.

"Silence! Let's have some order here," Mayor Bradford shouted above the crowd.

Jill shot up from her seat and pointed a finger at the mayor. "I demand that you shut that institution down immediately. The place is cursed!"

There was a commotion that followed. The gavel struck the desk once more.

"Order!"

Panic flooded the room.

"What's being done about that killer on the loose?" another woman cried out. "We're afraid to let our children play outside! How many innocent people must die before something is done?"

More voices were heard rising from the townspeople and it was starting to get out of control.

"I assure you, Mrs. Reed," Sheriff Freeman announced over the rising voices. "We are searching every field, forest, and structure for this man."

"That's not good enough," Jill cried out while wildly gesturing. "The institution must be shut down! Who's taking responsibility for the deaths of the patients in the east wing? My brother's dead! Why didn't the fire alarms sound? Why hadn't the sprinklers been discharged? Who's accountable?"

Howard lurched from his seat near the mayor and leaned over the microphone on the table where they sat. "The fire was an unfortunate incident started by the escaped patient," Howard said. "Somehow he'd managed to disarm the alarm and the sprinklers by the main box. There was no possible way we could've foreseen this tragic incident. Measures are being taken to prevent this. Any parties responsible will be dealt with accordingly."

"Who were the guards?" Jill shouted out. "They should be held accountable for the escape of this patient and the deaths of the people he's killed!"

"We're investigating the incident," Howard retorted firmly while digging his fingers into the table. "There's a possibility that Nurse Asher may have, for reasons unknown, released the patient from his bed."

"That will not do," shouted a male voice from the back above the crowd. The firm, harsh voice spoke with such sharpness, everyone fell silent and turned toward the back of the hall.

Howard straightened and stared at Asher as he slowly walked along the aisle toward the front. His piercing gaze was fixed on Howard standing behind the table.

"I will not permit you to tarnish my wife's reputation to save your own asses," Asher said forcefully and paused by the first row of chairs.

Howard held his breath then gently cleared his throat. "It's not tarnishing her reputation nor is it putting any blame on her for her actions, Mr. Asher. It's sometimes necessary to release patients from their beds."

"She was murdered in the file room," Asher stated firmly without emotion. "There was no struggle, just one, quick, deadly cut. The guard reported she was on her way to the file room just twenty minutes before her attack. Also, the patient was resident to the second floor, not the first floor. He wasn't even her patient. She wouldn't have had any reason to release him from his restraints." Asher raised his head proudly, and his eyes narrowed. "You will not breathe my wife's name nor make reference toward her again in this meeting. I will not permit it."

There was an odd silence from the entire room. Howard stared at Asher in silence with his mouth partially opened. He shut his mouth and gently cleared his throat.

"I'm sorry if I've offended you, Mr. Asher," Howard responded gently then returned to his seat, turned toward the mayor, and whispered, "I thought he was still in the hospital."

The mayor shrugged.

"I will repeat Mrs. Reed's earlier question," Asher announced sternly. His tone commanded the attention of every person within the hall. "What is being done to capture this monster? You really expect four baby-face deputies and one overweight sheriff to search this entire town and all its farms?" He looked at the crowd within the hall. "Gentlemen, I believe it's time you've called in some additional help."

Mayor Bradford straightened in his chair. "Mr. Asher," he announced firmly. "The police in other towns have their own crimes to worry about. Our police are competent enough to find this man. It's just a matter of time."

"People are dying," Asher hissed lowly. "How many more lives will it be until you've caught this butcher? Perhaps I must find some outside help myself." Asher looked past the six men on the council. "Offer a one hundred thousand dollar reward for the capture of this monster--dead or alive."

Voices began to murmur loudly from the townspeople as well as the council. Mayor Bradford struck the gavel to the desk then pointed the gavel at Asher.

"That would be an invitation for every bounty hunter and gangster to flock to our quiet, little town," Mayor Bradford snapped. "I will not allow you to turn this town into a battlefield."

Asher approached the table, placed his hands on it, and stared directly into the mayor's eyes. "You'd better hope your men get to him before I do, because if I find him first, there won't be anything left of him to identify."

Sheriff Freeman approached Asher. "Take a seat," Freeman growled lowly and reached for his arm.

Asher spun to face the sheriff and pulled his arm back. The look in Asher's eyes was enough to stop Sheriff Freeman. "Don't you fucking touch me," he growled then lowered his arm and relaxed. "I was just leaving."

Everyone watched in silence as Asher walked along the aisle and for the door. Derek glared after Asher as he left the hall.

†

*D*eputy Monroe drove along the dark, back road in the wooded hillside area of the county. The light rain sprinkled across the windshield as the wipers squeaked while moving back and forth. The headlights reflected shadows within the trees lining the road. Something moved to the right of the police blazer. A woman suddenly appeared in the headlights. Monroe stepped on the brakes and clutched the steering wheel. He let out a startled cry as the tires skidded on the wet, gravel road and came to a grinding halt. The woman collapsed across the hood then fell to the road. Monroe stared at the front of the blazer a moment with a look of horror in his eyes. He hadn't hit the woman. She hit him! He put the blazer into park and sprang from the vehicle. Monroe moved quickly, yet cautiously, to the front of the cruiser and looked at the fallen woman. Blood covered the teenage girl's shirt, arms, and hands. Her eyes were open with a fixed stare. Monroe lowered himself to her side and felt her neck for a pulse. She was dead.

†

*I*t was nearly dawn as the police blazer drove along the narrow lane and into the secluded clearing in the woods. An old, blue car came into view at the back of the clearing. The secluded location was a local hot spot for teenagers to park and fool around.

Monroe sat in the driver's seat of the police blazer with a young, newly appointed deputy alongside him. Monroe pointed at the car.

"That car belongs to the dead girl's boyfriend," he announced to his young partner. "She was with her boyfriend last night. His parents said he never came home."

The young deputy looked at the old, rusted vehicle. "Look at the window," he said softly while pointing a trembling finger.

The back driver's side window had been shattered. They drove closer to the old car. Despite the light rain, blood remained streaked along the shard glass. Monroe stopped the blazer. Both men climbed out and drew their weapons. They cautiously approached the vehicle and peered into the backseat. Blood covered the old, leather seat. The right, rear passenger door was open. The young deputy stepped around the broken glass just outside the car, indicating the glass had been broken from the inside. Monroe hurried around the back of the car and studied the surrounding area. There was blood on a nearby tree. The girl had apparently traveled the gravel road the entire distance. She was found just a mile from the secluded area. It seemed improbable that it was her blood on the tree. Someone had entered the woods by the vehicle, which was in the opposite direction. Both deputies followed a small deer path through the woodland. There was another tree with a large amount of blood on it. The rain hadn't been heavy enough to wash it away.

"Monroe, look," the deputy cried out with panic and pointed past the tree.

A young boy lie on his back in the thick brush beyond the tree. Insects and slugs covered his damp, blood-soaked body. He had several gashes on his arms and upper body, indicating there had been a struggle with his attacker. His throat had been slit, ultimately killing him. The telltale symbol was carved into his neck just like all the other victims. Monroe shut his eyes and lowered his head.

†

Five days later...

*T*he quaint general store was the original general store from the 1800's before the town was even known as Stony Ridge. It was reminiscing of an old cabin. The hardwood floors were all original and creaked with every step. The sounds of creaking floorboards were heard throughout the entire building. Jacey studied the rows of candy bars through the glass of the candy case. She wasn't often allowed chocolate, and she wanted a candy bar today more than most days. Her mother, Russell, and Jill, who owned the general store, were talking over one another without any pauses between sentences. Their conversation bored Jacey. Most adult conversations bored Jacey, and she easily blocked them out.

"What does it matter," Jacey's mother said firmly. "The killings have stopped."

"I'm just glad they're shutting down that damned institution," Jill huffed from behind the candy case.

"Personally," Russell interjected, "I don't care if someone grinded the bastard in their garbage disposal."

Jacey suddenly looked up and tilted her head with a look of surprise. "Someone did that?"

Her mother frowned. She picked a fine time to start listening to adult conversations. "No, darling. Uncle Russell was just making a bad joke."

The door opened with the jingling of a bell. Asher entered the general store and strolled along the aisle. Two other customers looked at him and whispered as he passed. He approached the counter and smiled cheerfully.

"Good morning, Jill," Asher said pleasantly. He then nodded to Russell and Jacey's mother.

"Morning, Asher," Jill said with a slightly raised brow. "What can I do for you?"

"Six bags of fertilizer," he announced. "The plants need some TLC. Katie would be furious if she saw the condition of her garden."

Jill flashed a fake smile. "Taking up gardening?" she teased.

"Little choice, I'm afraid."

She rang out his purchase and spoke casually. "So, have they found the guy yet?"

Asher's smile faded into a preoccupied smirk. He removed a lollipop from the box on the counter and handed it to Jacey. She accepted it without hesitation.

"Uh, no, they haven't," he replied and looked back at Jill. "I think he finally moved on. I'm sure they'll catch him one of these days."

Asher then gave a general nod and went to collect his bags of fertilizer. He carried the first two bags from the store and appeared oddly cheerful. Russell watched with a look of disapproval and shook his head as Asher walked out the door.

"There's no doubt in my mind," Russell muttered. "He killed him."

Jacey looked at the door with wide eyes. She then looked at the lollipop and quickly returned it to the box on the counter.

"Wouldn't doubt if he ate him," Jill remarked lowly under her breath.

Jacey suddenly gasped and covered her mouth.

Her mother glared at the woman behind the counter. "Jill," she scolded then looked at Jacey and squeezed her shoulder while smiling sweetly. "Honey, Mr. Asher didn't eat anyone."

Chapter Six

Ten years later...

*T*hree horse and riders galloped through a large, lush field in the warm afternoon sun. All three horses were neck and neck as they thundered through the field racing one another. The twenty-two-year-old woman was Jacey McMurray now grown. She rode her gray horse and attempted to pull ahead of the other two riders. A large, brown and white paint horse carried a blonde-haired, fifteen-year-old girl, Monique Harris. The black horse was ridden by another fifteen-year-old girl with dark hair, Coleen Cooper. At the last moment, the girl on the black horse pulled ahead of the other two. All three slowed their horses to a more relaxed gait.

"I win," Coleen proclaimed while grinning.

As they approached the woods, the horses remained excitable, but none of the three appeared to notice.

"I'm so glad you invited us to spend the week with you, Jacey," Monique said and patted her paint gelding.

"You're lucky, Monique," Coleen sulked. "None of my relatives have horses, and I'd certainly never be allowed to bring Thunder with me." She hugged her black horse as they rode.

Jacey entered the path in the woods ahead of them to lead the way then turned sideways on her horse to look back at the girls.

"I really wanted to have both of you here. My mom and Uncle Russell went on their two-week cruise, so we'll have the entire house to ourselves." She grinned at them. "Kind of like girls' time."

"I'm so glad you invited Coleen along," Monique said cheerfully. "You know we're practically twins."

Jacey laughed softly at her young cousin's comment. "You girls are lucky. I wish I had a close friend growing up. My best friend was my pony, Patches. None of the girls my age liked riding, and I usually showed up the boys."

"Us too," Coleen replied and appeared pleased about it.

"We're going to ride all day and watch scary movies every night, right?" Monique said excitedly.

"We certainly are," Jacey replied happily. "I took time off work at the library and the local paper."

"You're cousin is so cool," Coleen marveled.

They rode through the woods and peered along several other trails. There seemed to be never ending trails throughout the woods, providing hours of trail riding within the game land.

"What was that big, old building we passed when we drove through town?" Coleen asked. "The one behind the cemetery with the big fence around it."

"That used to be the nuthouse," Monique said dramatically.

"The place that burned all those years ago?" Coleen asked. "I thought it burned to the ground."

"No," Jacey replied. "Just the east wing."

"Didn't look burned to me," Coleen announced. "Just slightly abandoned."

"It's been abandoned for almost ten years," Jacey informed her. "But not for long."

"They're finally tearing it down?" Monique asked.

"No," Jacey replied. "They've been renovating it the last six months. They tore down the remains of the east wing a few months ago."

"Are they bringing more crazy people?" Coleen asked.

"No, it's going to be some sort of laboratory and museum for scientists," Jacey explained. "I intend to do a story for our local paper. They're supposed to be arriving next week and having some big, formal party. Shelly, the paper owner, promised I could do the story."

"That sounds cool," Monique said with excitement in her eyes.

Jacey attempted a smile then sighed softly. "It's tough competing against Brenda. She's been writing for the paper for a few years now and has seniority over me. She's aggressive when it comes to interviews." She then considered her own comment. "Brenda's aggressive when it comes to just about everything."

"Yeah, we have a girl like her at our school," Monique announced. "She's boy crazy."

"No boys for you, huh?" Jacey asked and smirked.

Both glared at her and made faces.

Coleen patted her horse's neck and grinned. "Thunder is the only man for me."

Jacey smiled knowingly. She had been the same way at their age. Actually, she hadn't taken an interest in boys until she was eighteen, and even then, it wasn't anywhere near the way other girls reacted around them. Honestly, she could still take them or leave them. A certain young deputy soured her on men. They rode for several minutes in the woods then came to a clearing. A large, modern cabin with an all-glass sunroom came into view. They were directly behind the home, allowing them to see the beautiful, well-kept garden with its stone wall, waterfalls, trees, bushes, plants, and marble statues.

"That's quite a garden," Coleen remarked. "My mother would love to see that." Coleen removed her cell phone and snapped a picture.

"That's Konrad Asher's house," Jacey informed them. "He leads a bit of a secluded life."

"Isn't he the guy who murdered his wife?" Monique asked curiously.

Jacey looked at Monique with some surprise by the comment. That rumor had gotten around town right after his wife's death, but they were never able to prove anything. Jacey just wondered where her cousin, who lived several counties away, had heard about it.

"He murdered his wife?" Coleen asked with wide eyes then made a face.

Jacey rolled her eyes and moaned. "Where did you hear such a ridiculous story?" she demanded to know.

"Uncle Dave," both replied simultaneously.

Jacey shook her head with disapproval. "Should've guessed." She looked at Coleen while cleverly raising her brows. "No offense, Coleen, but you're Uncle Dave is clueless."

"We know," both once more replied together.

Although not related, Monique and Coleen were closer than most sisters, having been best friends since birth. Coleen's Uncle Dave was one of those relatives everyone dreaded knowing.

"Last time my mother and I visited, your Uncle Russell told us all about Mr. Asher," Monique informed her. "He said no one in town talks to him, he never leaves his house, and everyone is afraid of him."

"I'm not," Jacey announced firmly. "Since the death of his wife, I've heard all sorts of stories. Some claim he killed his wife using the escaped mental patient as his scapegoat; some are even convinced he set the fires himself. I will admit people in town do fear him, but that's because they're narrow-minded fools. I've never believed any of it."

"Your uncle seemed to believe it," Monique added.

Jacey sighed sadly. "I'm afraid my family's been sucked in as well. You'll find this town is filled with skeptics and superstitious ninnies."

The sound of hedge clippers could be heard from the garden. Monique and Coleen jumped then looked toward the stone wall surrounding the garden.

"We'd better get out of here," Coleen nervously suggested.

Monique nodded in agreement.

Jacey reluctantly sighed and forced a tiny smile. "Why don't you take the old mining road back to my house and find something for lunch," Jacey suggested. "I don't want to seem rude and not say hello."

Both girls appeared horrified.

"No, he'll kill you," Monique gasped.

She laughed softly. "Don't be silly. Go on--go home."

Jacey rode up to the garden as the girls turned toward the wide, dirt road. Without fail, they sent the horses into a gallop and raced each other down the road. Jacey dismounted and tied her horse to the old, iron hitching post, which seemed oddly placed in such a remote area. She walked around the stone wall and nearly ran into a man leaning casually against the large, oak tree holding a hedge clipper. She jumped with some surprise then relaxed and smiled. A much older Konrad Asher smirked appearing pleased to have startled her.

"You startled me," she said with a tiny sigh.

His smile was fixed and unchanged. "And you me," he said in a calm, monotone voice.

Jacey somehow doubted that. He probably heard them coming a mile away.

"I wasn't expecting any visitors today." His smile brightened. "I was actually anticipating a peaceful day at home alone for a change." He chuckled lowly at his own witticism.

Jacey smirked and held back her laugh. "I bet you were."

Every day was a quiet day at home alone for Asher. He rarely left his house. Asher turned his head toward the woods then looked back at her with the same, solemn smile.

"Your friends didn't care to stop for some lunch?"

"That's my cousin, Monique, and her friend, Coleen. They'll be staying with me for the week."

"While your mother and uncle are on their cruise, no doubt," he replied.

She nodded slowly.

"Your cousin and friend could have stayed for lunch. I do enjoy entertaining," he said with a mocking smile.

Jacey forced a nervous smile and covered by running her fingers through her long hair. "You know how kids are. They wanted to get back to the house and watch movies."

Asher smirked with a humored laugh. "You don't need to lie to me to spare my feelings, Jacey. I don't have any worth sparing."

He turned and walked back into the lavish garden. Jacey followed him through the extensive, carefully manicured garden. They passed a massive weeping willow tree with a marble placard dedicated to Katie. Asher had planted the tree in her memory after her death and buried her ashes along with it. They approached the patio. He set the hedge clipper on the patio table.

"My reputation precedes me even to strangers," he announced as he approached the glass, patio doors. "Young girls fear what they perceive to be real life monsters."

"You're not a monster," she stated firmly and followed him into the sunroom filled with various hanging plants. She closed the glass door behind her.

Asher turned in the archway to the kitchen and leaned his shoulder against the frame.

"Even you weren't so easily convinced," he said simply with a tiny, knowing smile. He placed his hands in his pockets. "You wouldn't even speak to me until that day your horse tossed you in the woods, and I helped you catch the beast. You were what? Thirteen?"

Jacey nodded.

"You'd stop by and say hello after that and even had soda on my patio." His smile brightened and almost mocked her. "Yet you wouldn't enter my house until you were nearly eighteen."

She smiled with some embarrassment. "Okay, you've made your point," she announced. "I was young and still believed some of what I'd heard."

He laughed, straightened, and entered the kitchen. "Yet part of you still believes some of the stories."

She followed him into the elegant, modern kitchen with marble countertops and tile floor. "Of course not," she scoffed. She didn't know why he enjoyed tormenting her. He obviously got some sort of sick pleasure out of it.

Asher chuckled softly. "I'll believe you, if it makes you feel better."

✝

*T*he McMurray farm appeared unchanged ten years later. There were several new horses in the pasture along with Coleen's black horse and Monique's brown and white paint. The house appeared freshly painted, and there were several new plants hanging around the wraparound porch. It was a clear summer night with a bold, nearly full moon. Despite the bright barn light, the house appeared mostly dark. Eerie, dismal music could be heard within the house. Jacey, Monique, and Coleen sat on the floor in the dark living room watching a horror movie while eating large bowls of ice cream. There was the chilling sound of someone being stabbed in the movie, and it echoed throughout the room. All three cringed and moaned with disgust at the gruesome gory scene on the television.

"The boyfriend's toast," Monique chuckled.

"The boyfriend always gets killed in these movies," Coleen remarked simply.

"Speaking of boyfriends," Monique said and grinned at Jacey. "I was told you had one."

Jacey laughed softly without looking at the young girl. "*Had* is the appropriate word choice. I've tried dating a couple of times. I dated Deputy Jameson for nearly two weeks, but that's a recurring nightmare. I've concluded that horses are more understanding and less demanding. I can't seem to find attraction toward any man in this town."

"I want to marry a rancher," Monique said cheerfully. "With lots of land to ride."

"I'll only marry a guy if he can out ride me," Coleen said with a tiny laugh.

Monique looked at Jacey. "What about you? Do you have a dream man in mind?"

"I'd say a combination of your dream men put together, but I've already met him, and we didn't get along." Jacey sighed then smiled. "But he definitely needs to be a country boy, none of those stuffed and pompous city types. He should like horses and know how to ride well." Her smile brightened. "He should be strong, bold, and outgoing--rugged and manly."

The woman in the movie screamed hysterically, causing all three to jump with surprise. There was a harsh pounding on the kitchen door. All three screamed. Jacey sprang to her feet and hurried to the kitchen door. She looked through the window, groaned, then unlocked the door and opened it. Deputy Jameson Ramos, the former institution security guard, looked past her and into the kitchen with concern. He looked very handsome in his deputy uniform and official police cowboy hat.

"Are you okay? I heard screaming," Jameson announced.

Jacey smiled with some embarrassment. "We're watching a horror movie."

"I thought your parents left yesterday for their cruise," Jameson remarked then strained to look past her toward the living room.

"They did," she replied while glaring her disapproval of his curiosity. "My cousin and her friend are staying with me."

Monique and Coleen entered the kitchen with their dirty dishes but appeared more interested in the uniformed stranger. Deputy Jameson looked at them with mild relief, smiled warmly, and then focused his attention on Jacey.

"I thought I'd check on you, since your parents were gone," he informed her. "I was concerned about you being out here by yourself."

"I appreciate your concern, Jameson, but it's not necessary," she informed him with a tiny, humored laugh. "I'm old enough to take care of myself."

He smiled with embarrassment. "I know you are, Jacey, but I'm still allowed to be concerned, you know, with some of the characters living in this area."

Jacey frowned and folded her arms across her chest. "I know how to use a gun, which I have several," she informed him in a matter-of-fact tone. "There's never been any problems on our property before. And if there is trouble, Asher lives just a short ride down the road." Her words were arrogant and bitter to Jameson's insinuation obviously directed at Asher.

He looked past her at the two girls, who cleaned their dishes a little too thoroughly, indicating they were possibly listening to their conversation. He looked back at her.

"Could I speak to you a moment outside?"

Jacey sighed and followed him onto the porch. He turned to face her and shook his head while studying her.

"You know how I feel about you associating with Konrad Asher," he announced. "You were too young to understand what happened, but you have to trust me when I tell you to stay away from him. At the very least, he's insane."

Jacey cocked her head to one side. "You're a lawman, Jameson. Surely, you understand innocent until proven guilty. They've never been able to prove Asher murdered his wife."

"I know they haven't," he replied. "I never believed he killed his wife, but I do, however, believe he killed Hal Burgess."

"I don't know how you can assume there was a killing. They never found the guy--dead or alive." Her brows raised. "Or do you think he ate him too?"

Jameson sighed and shook his head. "I've known Asher for a long time. He's very intelligent and rather tricky. And since his wife died, I'd say he's very dangerous."

"I'll keep that in mind," she muttered with disinterest. "Thanks for stopping by, Jameson, but I'd better get back to the movie before I miss the ending."

"I'll talk to you tomorrow," he said with a tone of defeat.

Jacey entered the kitchen and saw both girls straining to look out the window by the sink as the police blazer drove away from the house and up the long, dirt driveway. Monique and Coleen spun to face Jacey with matching grins.

"It would seem the deputy is still an interested party where you're concerned," Monique said with a giggle.

"He's kind of cute too," Coleen added.

"Smothering and possessive would be the description I'd choose," Jacey replied. "In the two weeks we'd dated, he was here four times a day while on duty, and then he'd spend the entire evening here. I couldn't make a move without his knowing about it, and there were constant questions if I happened to slip out of his sight."

"Too bad," Coleen said. "I think it'd be cool to date a country cop. They all look so handsome wearing those gun belts and cowboy hats."

Jacey laughed and shook her head. "Yeah, that's probably the reason I went out with him too."

Chapter Seven

$\mathcal{T}$he rain poured down over the small town. It was a little before noon when Jacey and the two girls ran into the quaint little diner. They stopped just inside to remove their soaking wet jackets. The waitress, Tiffany, approached them by the coat rack.

"Afternoon, Jacey," Tiffany said cheerfully. "Bit dreary out today."

Jacey moaned and forced a tiny smile. "Hasn't stopped since late last night," she replied to the waitress.

"I just hope we have good weather for the town fair. Hot cocoa?" Tiffany asked.

All three nodded then sat down at an empty booth. The diner was particularly busy that afternoon. It was always its busiest on rainy days. The diner seemed to turn into a social gathering for farmers and housewives when it rained. The waitress was prompt with their hot chocolate despite the small crowd. Jacey stared out the window at the heavy rain and shook her head.

"I guess we were due for some rain," she announced with a defeated sigh.

"No riding today," Coleen muttered with a frown.

Jill Sutten, now in her late thirties, approached their table appearing cheerful. The last ten years had taken their toll on Jill. She almost looked older than she was, but there had been rumors that she took up drinking as a hobby after the death of her brother. Jacey never understood Jill's relationship with her brother. From what she heard, her brother had been committed before he even reached puberty. Her family moved to town when her brother was transferred to the infamous institution. By all accounts, her brother was a known threat to himself and others.

"Good morning, Jacey," Jill said with a pleasant smile and looked at the two girls. "These young ladies must be your houseguests."

Jacey wondered how Jill knew she even had houseguests. The gossip grapevine was faster than the internet in Stony Ridge. She introduced both girls to Jill, who appeared pleasant but promptly returned her attention to Jacey. Her expression became serious with a look of desperation. She extended a folded paper.

"Would you sign this petition to stop them from reopening the institution?" Jill asked.

Jacey eyed her skeptically. "I don't think that'll matter at this point. The building's already been sold and renovations are mostly complete."

Jill frowned with apparent disgust. "That place must never be opened again. It's cursed," she insisted. "If they open it, more people will die."

Jacey rolled her eyes and looked away a moment. Monique and Coleen looked at each other with apparent doubt to the woman's sanity. Jill was becoming more paranoid with each passing year. She often spoke of curses. Jacey looked at the paper briefly and noted the signatures on it. She looked back at Jill and returned the paper unsigned.

"I heard there's a group of scientists moving into the old institution," Jacey announced with a tiny smile. "They'll be studying the stars, fossils, and other scientific areas. The main building is going to be made into a museum with archaeological finds, dinosaur bones, and educational displays."

"They're going to do experiments on animals, make chemicals that could harm our town, pollute our water, and kill organic life," Jill insisted. "No good will ever come from that place. It should be torn down and made into a park to remember those who'd died there."

Jacey raised her brow. "A park behind the town cemetery? Hardly. Besides, we already have a big park just three blocks down the road."

"Do you approve of animal research, Jacey?" Jill demanded to know. "If your father was alive today, he'd be helping to fight this atrocity."

Jacey inhaled deeply then leaned toward the woman. "If my father was alive today, he'd tell you just what I'm about to tell you. The new institution will be highly educational and profitable for both the town and future generations. There will be no chemicals to speak of and certainly no experiments on animals. There'll just be old fossils and a huge telescope sticking out the top of the building, which I assure you won't transmit radiation or signal alien attackers. The building isn't and never was cursed."

Jill appeared annoyed. She huffed, snatched the paper, and glared at Jacey. "I should've expected that from a friend of *his*," she hissed as her temper quickly rose. "You just wait and see. When more people die, you'll be just as responsible as the others who allowed them to open that place."

All three watched Jill storm across the diner and to a small table with four other women. The five women were the town's busybodies, known for causing trouble. They were also partially responsible for the town's attitude toward Asher. If it were up to them, Asher would've been lynched from the tallest tree in Town Square.

"She's a bit eccentric," Monique said under her breath.

Jacey shook her head and sighed. "Her brother died in the institution fire ten years ago. She couldn't find anyone to hold accountable, not for lack of trying. Now she's blaming some curse for the trouble there. If you ask me, she's more insane than her brother ever was."

"So we see," Coleen replied dryly.

Tiffany approached their table with a tiny smile on her face. "You could've saved yourself her wraith had you just signed her stupid paper," she remarked. "Half the people who signed it just wanted to get her away from them. It's not going to matter anyway."

"I'm sure it won't, but I don't want anyone to think I support that rubbish."

"It's always entertaining to watch a confrontation with Jill," Tiffany giggled. "She's pretty amusing when she starts with that curse stuff."

"Unfortunately, there are many people in this town who are crazy enough to believe her," Jacey replied.

"This town never was high on intelligence," Tiffany said. "They'll believe just about anything."

She took their lunch order then left the table. Jacey glanced around the crowded diner. She saw Roseanne Pierce, now in her mid-thirties, approach the crowded counter. Roseanne wore a conservative nurse's scrub uniform with cartoon animals on her scrub top. She had been working the last nine years as Dr. Talbert's nurse. Dr. Talbert was now the town's general practitioner. He had an excellent practice since the institution closed. Derek Falcone, the diner's short-order cook, approached Roseanne and appeared cheerful.

"Here for your take-out?" he said a little too cheerfully. He was obviously smitten with the still beautiful nurse.

Roseanne returned the smile with less interest in him despite his attractiveness. "Yeah, I'm here for Dr. Talbert's usual."

"Liverwurst," Derek remarked with a look of distaste. "I don't know how he can eat that stuff every day." His smile broadened. "I'll get your order. Give me a minute."

Roseanne nodded and looked around the crowded diner. Her eyes suddenly rolled back. Jill was standing directly in front of her with her petition clutched firmly in hand.

"Hey, Rosy," Jill announced with a smirk chiseled on her face. "I'm trying to get a petition passed against the reopening of--"

"I know what you're peddling," Roseanne suddenly snapped with hatred in her eyes. "Get away from me with that paper!"

Several patrons suddenly turned and looked at Roseanne, having heard her raised voice. Jill looked stunned by the hostility.

"But you don't even--"

"I don't care," Roseanne retorted. "You and your little petitions nearly cost me my livelihood. I lost my job when you and your cronies petitioned to have the institution shutdown. I was lucky enough to become Dr. Talbert's nurse, but some of my friends weren't so lucky. It's because of you they all moved away to find work. So you just stay the hell away from me."

Derek approached the inside counter with Roseanne's take-out bag and eyed Jill sternly.

"I think you'd better go back to your table and mind your own business, Jill," Derek informed her. "This is a diner; not your personal forum."

Jill sneered at Derek and returned to her table. Roseanne frowned and shook her head.

"I'm sorry, Derek," she said softly while running trembling fingers through her hair. "That woman just brings out the worst in me."

"You and everyone else," Derek chuckled. "Don't worry about it."

Roseanne smiled her appreciation, paid for her lunch, and left the diner. Derek stared after her until she was gone. Jacey glanced at Monique and Coleen and held her breath.

"Tensions are certainly high today," Jacey muttered.

"I'm surprised someone hasn't whacked Jill," Monique casually remarked and immediately received stares from Jacey and Coleen. She saw them staring at her and apparently realized she'd spoken aloud. She smiled with embarrassment. "Sorry, I've read one too many detective novels."

The door to the diner opened and several men in suits and trench coats entered. Several heads turned to watch them, indicating they were strangers. Jacey followed tradition and looked as well. They hung up their wet trench coats, proceeded past her table, and took a larger table near the back. There were five men and one woman all dressed for business. Tiffany scurried to their table with typical curiosity on her mind. Most strangers came to their town purely by accident. The five gossiping biddies were only two tables away, stretching their necks to have a look at the newcomers. Their lack of discretion was almost humorous.

"Plenty of interest in that group, huh, Jacey?" Coleen said with less interest now. "They look like a bunch of pompous scientists to me."

Jacey nodded then minded her cocoa. "Might be just that," she replied.

"Not a bad looking bunch," Monique remarked while sipping her hot chocolate. She purposely left the whipped cream on her upper lip and tried to make Coleen laugh.

Coleen rolled her eyes at her friend's warped sense of humor. "The waitress seems to think so too," Coleen added and watched Tiffany flirt with the men.

Jacey felt compelled to look in the direction of the table full of strangers. Tiffany was using her standard body language on a particularly handsome man with a clean-cut, youthful face. He had a modern haircut, which was short on the sides and slightly longer on top with stray locks falling into bangs. Jacey had to admit he *was* handsome. She had a sneaky suspicion about handsome men. Too often, they knew they were handsome and reeked of arrogance. Jacey now felt compelled to scan the other four men and woman. The woman was rather serious looking and refined adding an odd sort of attractiveness about her. She wore her nearly black hair back in a bun. Her lips were red and pinched in an almost prudish manner. She was more than likely stuck on herself. There was a definite class about the woman, which almost made Jacey envious. She was undoubtedly respected, which was something Jacey couldn't seem to achieve but desperately sought. Men seemed to come on hard then react defensively when she'd turn them down. It appeared some thought country girls were easily had.

One of the other men was in his fifties. He was distinguished looking with gray hair, a gray beard, and a pleasant smile. He appeared to be the typical grandfather type. There was a heavyset man with slightly longer hair. He appeared pleasant and smiled most of the time. He also did most of the talking and was rather loud. Another man was thin, tall, and lanky with light brown hair. He appeared fairly serious. He seemed to order something Tiffany couldn't comprehend. The last man wore black rimmed glasses that screamed computer nerd while he read the menu. He had short, dark hair and the darkest eyes she'd ever seen. When Tiffany spoke to him, he appeared shy and barely made eye contact. He removed his glasses and spoke to the prissy woman beside him. Before Jacey could mind her own business, the handsome first man caught her gaze. She forced a tiny, embarrassed smile then looked back at Monique and Coleen.

"So what would you like to do today since riding is out?" Jacey asked curiously.

The table with the six scientists became slightly loud with laughter, mostly caused by the heavyset man. Most of the locals stared at them and talk quietly. The rumor mill would be working overtime tonight.

"I want to tour the institution," Monique chirped.

"You what?" Jacey asked with some surprise.

"Yeah, let's check it out," Coleen agreed. "It's kind of like a historical site--rich with culture and scandal."

"They don't give tours," Jacey informed them firmly.

"Oh, come on," Monique whined. "Surely you know someone who could get us in. You said you were going to do a story for the paper."

"Yeah," Coleen jumped in. "If those are the scientists, you could arrange to do an interview or something."

"Okay," Jacey said with a sigh. "After we eat, I'll go over there and introduce myself. I'll see if they're who I think they are and see about an interview, but you can't possibly expect that to happen today."

Before their food arrived, the handsome man of the strangers, Brian Murdock, approached their table. He smiled charmingly at Jacey.

"Excuse me, but I'm sure I know you from somewhere," he said with conviction.

Jacey stared at him with astonishment. How stupid did he think she was? She then forced a tiny smile and decided to play along for the sake of the girls and the article.

"I don't believe we've met before. I never forget a face," Jacey announced.

He laughed softly. "Perhaps it was in one of my fondest dreams," Brian said warmly and perfectly timed his charming grin. "I've been searching for you my entire life."

Jacey couldn't believe the old pickup lines he was using. She thought she at least deserve some fresh lines. She held back her laughter, though her smile mocked him.

"How interesting," she replied and was unsure if she was more humored or insulted by the pickup line.

"It's destiny that brought us here together," he continued with a warm smile.

Monique and Coleen giggled softly. Obviously, they read him loud and clear also. If he couldn't fool teenage girls with his bad pickup lines, how did he ever expect her to fall for them? Again, she continued to play along. She was actually starting to enjoy this game they were playing. It seemed inconceivable that he was a scientist. He didn't sound very intelligent. Maybe he was so smart; he didn't think some simple, country girl could comprehend his game.

"Maybe it is," Jacey announced simply, throwing it back at him. "You wouldn't happen to be one of the scientists moving into the old institution, would you?" she asked.

He appeared surprised, though he wouldn't if he'd lived in their town. Everyone knew everyone else's business. Almost everyone within the diner knew who they were the moment they walked through the door, even if they were a week early.

"Yes," he replied more naturally. "We just arrived in town last night." His sincerity was immediately replaced with his failed attempt at charm. "Ironic that we should meet the very moment I enter town. You must see it too."

Jacey normally would've laughed and walked away by this point, but she had a mission in mind and two teenage girls to entertain on a rainy, dreary day.

"Yes, I do," she replied in all seriousness and added a slightly dreamy smile to lure him into her web. "Actually, I've been waiting for your arrival."

The man was again surprised then smiled with arrogance. "You have?"

"Yes," she replied in her best sexy tone then immediately turned professional on him. "I'm a journalist with our local paper. I'd like to come to the institution today, if it's convenient for you and your colleagues, and conduct an interview on your current and future projects. It's also been about ten years since anyone's set foot inside the old building. I'd love to have a look around and see what changes have been made."

Brian was completely astonished. Jacey was beginning to think she had him almost convinced it was destiny that brought them together.

"Talk about fate," he said with conviction in his tone. "I'm sure Dr. Zellner wouldn't mind. In fact, he'd welcome any good publicity connected to the institution."

"It's going to be a story to help put the fears of the town aside," she informed him. "This town has a tendency to be very narrow-minded."

"So I've heard," he replied with a genuine smile. "We'd appreciate some positive response on our research. Public relation is very important in these small towns. When will you be dropping by?"

"Would this afternoon be okay?" she asked with some apprehension.

"It'll be a bit cluttered. We haven't really had a chance to go through a lot of things, but today will work just fine," he said with a soft laugh then extended his hand. "I'm Brian Murdock."

"Jacey McMurray."

"Are these your sisters?" he asked and looked at both girls seated in the booth.

He had to know they weren't. She laughed softly and marveled at this man. He missed his calling selling snake oil. "My cousin, Monique, and her friend, Coleen."

He nodded politely to both of them.

Chapter Eight

$\mathcal{T}$he local newspaper press was barely two rooms attached onto the pharmacy next door. Monique and Coleen poked around the old-fashioned press while Jacey talked to the blonde woman, Shelly, by the counter. The business was still run as it had been for decades and the old press was still used on occasion, although Shelly, the owner's daughter, was slowly transferring the press into the digital age. Jacey looked at the moderately large digital camera then to Shelly and frowned.

"I'm not sure about taking my own photos," Jacey informed the woman. "You should see the photos I took last Christmas. I couldn't tell the tree from my mother."

Monique sprang forward eagerly and grinned. "I can take pictures. I'm an excellent photographer."

Coleen nodded. "She takes great pictures of our horses."

"I really want some pictures of the inside of the institution," Shelly said. "No one's been inside for ten years. I'm sure seeing it will change some opinions, once they see there aren't any ghosts or demons."

Jacey jotted some notes on her tablet then sighed. "Should I interview the man in charge or all six?"

"All six, if possible," Shelly replied. "Have them tell you what their special area is and what they'll be contributing to the foundation on a whole." Shelly's look was serious. "Make sure there's a positive side to benefit the town."

Jacey nodded and checked the small tape recorder. "I'm not used to interviews with actual people. I hope I don't stumble over myself."

"You can't write about the collapse of old mines all your life, Jacey," Shelly said firmly. "You have to graduate to actual people eventually. I'm getting tired of the same old interviews from Brenda." Shelly's eyes suddenly strayed to the front of the press as the door opened. Her smile faded. "Speaking of the she-devil--"

Jacey glanced toward the front of the press. An attractive woman in her late twenties with raven black hair and milky skin entered the press. She had a flawless figure with proudly displayed cleavage that screamed 'squeeze me'. It's not as if Jacey and Brenda were rivals in the sense that they liked the same men, they were just rivals over top stories for the paper. Jacey's stories almost always played second fiddle to Brenda's stories. Of course Brenda's stories were better; there was usually a lot of pillow talk involved in her interviews.

Shelly pat Jacey on the back. "Good luck. I won't tell her about the scientists arriving early, but she's bound to find out on her own pretty fast, so get your article to me as soon as possible."

Jacey nodded but wasn't sure she liked the added pressure. As they turned to leave, Brenda smirked at Jacey and gave her the standard, disinterested nod. She obviously felt she was above Jacey, and Jacey was pretty sure she was right.

"Soliciting another article about the mayor's garden?" Brenda mocked with a twisted smile on her nearly perfect face.

Jacey found dealing with Brenda exhausting. She smirked without comment and ushered both girls from the press. She didn't want to admit how much she hated Brenda, because she refused to believe she hated anyone, but there were days she wanted pluck every black hair from her head. Judging by the looks she received from both girls, they were silently wondering why she didn't do just that. Truth was, Jacey could have a headline article that would stun and shock the town while shutting Brenda's mouth once and for all, but she wasn't about to act on it. Asher had offered to do an interview with Jacey to further her career, but she refused to print anything about him that would stir more controversy and cause problems for him. It was generous of him, but she couldn't do that to him. If the town knew her true relationship to Asher, they'd be shocked. The three left the press with the professional looking camera. Jacey could see several people standing on their porches, gawking at the scientists leaving the diner. She immediately wondered if Brenda had noticed or not. Of course, she noticed. How could she not notice? The scientists piled into a white, luxury van. It was still raining quite heavily, but that didn't stop the nosy townspeople from standing around and gossiping.

"What does this town do for fun?" Coleen asked. "Watch paint peel?"

"Oh, no," Jacey said cheerfully. "Their main objective is to persecute the innocent, ridicule the weak, and condemn those who dare think differently."

Monique aimed the camera at two older women on their porch, staring intensely at the van as it pulled away from the diner. She snapped a picture. The older women appeared to notice their picture being taken.

Monique grinned proudly. "I'll call that one 'portrait of a busybody'," she said loud enough for the women to hear.

Both women huffed and went inside the house. The door slammed shut.

"Stop that," Jacey scolded then secretly smiled.

†

The mayor's office was nestled in the corner of the top floor of Town Hall. The town had come a long way since the days of mayor being an unpaid position taken by locals who held other full-time jobs. Ten years ago, Mayor Bradford used the conference room to conduct any official business, of which there was very little. The new mayor's office, renovated nearly a decade ago for the new mayor, was as old as the building itself but had a regal appeal to it. The large, old-fashioned desk was elegant and possibly antique with sculpted edges and fancy legs. Howard Norad sat behind his desk in the large, leather chair and rubbed his sore temple while holding the phone to his ear. When the position of mayor became a full-time paid position, Howard leapt at the opportunity to secure it. With the shutdown of the fire riddled mental institution, Howard needed a new position to command.

"I know you're concerned," he muttered into the phone. "But the institution opening is completely out of our hands." He became silent then groaned and sat back in his plush chair. "That's impossible, it can't be done," he said and sat forward while quickly losing patience with the caller. "I've had fifty phone calls today from our citizens. All of them want the institution plowed to the ground.

My personal thoughts are of no importance here. There's nothing I can do about it. I've fought, I've begged, and I've even groveled, but there's nothing more I can do." He groaned and listened while rolling his eyes. "Okay, okay. I understand your point."

There was a knock on the door and the secretary entered. She leaned on the doorknob. He looked at her, rolled his eyes, pointed to the phone, and shook his head.

"If you have another idea, I'd be more than willing to hear you out." The mayor was silent. His brow raised sharply, and he eyed his secretary. "No, that's not a good idea. You'd better think of something else. Listen, I have to go," he announced firmly. "There's a meeting I need to attend." He was finally able to put down the phone. He allowed his head to drop to the desk then lifted it with a groan. "No more phone calls on the institution subject. I can't handle anymore."

The secretary smiled sympathetically. Howard motioned for her to come to him with both hands and a warm, inviting smile. Her smile faded into something resembling a sneer.

"Your wife is here with Jill Sutten," she said firmly.

Howard's head once more dropped to the desk. "No, not Jill," he moaned. "Tell them I'm dead."

"I told your wife that the last time," she replied dryly. "She didn't believe me." Her eyes swept over him as he straightened and rubbed his eyes. "You said you were going to divorce her."

"Soon, darling," he said with a moan. "One crisis at a time, please."

The secretary gave him a cold glare then left the office. A few minutes had passed before a stocky woman entered Howard's office with Jill.

"Damn it, Howard," his stocky wife lurched. "I want that institution shut down--today!"

He smiled wryly and barely attempted to humor her. "Honey, I can't shut the place down. It's out of my hands," he insisted. "Don't you think I've tried?"

"You'd better try harder! They're going to do experiments on animals," she complained. "I have it on good authority. Shut it down!"

†

*J*acey's jeep drove through the gates to the institution just beyond the cemetery. All three stared at the headstones as they passed. Jacey looked at the recently mowed lawn. There were tall weeds near the fence that needed tending and the hedges were in need of trimming, but it looked better than it had in years. Both girls looked out the window with great interest and awe. The Stony Ridge Institution was just as impressive as it had been before the fire-- and twice as creepy. Jacey inhaled deeply with some apprehension.

Coleen looked at Jacey. "You aren't nervous about the interview, are you?"

Jacey slowly shook her head and stared at the institution ahead of them. "No, not the interview," she replied. "I suppose I'm a little skeptical about setting foot inside. All those years and having heard all the stories; it's like entering a haunted house."

"Yeah, cool, isn't it?" Monique said excitedly.

Jacey looked at her young cousin then smiled with a feeling of relief. "You're right," she replied. "It's an amazing opportunity, and it'll be exciting to be one of the first locals to see the place in ten years."

The rain continued to pour, giving the institution an even more eerie presence. Jacey's jeep pulled up to the front doors just alongside the familiar white van. They hurried from the jeep and ran through the pouring rain to the large, stone porch before the double doors. The building itself was elegant in design with its fancy porch and sculptures, though they were in desperate need of a scrubbing. Jacey knocked on the double doors and waited several minutes before the door was opened by Brian and the heavyset scientist, Timon Bennet.

"Glad you could make it," Brian announced while retaining his charming smile. "Come inside."

All three entered the large foyer just before the spacious solarium. Brian shut the door and turned to face them. "This is Dr. Timon Bennet," Brian announced pleasantly. "Timon has a PhD in Astrophysics, same as me. Timon, this is Jacey McMurray."

Timon extended his hand to Jacey. "Timon," he announced with a pleasant smile.

Jacey shook his hand. He then looked at both the girls and appeared enthusiastic.

"And you two young ladies must be Monique and Coleen," Timon said with a daring smile. He shook their hands suavely. He tilted Monique's hand and examined her braided bracelet. "Hey, cool bracelet. What's it made from?"

Monique giggled. "My horse's tail. I made it myself."

"The others are in the lab in the back of the building," Brian announced. "It's such a large place, we barely heard you knock."

"I still can't find my way around," Timon announced with a soft chuckle. "I wanted to try leaving breadcrumbs, but I still haven't found the kitchen." He then grinned and raised his brows. "Of course, we have rats the size of dogs, so breadcrumbs would probably be counterproductive."

Both girls smiled at him. Timon was the typical comedian type.

Jacey grimaced and looked around. "I'm not a fan of rats."

"Ah, don't worry about the rats," Timon said cheerfully. "The snakes are keeping them under control."

Monique and Coleen suddenly looked around the floor as well. Timon laughed heartily, startling all three. Brian rolled his eyes then led the way along the large hallway. Jacey walked more slowly and studied the walls and floor. She felt a little uneasy. The building was almost mansion-like. It was truly elegant and rich. The tables were antique and old paintings lined the walls. There was a library, dining room, and several offices. They passed an old, sculpted elevator. Timon pointed out that the elevator didn't work, like most things in the institution. They entered a large room in the back, which was one of two ballrooms now converted into a sprawling lab. There were rows of tables with fossils and various other finds lying about. Some, oddly enough, just looked like piles of dirt.

Brian fell back and walked alongside Jacey. He casually placed an arm over her shoulder. "Timon and I study the stars. Our observatory is upstairs in the attic. It's far from being finished, but we do have our planetarium erected."

"Yours always is," Timon muttered softly.

Both girls looked at him and appeared slightly puzzled. He gently cleared his throat and appeared to estimate the age of his audience. He quickly fumbled for something more appropriate to say.

"The telescope won't be along for several weeks," Timon added and turned his head to look back at Jacey. "Wait until you see the size of that baby." He laughed in his throat. "The monster of all telescopes. We'll be the envy of every nerd this side of the Rio Grande."

The other four scientists were at their respective workstations, looking through microscopes and documenting their discoveries. The gray-haired man, Dr. Zellner, looked in their direction, smiled brightly, and stood.

"Ms. McMurray," he announced pleasantly and approached her with hands extended. He grasped her hand with both of his. "It's a pleasure to meet you. I'm Dr. Zellner, but you can call me Doc. Brian mentioned you'd be here for an interview. I'm so glad you could make it." He then released her hand and looked at both girls. "And who are these young ladies?"

Jacey introduced Monique and Coleen. They exchanged pleasantries. Doc was even more pleasant than Jacey had imagined. Doc linked Jacey's arm onto his and guided her toward the other three. They paused near the tall, lanky man.

"This is Dr. Ted Fuller," Doc announced proudly. "He has a PhD in Paleontology. We stole him from a very prestigious college."

"Everyone calls me Professor," Professor said with a warm smile and shook their hands. He seemed a bit fidgety and awkward to say the least.

Doc then led them toward the sole woman on their team. For some strange reason, Jacey was interested in meeting this woman. She struck Jacey as being mysterious, and she wanted to know more about her.

"This is Dr. Angela Cimarron," Doc continued. "She has a PhD in Palaeobiology."

The black-haired woman forced a tiny smile and barely shook their hands. She appeared to eye Jacey with some secret loath. Jacey felt uneasy around the woman almost immediately. So much for the intrigue of the mysterious woman. Monique and Coleen seemed to sense the woman's lack of interest as well. They both ignored her and talked between themselves over one of the fossils on the table before them. Doc then guided them toward the strange man with the dark eyes. He wore a white lab coat and looked the part of a nerdy scientist, although now without the glasses. "And this is Dr. Maxwell Alvord," Doc announced proudly with a broad smile. "He also has a PhD in Paleontology. He's just had his third book published on ancient artifacts and archaeological finds."

Dr. Alvord appeared slightly awkward and shy as he shook Jacey's hand. "It's a pleasure, Ms. McMurray," he said in a refined, British accent.

Jacey was slightly surprised by the accent. She'd never met a real Englishman before. Stony Ridge didn't see many foreigners. She looked into his dark eyes and felt herself smile helplessly. He had a refined style about him. It was almost superior without seeming arrogant. She slowly pulled her hand away from his but didn't take her eyes from him. His smile was warm and almost boyish. Without the nerdy glasses, he was rather handsome. Maxwell then shook Monique and Coleen's hands in a polite gesture.

"I assume you'd like to start with a tour," Doc announced cheerfully.

Jacey slipped back into reality and looked at Doc with an embarrassed smile. Monique and Coleen were about ready to bubble over with glee.

"Yes, we'd love to have a look around," Jacey announced, almost sharing the girls' enthusiasm. "I've never been inside the institution before."

He patted her hand on his arm. "I'd be more than happy to answer all your questions. We really would like the support of the town. I've felt the tension from the moment we arrived, and I'd like to dismiss their fears."

"Just ignorance, but I'd like the chance to rectify that," Jacey replied.

"I'm glad to hear," Doc said with a sigh. "I've received much hate mail and even some death threats from this town. I was tempted to discontinue our project here, but the school administration persuaded me to proceed." He forced a tiny laugh. "You'd think we're making monsters in the basement or something." He laughed at himself then smiled. "We won't be discouraged, but we would prefer the support."

Jacey managed to smile warmly. "On behalf of the sane people in town, I'd like to apologize for what you've been put through. It sounds much worse than it is," she informed him. "Your biggest problem is a small handful of townspeople led by a spiteful woman with too much time on her hands. The others are just easily swayed."

"And you're going to set them straight, I trust," Doc chirped.

Jacey laughed softly. "I hope so," she replied. "A few good articles, some public relations, and they'll be cheering for the benefits to our town."

"Great. Then we'll start our tour right here," Doc announced cheerfully.

Brian was directly behind them and had apparently been following them the entire way. He placed a hand on Doc's shoulder. "You're busy, Doc," Brian said with a bold smile. "I'll show the ladies around."

"I'm not busy," Timon chirped and stepped forward with a bright smile as his eyes swept over Jacey. "I'd be more than happy to show them around."

Doc clung to Jacey's arm and lifted his head proudly. "My building; my interview; my young ladies."

Doc led Jacey from the lab and talked the entire way. Monique and Coleen hurried after them.

Chapter Nine

*T*he interior of the institution was the same as it had been
nearly ten years ago. Most of the furnishings were the same with the
exception of the lab and the attic, now turned into a planetarium.
The west wing still contained all its patients' beds and electronic
locking doors. The building had been sold with everything intact.
None of the furniture was removed in the hopes that the doors would
again be opened, but that never happened. Doc omitted the
basement from the tour, claiming it was dirty, cluttered, and a maze
of rooms filled with old mattresses and boxes of useless items. They
would eventually be sold at an auction to be held later in the month.
Doc told Jacey in great detail about their research and their plans for
the future of the lab. He explained how it would benefit the town
with culture, knowledge, and a large telescope to enlighten children.
It all sounded wonderful, though Jacey wondered if there was
something he neglected to mention. Doc told her about his life, his
work, and his life goals. He was a very intelligent man with much
greatness and many degrees attached to his name.

Monique took many pictures while they toured. The institution
no longer appeared frightening to Jacey. Even the tour of the west
wing didn't bother her. They finally returned to the lab. Monique
took pictures of the other five scientists while Coleen helped pose
them for quality photos. Jacey found the girls' professionalism slightly
amusing. Brian volunteered as the first to be interviewed. Since it

was obvious he wasn't leaving her side, Jacey accepted his offer. Brian explained many aspects of astrophysics and told her what he'd be doing for the good of the team. After only ten minutes, he swiftly changed the subject to his personal life.

"I'm twenty-nine and single," he added with a smile. "I also have other interests beyond just stars and nebulas. In fact, I love dancing and going to nightclubs. Maybe you'd be interested in showing me some areas of interest. I could pick you up at your house tonight around seven for dinner," Brian announced and warmly took her hand in his.

Jacey smiled with some embarrassment and slowly pulled her hand away. "That sounds very nice, Brian, but I'm afraid I have a prior commitment with Monique and Coleen. I wouldn't feel right leaving them alone."

Brain looked at the two girls who giggled at something Professor showed them on one of the tables. He looked back at Jacey and smiled daringly.

"You can leave them here," he informed her with a little too much charm. "Doc loves kids, and Professor will educate them. It'll be like summer school."

Despite his pleasant smile, Jacey still thought Brain was a womanizer. She didn't particularly trust him after their first meeting. A date with him just sounded all too exhausting.

"I don't know," she said with some apprehension. "They are my responsibility the entire week."

Monique and Coleen ran toward Jacey and Brian with a look of excitement on their faces.

"Professor's going to show us the padded cell on the third floor on the west wing," Monique announced with morbid enthusiasm. "Can we go?"

Jacey smiled wryly. "How exciting," she said with distaste. "Sure. Have fun."

Brain stopped them. "How would you ladies like to spend the evening with Professor and Doc? They could show you some really fun things."

Professor approached and eyed Brian skeptically. Jacey looked at Professor and appeared sympathetic. She knew what Brian was up too. She was certain Professor knew it too.

"I don't want to trouble you, Professor," she said gently.

"No trouble at all," he replied then looked at both girls with a smile. "We have access to the large movie screen in the west wing. We could watch some classic horror movies I brought along then scare Dr. Alvord half to death afterwards."

Both girls looked at Jacey for approval.

"Could we, Jacey?" Monique begged.

"We'd love to explore the institution some more," Coleen added. "It'll be really creepy at night."

Jacey smiled with a look of defeat and sighed. "Sure," she said. Of course, it also meant she would be going on a date tonight with the overtly charming Brian.

"That's great," Professor said cheerfully. "We'll have pizza delivered, if they'll deliver it here. My treat."

"I'll pick you up around eleven," Jacey informed the girls.

"Uh, midnight," Brian said to Professor with a cheap grin on his handsome face.

Professor managed a smirk, nodded, and then led the girls from the room. Brian looked back at Jacey and placed a hand on her shoulder.

"Problem solved. That was easy enough," he said and gently rubbed her shoulder. "Where can I pick you up?"

Jacey was already uncomfortable with his frequent touching and wondered if it'd be an evening of prying him off her. "It'd be easier if I just met you here after I've changed," she replied with a tiny smile. "My house is hard to find even when you know where you're going."

She also didn't need him picking her up and dropping her off at her secluded home when there was no one around. That would be an indecent proposal waiting to happen.

"Okay," he replied. "I'll look for you around seven. And don't worry about the girls; Professor is great with kids." His eyes swept over her again. "See you later."

Brian kissed her quickly on the lips, nearly startling her. He then darted away before she'd even realized what had happened. Jacey collected herself and nervously ran her fingers through her hair. When she looked up, she noticed that the others were staring at her. She felt her cheeks immediately redden. Timon sat on the table near her and grinned.

"Looks like Brian, the kissing bandit, strikes again," he said and laughed loudly. "You still want to interview the rest of us, don't you?"

Jacey gently cleared her throat. "Uh, yes, I do."

Timon proceeded to tell her about his education, degrees, and special achievements. It was unnecessary for her to ask any questions, since he answered everything without being asked. He was a very interesting man, though he didn't look much like a scientist. He still had a comedian appeal about him. Jacey couldn't help but wonder if he was as much fun to work with as he appeared. Jacey found herself laughing at most of what he said. He liked to poke fun at himself and his own intelligence. Despite his outgoing nature, he was well-mannered and seemed very respectful toward her. Once he had finished, his smile brightened and he nodded toward the door from the lab.

"Are you going out with Brain?" he asked inquisitively.

Jacey felt her cheeks redden and forced a tiny smile. "Uh, yes, I suppose I am."

Timon nodded with a look of defeat. "I thought so," he replied simply. "Brian doesn't waste any time when it comes to attractive women." His eyes met hers, and he smiled in a knowing sort of way. "He gets around."

Jacey starred at Timon a long moment. Neither said a word. She then understood what he was telling her in that last sentence. He must have thought he was telling her something she didn't already know. She knew the sort of man Brian was. She'd met plenty of guys like him in her limited dating career.

Timon smiled with sincerity and shrugged. "Just thought you'd like to know."

"I appreciate your concern, Timon," she replied with a knowing smile. "But I'm not easily seduced by a handsome face and witless charm."

Timon's eyes brightened as he laughed heartily and slid off the table. "Witless charm! I love it! Enjoy your date," he announced and continued to chuckle. "I'm sure Brian will be in for a real eye-opener." He continued to laugh as he walked away.

Jacey wished now, more than ever, that she could get out of her date. She approached Angela next to interview her. Angela wasn't very interested in talking to her, so the interview was very quick and impersonal. Jacey didn't really mind either. Angela had a very casual way of making her feel small and insignificant. Angela told of her prestigious achievements with an amazingly unique, snobbish appeal. She also flaunted the fact that she was top in her field. Jacey never even went to college. Once the interview had concluded, Angela approached Dr. Alvord and clung to his arm. She spoke quietly to him and laughed softly. Dr. Alvord smiled warmly. Angela nodded toward Jacey then released his arm. Jacey pretended to jot something down in her notebook and avoided looking at them. They were obviously talking about her. She could see where this next interview was going to go. Dr. Alvord approached her and casually sat on the table across from her. He shifted uncomfortably and managed a smile.

Jacey remained leaning against the opposite table. "Nice woman, that Angela," Jacey said politely though she intended it to be sarcastic. She almost wished she hadn't commented at all. She wasn't going to win any points by insulting the woman to her boyfriend.

"Yes," Dr. Alvord said with a tiny smile.

Jacey had to ask the questions directly. It took him several minutes to become comfortable enough to talk freely. Once he started, he told her about his work in great detail. Most of what he said was so technical and above her, she could do little more than nod and smile. She felt insignificant to his superior knowledge and accomplishments. When it came to his personal life, he hesitated and once more became uncomfortable.

"There's, uh, not much to tell, really," he announced and shifted. "I pretty much keep busy with research."

Jacey couldn't help but wonder if he really was a snob, or if he was just so smart that he didn't know how to relate. When it came to his personal life, he was incredibly shy.

"No hobbies? Wife? Children?"

He then laughed softly and looked down with an innocent smile. "No--to all of the above. My work keeps me extremely busy." He then looked up and their eyes met.

Jacey stared at him in silence, as if reading what lie beyond his dark eyes. She found herself wondering what sort of relationship he had with Angela. She had to admit, he looked almost sexy in his white lab coat, neatly pressed shirt, tie, and brown pleated pants. Dr. Alvord again shifted and both looked away.

"Would you mind if I asked you a couple of questions, Ms. McMurray?" he asked and looked at her.

Jacey straightened and smiled. "Please, call me Jacey. This town's not very formal."

He sat forward with a puzzled look. "What has this town so upset about our presence? Why would Doc receive death threats, or any threats for that matter? I'm afraid I don't understand."

Jacey inhaled nervously. "Well, Dr. Alvord--"

"Please, call me Maxwell." He smiled timidly. "We're not formal either."

Jacey blushed with embarrassment. "Okay, Maxwell," she replied warmly then became serious. "Certainly you'd heard what happened here ten years ago--with the fire."

"Yes, I did some research on the institution after Doc announced our transfer here," he informed her in his sexy, British accent. "The east wing burned to the ground and killed twenty-five patients, two nurses, and one guard, I believe."

"Yes, that was the article from the city paper, but the articles from our paper told more about the people in town who had loved ones in the fire," she informed him. "There were also rumors that one of the patients had set the fire to create chaos while he escaped. But the story didn't end there."

He tilted his head with great interest.

"The same patient had brutally murdered one of the nurses and escaped in an orderly's uniform. Four more townspeople were murdered in the days that followed. The townspeople protested the institution, and the mayor shut it down. There are still some people in town who believe this place was cursed by the souls of the dead patients. They also believe if this place is disturbed, the killings will start again." She forced a tiny smile. "I'm sure it sounds ridiculous that grown people should--"

"No, not at all," Maxwell remarked simply. "Superstitions and curses have been a belief for many centuries. Witch burnings are a prime example of the power of fear. Either something isn't understood or they don't want to believe it, so alternate explanations are created."

Jacey nodded with some relief. "It's not everyone in town. It just happens to be the loud, opinionated ones who have the problem. They carry much influence on the others."

"Do you suppose the town library has any information on what you've told me about the institution? I'd like to do my own research on the subject."

"I'm sure there are plenty of articles on the institution and the murders," she replied and smiled lightly. "I work there. You'd think I'd know."

"Then you'd also know where the library is," he said with a tiny, mocking smile. "I have some free time this afternoon. Is it far? Maybe I could walk there."

"In this rain?" she questioned then smiled. "I could take you there, if you'd be ready in the next twenty minutes. I still need to interview Professor. It's more or less on my way."

"That's kind of you," he announced warmly. "I just need to tell Doc I'm leaving for the afternoon. I'll meet you out front in twenty minutes."

As Maxwell hurried across the room, Jacey couldn't help but watch him. Something about him drew her to him. She didn't really understand it. He was obviously out of her league. Even his degrees had degrees. Still--? Jacey noticed Angela staring at her. She'd obviously noticed her staring after Dr. Alvord. It became even clearer that the two were in some sort of relationship. A few hours ago, she would have understood it. Angela seemed the perfect woman. Attractive, smart, and refined. Now that she'd gotten to know her, more or less, she realized she was bitter and clingy with a superiority complex larger than the entire institution.

Chapter Ten

*J*acey drove along the back road toward town and the library, which was on the opposite end of town from the institution. Despite the pouring rain, Maxwell was interested in the buildings they passed. There was a black station wagon alongside the road with its hood up. A woman dressed in a scrub uniform holding a large, black umbrella flagged them down.

"That's Roseanne," Jacey informed Maxwell. "She's Dr. Talbert's nurse. That's his car. We have to stop and see if he needs help." She pulled to the side of the road.

Dr. Talbert slammed down the hood, grabbed a black bag from his car, and both ran to Jacey's jeep. They piled into the back, wet and out of breath.

"We have an emergency, Jacey," Dr. Talbert announced while looking exhausted. "Konrad Asher took a fall. I don't know how serious it is. His cell phone cut out."

Jacey's heart pounded with concern, and her mouth fell open. "I'll get you there right away."

Despite the standing water on the road, Jacey sped down the back roads through the pouring rain. Her jeep could handle the terrain. It took nearly twenty minutes to reach Asher's secluded house along the private, wooded, dirt lane. It was a shorter ride from her house through the woods and fields. She stopped in front of the house. Everyone hurried from the jeep, avoiding becoming soaked, and ran to the front porch. Dr. Talbert knocked on the door then tried the knob.

"It's locked," Talbert said with concern. "If he's unable to move, he won't be able to get to the door."

"We could check the back door," Roseanne suggested.

"Wait," Jacey announced and approached the porch railing.

She removed the railing ball, took out a hidden key, and hurried back to the house. Dr. Talbert and Roseanne stared at her with silent concern. She unlocked the door and hurried inside. Dr. Talbert, Roseanne, and Maxwell entered the tastefully decorated, unusually clean living room behind her. Asher was an amazing housekeeper, but considering his reclusive lifestyle, he did have to live in the home day in and day out.

"Asher," she called nervously and walked slowly through the living room. "Asher, the doctor's here!"

"Jacey," came Asher's voice with the sound of agony. "I'm out here."

Jacey ran toward the sunroom. A ladder lie on the floor along with a broken hanging plant. Asher sat on the floor against the wicker coffee table with his legs casually outstretched in front of him. He smiled warmly with a look of embarrassment and held a handkerchief to his temple.

"Nice of you to stop by," he said pleasantly. "Sorry I don't have any coffee made."

Jacey hurried to his side along with the doctor. He lowered his bloodied handkerchief to reveal a cut that bled freely in his slightly graying hair.

"You idiot," Jacey scolded. "What do you think you were doing?"

He eyed Jacey with a surprised look and blinked innocently. "Watering my plants." He looked from Talbert and Roseanne to Maxwell then smiled. "I haven't had this many visitors since the last lynch mob passed through."

Dr. Talbert put a cloth on Asher's head and had Jacey hold it in place. "Can you move? Where do you have pain?" he asked while preparing some solution on a pad.

"Just my head and my left ankle," he replied.

Roseanne removed his left shoe, causing him some agony. She then removed the sock.

"Careful," he said then smiled. "I'm ticklish."

She felt his ankle, probing him. "It doesn't appear broken," she announced then gently turned his foot.

He jumped in pain and winced. "Easy, Rosy."

Roseanne frowned with disapproval. Considering her feelings for him many years ago, it was obvious she despised him now. "Wiggle your toes," she ordered.

Asher did as she commanded.

"You took a nasty bump to your head," Dr. Talbert said with a sigh and straightened on his knees. "We should take you to the hospital for some tests."

"No, no hospitals," Asher said firmly. "They poke and prod every crevasse on a man's body. I'd rather not be violated tonight, if it's all the same to you."

"This is serious, Asher," Talbert said sternly. "You could have a concussion or worse. I won't allow you to stay here alone. Someone needs to keep an eye on you. The hospital is your only choice."

"I'll look after him, Dr. Talbert," Jacey announced almost immediately.

Roseanne and Dr. Talbert eyed her with their mouths hanging open. Her unusual friendship with the infamous Konrad Asher had been kept a secret for a very long time, although there had been rumors of their association. Her willingness to stay with him almost confirmed their closeness.

"Jacey, I don't think that's--" Roseanne began then fell suspiciously silent.

Asher struggled to pull himself upright and glared at Roseanne with narrow, evil eyes. "And why not, Rosy?" he hissed coldly. He obviously knew what she meant.

There was silence in the room. Dr. Talbert cleared his throat and caused both Jacey and Roseanne to jump.

"Let's get you patched up first," Dr. Talbert said gently and worked on placing surgical tape across the cut to his head then taped a patch to it. "Help me get him onto the couch."

Maxwell immediately came forward, helped move the coffee table while Jacey supported Asher against her, and then helped Dr. Talbert lift Asher to the nearby sofa. They propped his foot on the cushion. Both doctor and nurse worked on his ankle while Jacey sat on the edge of the sofa near Asher's side.

He patted her hand and strained to look at her. "I'm glad you came, Jacey," he said softly. "I need someone to look out for my best interest. I called you first, but you didn't answer."

"I'm sorry. The girls and I were doing an interview for the paper. I must have left my cell phone in the jeep."

"Not your fault. You didn't know I was having a clumsy day," he teased.

Once his ankle was wrapped, it was insisted he not move around much. He patted Jacey's arm. "Would you mind going to my desk and fetching my checkbook?"

Jacey left the room and went into Asher's study. She found his checkbook and a pen then returned to the sunroom. She handed them to Asher.

"I insist everyone stay for some coffee," Asher announced more cheerfully.

Roseanne glared at Dr. Talbert. He nodded slightly. She rolled her eyes then forced a tiny smile. "I'll make some." Roseanne was quick to leave the room.

"Rosy really needs to work on her bedside manner. I remember her being *friendlier* in the past," Asher said with a sly smile.

Roseanne stopped in the kitchen doorway and cast a glare at Asher. She obviously didn't care for the reminder of her behavior in her younger years. If Asher caught her stare, he didn't acknowledge it. Asher again eyed Maxwell and offered a charming smile, although he was obviously attempting to figure him out with a single look.

"I don't believe we've met," Asher announced.

Maxwell approached the sofa and extended his hand. "Maxwell Alvord," he announced with a pleasant smile.

"Konrad Asher; local legend. Pleasure to meet you," Asher announced with a cheap grin.

"Pay no attention to him," Jacey scoffed.

Asher frowned. "Only telling it like it is, right, Doc," he called to Dr. Talbert, who cleaned up the paper packaging.

Dr. Talbert attempted to smile. "I assume you're feeling better," he remarked simply and straightened. "With your thick head, I'm not surprised. I think you'll be fine being on your own tonight."

Maxwell gave Dr. Talbert an odd look. "Do you think that's wise? He obviously has a concussion, it could be dangerous to leave him by himself."

Dr. Talbert eyed Maxwell with some annoyance then smiled gently. "As a doctor, I think I know what's best for my patients," Talbert chirped.

Jacey glared suspiciously at Dr. Talbert then smiled pleasantly at Maxwell and offered a gentle tilt of her head. "A second opinion never hurt, *Dr.* Alvord."

Dr. Talbert looked sharply from Jacey to Maxwell and fidgeted slightly. "You're a doctor?"

"Scientist, actually," Maxwell replied. "Though I do know enough about medicine to keep this man under observation. It would be best if Ms. McMurray stayed with Mr. Asher tonight."

Dr. Talbert looked back at his bag with embarrassment and slowly closed the bag. "Of course, you're right," Talbert replied softly, almost under his breath.

"You'll have to forgive Dr. Talbert," Asher announced cheerfully with narrow eyes on the doctor. "He's just afraid I might have the young lady for dinner, *literally*."

Talbert spun to face Asher with reddened cheeks and anger in his eyes. "That's not funny in the least!"

Asher chuckled in his throat. "It would've been, if you didn't actually believe it."

Maxwell looked at both men with apparent confusion. "Did I just miss something?"

Asher looked at Maxwell with a broad smile. "The rumor about town is I'm some sort of monster. Supposedly I killed a man, but since they never found a body, it's assumed I ate the poor bastard."

Maxwell stared at Asher without expression. The look of concern was enough. Maxwell then smiled and appeared humored. "You didn't, of course."

He laughed lowly. "Of course not. I'm practically a vegetarian. And if it wasn't for pork, beef, and chicken, I would be one," Asher teased.

Maxwell laughed as well and appeared relieved. Jacey frowned and smacked Asher's arm then looked away with disgust. She hated when Asher poked fun at his tainted reputation.

"Your reputation is no joking matter," Dr. Talbert said firmly and with annoyance.

"Of course it is," Asher remarked. "No one in this town will give me the time of day no matter how nice I've been to them. Before my wife's death, I was a respected man. Fate cursed me twice in one night. I don't give a damn what anyone thinks of me anymore." Asher relaxed, inhaled deeply, and then smiled. "At the risk of offending you, Dr. Talbert, I would think you could sympathize. The same tragedy that ruined my life nearly ruined your career and reputation as well. There was that scandal about your part in the fire."

Roseanne paused in the sunroom doorway and appeared to listen to their conversation. Dr. Talbert snatched his bag and turned to Roseanne.

"Call Deputy Jameson and ask him if he'd give us a ride back to the office."

Roseanne uncertainly nodded and removed her cell phone from her scrub top pocket.

Dr. Talbert spun back toward Asher. "I don't care to discuss this with you any further," he snapped. "Unlike you, I'd like to preserve my reputation!"

"Is that what you were doing when I saw you running into your office when you were supposed to be saving patients?"

Everyone now stared at Asher and Dr. Talbert. Dr. Talbert glared at Asher with a look of confusion and impatience.

"What?" he demanded to know.

"Just before midnight on the night of the fire," Asher remarked simply and cleverly raised his brows. "I was leaving the lounge, and I saw you running into your office. I called to you, but you didn't seem to hear me."

"I went to call the fire department," Dr. Talbert snapped. "If you were in the second floor hall near the lounge, you should've seen the smoke from the fire. Why didn't you help?"

"I wasn't aware there had been a fire until I was in the stairway heading toward the first floor. From the crossing hallway to the stairs, I could see your office but not the linen closet." He shifted on the sofa and appeared curious. "And who disconnected the fire alarms?" Asher asked coyly and cocked his head to one side. "Certainly not Hal Burgess. Where would a mental patient get the codes to disconnect the alarms? Let's face it, for a psychotic serial killer, the boy wasn't too bright."

"That's no joking matter," Roseanne scoffed. "That bastard killed my best friend."

Asher wasn't even affected by Roseanne's remark. He kept his attention focused on Dr. Talbert, who was growing more furious and enraged.

"Don't drag me down with you, Asher," Dr. Talbert lashed out hotly. "I won't be a part of your sick analogies."

The doctor turned, stormed past Roseanne, and hurried into the kitchen. Roseanne stared at Asher a long moment then realized someone was speaking to her on her cell phone. She quickly turned and followed Dr. Talbert. Jacey glared at Asher through narrow eyes and frowned. Asher raised his brows sharply in response to her disapproving look and seemed almost humored.

"What's that look about, my dear? You don't approve of the truth?" Asher asked simply. "I know in the perfect world you'd like to see the town embrace me with open arms, but that'll never happen."

Jacey looked away and frowned. She caught Maxwell's stare and forced a tiny smile. "Perhaps it'd be best if you rode back to town with Deputy Jameson," she said gently. "Do you think Professor would mind keeping the girls overnight?"

"I'm sure he wouldn't," Maxwell replied in a soft tone. "Should I tell Brian you won't be able to make it tonight?"

Jacey was slightly surprised that he had known about their date as well, but Timon seemed the gossiping type. Actually, Asher's unfortunate accident worked out to her benefit as far as Brian was concerned.

"I, uh, suppose you should tell him what happened," she replied.

Asher touched Jacey's arm. She glanced at him and noted the concerned look on his face.

"You had a date tonight?" Asher asked with surprise. "Why didn't you say something? I'm sure I'll be fine by myself. I don't want you to miss an opportunity."

Jacey forced a tiny smile. "It's okay, Asher, *really*." She meant that. She leaned on Asher's shoulder and moved closer to his ear. "I don't mind getting out of it."

Asher patted her leg and chuckled softly. He then shifted on the sofa and smiled cheerfully at Maxwell. "I have an idea. Why don't you stay with us for a while, Dr. Alvord? I have some lobster tail in the freezer, and we can discuss the plans for the institution. It's not often I have visitors who aren't afraid of me."

Maxwell smiled lightly then laughed. "I'm sure the two of you would have a better time without me. I'd just bore both of you with fossils and finds."

"I insist," Asher announced firmly. "I'll give Jacey a crash course in cooking, and you and I can talk scientifically while Jacey amuses us in the kitchen."

Jacey smirked and folded her arms across her chest. "I know how to cook."

"Darling," Asher said and tilted his head. "Pushing numbers into a microwave isn't cooking; it's preventing starvation, and lobster can't be microwaved."

Jacey blushed with embarrassment. "I knew that," she snapped then looked away and nervously bit her lip.

"Alright," Maxwell said with a smile. "You've talked me into it. But if it's all the same, I'd like to do the cooking. I'm not a half bad chef."

Dr. Talbert entered the sunroom without Roseanne. "Roseanne and I will wait outside for Jameson," he said firmly. "Despite your horrendous attitude, Asher, I'll be by in the morning to check on your condition."

Asher frowned. "I'm sorry for offending you, Doctor. I do appreciate your coming out here. Not everyone would have done that for me. You're a good man."

Talbert then managed a tiny smile. "You were right. I do understand what you've been through."

"Are you sure you won't stay for coffee?" Asher asked more gently.

Talbert smiled more naturally. "Really, I can't. I have a dinner engagement with young widow Glease. I wouldn't want to keep her waiting."

Asher snickered lowly and grinned. "Young widow Glease? Rumors will fly."

"Maybe so," Dr. Talbert said with a sly smile. "But I don't mind. She's the best looking widow I've ever seen--and a damned fine cook too."

Chapter Eleven

*J*acey couldn't believe how well Maxwell and Asher got along. By the time dinner was finished, they sounded like old friends. Jacey insisted upon cleaning up after dinner, since she felt she did very little to help prepare the meal. She took her time and listened to the laughter from the sunroom. She was certain Asher was showing Maxwell photos of his wife. Katie had been gone ten years, and he still spoke of her with great affection. It made her happy to hear Asher enjoying the company of someone other than herself. She finally joined them in the sunroom. Asher smiled happily and returned Katie's picture to the fireplace mantle. He limped back to the sofa with the use of an old, carved cane with a gold top. When he saw Jacey, his smile brightened.

"There she is," Asher announced cheerfully and greeted Jacey with a hug and a kiss on the cheek. He proudly turned her to face Maxwell. "Just as beautiful as my Katie, don't you think?" Asher announced.

Both Jacey and Maxwell looked down with embarrassed smiles to the comment.

"Stop it," she said firmly as the color rose to her cheeks. She helped him to the sofa, propped his foot on the coffee table, and then sat alongside him.

Asher eyed Jacey with a broad grin on his face. "Did you know this young scientist wrote three books? I've read them and didn't even place the name."

Jacey wasn't surprised that Asher had read them. He was more intelligent than people ever gave him credit. His earlier conversations with Maxwell had proved that much. She hadn't understood half their conversation.

"Almost had you married," Asher announced boldly. "But the bastard wouldn't allow me to smoke my cigar or have a brandy, so I had to put it to a stop."

"Asher," she scolded while blushing. "You're embarrassing Maxwell."

"It's all in good fun, darling," Asher said with a soft laugh and patted her leg.

Jacey shook her head and rolled her eyes. "I see you're feeling better. Where'd you get the cane?"

Asher looked at the cane a moment then smiled brightly. "It was a gift from a Scott. A small token for something I'd done." He studied the design on the metal top. "Can't remember what I did anymore." He laughed and looked back at Jacey. "Knowing me, it must have been something courageous."

Maxwell stood and examined the cane a moment. "Must have been. This is an antique," Maxwell said. "Possibly dating back to the seventeenth century. That's a royal symbol." He tapped it. "Solid gold too."

Asher's smile faded into a slight smirk. He accepted the cane's return. "Wish I could remember."

Jacey gave Asher a strange look. It was unlike him to forget much of anything. It seemed more likely he didn't want to give any details of how he acquired the cane, which, in itself, was odd. Maxwell returned to his seat.

"How's the ankle?" Jacey asked curiously.

Asher's smile once more brightened. "Good enough to hobble about. I suppose I have a high tolerance for pain."

"Not me," Maxwell remarked then smiled. "That might explain why I'm not much of a fighter."

Asher laughed lowly. "World needs more lovers anyway," he teased.

"That's never been one of my stronger areas either," Maxwell said with a soft chuckle while insecurely scratching his brow.

"What is your strong area?" Asher finally asked with some frustration.

"Well, you know," Maxwell replied and shifted uncomfortably in his chair. "I'm your typical genius geek. I can invade the FBI's top-secret computer files, tell you everything you've never wanted to know about fossils, and bore you with the meaning of life. Ask me to tie my shoes, and I'll need to research it."

"You," Asher said and pointed his cane, "need a self-esteem lesson. You can't be quiet and shy all your life. This town will swallow you whole." He leaned his cane against the sofa and placed his hands over Jacey's ears.

Jacey groaned and rolled her eyes with embarrassment.

Asher looked at Maxwell with all seriousness. "This town will fuck you over just as they've fucked me." He casually removed his hands from her ears and smiled lightly.

Jacey shook her head. She didn't know why she played his games when he knew she could hear. It was almost amusing how he attempted to protect her from his foul language, even though he had used expletives around her many times in the past.

Asher's look became serious. "After the murder of my wife, the entire town jumped on the bandwagon and practically accused me of killing her," he said then leaned forward. "I loved my wife more than life itself. When I found her butchered in a room filled with flames, I didn't think I could ever go on without her. When you truly love someone, you'd gladly give your own life if it'd bring them back." He shut his eyes and sank back into another time. "I was there that night. I could have saved her," he said softly. "The time of death was estimated after my arrival." His eyes opened and he stared at a scratch in the coffee table. "Sometimes I hate Roseanne for not telling me that Katie wanted to see me the moment I'd arrived. I don't know why she kept it from me. A couple of minutes sooner, and maybe I could've saved her." His eyes lifted and met Maxwell's with a secret smile. "Or at least have died while bravely protecting her. There are certain women in life, my friend, that a man would be honored to die protecting."

Neither Jacey nor Maxwell said a word while staring at Asher. Jacey had heard Asher tell the story of his wife's death on more than one occasion, and it chilled her each time she'd heard it.

Asher studied Maxwell and smiled oddly. "I would've died one hundred times if it would've saved her." His smile twisted into something more sinister. "I'd have killed a dozen men if it would've brought her back."

Maxwell inhaled deeply and shifted in his chair. "She was a lucky woman to have been so loved."

"No," he said softly and with bitterness. "I let her down." His eyes returned to the coffee table. "I should've been there to save her; I should've perished with her." His eyes then lifted, and he looked into Jacey's eyes with a strange seriousness. "That will never happen again."

Asher then smiled and looked at Maxwell. He stood from the sofa with the use of his elegant cane, leaned toward Maxwell, and extended his hand. Maxwell stood as well and accepted his hand with uncertainty.

"It was a pleasure, Maxwell. Stop in again sometime." He released Maxwell's hand and turned toward Jacey with his usual, warm smile. "Get your girls and go home. I'll be fine on my own. I'd really like to be alone anyway." He kissed her on the cheek then limped from the room in the direction of his bedroom.

Jacey watched him disappear into his bedroom just down the hall and shut the door. She rubbed her chilled arms then smiled nervously at Maxwell.

"Do you think he'll be okay?"

"Probably not," he replied then looked at her with a tiny smile. "But he'll survive."

She looked at her watch and sighed gently. "Nearly one A.M. I should take you home while I'm still alert enough to drive."

t

*J*acey's jeep pulled up to the front of the institution a little after one in the morning. Maxwell and Jacey walked in silence toward the front door. Maxwell opened the door and allowed Jacey to enter the dimly lit foyer then followed after her. Timon appeared in the lounge with a bowl of popcorn in his hands. He paused when he saw them then smiled and laughed loudly with great humor.

"You are in so much trouble," Timon said to Maxwell. "If Angela doesn't kill you, I'm sure Brian will."

Maxwell frowned and rolled his eyes. "Where are the girls?" he asked sternly.

"Locked in one of the padded cells," he said with a laugh. "They got a little out of hand."

Maxwell didn't appear humored.

Timon snorted with annoyance. "You're certainly sour tonight," he snapped. "They're sleeping in the west wing somewhere. Professor is close by. They're safe, I promise." Timon then walked away and grumbled something under his breath.

"I suppose we should look for them," Maxwell said with a weary sigh. "It's a large wing."

"There's no point," Jacey said and wearily raked her fingers through her hair. "I'm sure they're fine wherever they've locked themselves. I'll come back in the morning for them."

"If you're not going to take them home then why not stay?" he asked then immediately fidgeted to his comment. "I mean, there are plenty of beds to be found. No one will care if you spend the night."

She forced a weary smile. "I think I'll take you up on that offer."

"I'll take you to one of the rooms in the west wing," Maxwell announced pleasantly with a boyish grin. "There are some musty smelling sheets in the linen closet."

They found the west wing on the second try and stopped in the first floor linen closet. Maxwell removed some sheets for her, and they approached the closest room. Maxwell checked the door and made certain it wasn't electronically locked. He opened the door, turned on the light, and looked over the bland, cramped room. It resembled a slightly more cheerful prison cell. At least the walls weren't made of stone or concrete.

"Not exactly the presidential suite," he teased with a tiny smile. He checked the lock again just to be sure. "Don't want you getting locked inside."

They entered the room and approached the small bed. He helped her with the sheets. Once they'd finished, she walked with him to the door. He opened it and turned to face her with a timid, boyish grin. Jacey found his boyish charm refreshing and returned the smile. As she stared at him, she suddenly felt a strange attraction toward him. She fidgeted and tried not to stare.

"You won't have any problems with Angela, will you? I don't want to get you in any trouble."

Maxwell appeared humored and laughed softly. "No, it's not like that at all. Timon likes to over-dramatize." He appeared to consider. "He's very good at it." He stared into her eyes a brief moment then smiled warmly. "Good night, Jacey. I'll return to wake you in the morning."

Jacey held her breath while staring into his eyes with a soft look. "It meant a lot to me," she whispered softly.

He tilted his head as if confused. "What did?"

"Your kindness toward Asher," she said gently. "He was serious. Most people in this town are afraid to even look at him or utter his name. He really enjoyed himself tonight, I could tell."

Maxwell smiled more naturally. "You're really fond of him, aren't you? No matter what the popular opinion."

She nodded in response. "I love him like my own father," she said softly.

Jacey placed her hands on his hand and kissed him quickly on the cheek. When she pulled back, he held her fingers firmly and stared into her eyes with a look of surprise. His smile brightened considerably and some color rose to his cheeks. Without hesitation, he lifted her hand and kissed the back of it with warmth and affection. When he pulled away, he contained his boyish grin and backed to the door. He released her hands and fumbled for the doorknob.

"Good night," he half whispered then slipped from the room.

Jacey stared at the closed door a long moment with her mouth hanging open. She shut her mouth and gently caressed her hand that he'd kissed. She could still feel his warm lips on the back of her hand.

"My God," she gasped softly then sighed romantically.

†

*R*oseanne's small ground floor apartment was cozy and quaint despite its odd location alongside the alley. It was almost two in the morning. Roseanne, in her white nightgown, turned over in bed and lay on her back a moment while groaning with disgust. The night was damp from all the rain, and a gentle breeze through the open window chilled her. She looked at the bedside clock, saw the time, and rolled her eyes. She finally got up and closed the old, single pane window. She wearily walked out of her bedroom while raking her fingers through her mussed hair. Roseanne passed through the living room and entered a small sitting room to the right of her old, worn apartment. She sat at a small, cluttered desk and opened the bottom drawer that was piled with old papers, files, and various objects of no value. She removed an envelope containing a copied note created from tiny, cutout newspaper letters. She scanned over the paper then carefully folded it and placed it inside the envelope without an address on it. She removed three instant photos from the back of the drawer and shuffled through them.

"What had you so upset that night?" she whispered softly while studying the photos. "If I only knew what you'd found."

There was a sound from the back yard near her apartment. Roseanne jumped slightly then groaned and shook her head. She stood, removed a book from the shelf and placed the envelope and photos in the book. She returned the book to the shelf then went to the kitchen and found some pills in the cupboard. She was about to take the pills when there was a faint knock on the door. Roseanne jumped with surprise and turned toward the door.

"Who the hell could that be," she muttered and walked toward the door.

She pulled back the curtain and looked outside. There was no one there, just the dark alley. Roseanne raised a skeptical brow and allowed the curtain to fall back into place. She looked at the locked door then hastily placed the dead bolt across it. She seemed a little more anxious than usual tonight. Roseanne remained still a moment longer and stared at the door. She finally relaxed, approached the sink, and took her pills. She walked back into the bedroom and paused just inside the dark room. She suddenly stopped and stared with surprise at the open window as the curtains blew gently inward. Her mouth slowly opened with concern. She quickly turned for the bedroom door. It suddenly slammed shut. Roseanne let out a startled scream and bolted for the open window. She was suddenly grabbed from behind and was tackled face first onto the bed. The intruder was on top of her. She attempted to fight her attacker while screaming, but she was pinned face down on the bed. She had no leverage and her screams were partially muffled from the covers. A cloth was suddenly placed over her nose and mouth. Roseanne struggled but rapidly became weak. Her body went limp.

✝

*J*acey tossed under the musty smelling sheets in the creepy institution chamber. Her pleasant dream changed into a horrible nightmare, causing her to jerk with a slight gasp as she clutched the sheets. Jacey looked around the plain, dark room with some disorientation. She suddenly remembered where she was. A chill swept over her, and she rubbed her cold arms while sitting up in the musty, old bed. She finally sighed and ran her trembling fingers through her hair. The nightmare seemed to stick with her several minutes after she'd been awake and her unpleasant sleeping quarters didn't help minimize the effects. She heard movement from the corridor then became still and listened a moment longer, questioning if it was someone else unable to sleep. A small part of her feared it was the ghosts of the mental patients who died in the fire, even if it was a silly notion. She didn't believe in ghosts. The footfalls grew louder, but they seemed slow, as if someone were pausing for some reason. She didn't believe in ghosts, but she did believe in crazed, psycho killers! Jacey quietly slipped out of the bed, wearing just her shirt and underwear, and crept toward the door.

There was no lock on the inside of the door, which didn't ease her concerns any. She listened to the person walking the hallway then heard the footfalls stop. She could hear the metal slide window open on several doors along the hall. It was possibly the most chilling sound she'd ever heard. Jacey held her breath and firmly grasped the doorknob with both hands while remaining to the side of the door. She heard the person within the corridor continue to walk along the hallway with the metal window sliding open and close on each door. She looked at the small window then to the unmade bed just across the small room. She bit her lip nervously. What was the person in the hall looking for? Jacey could hear the footfalls stop just before her door. She looked at the small window on the door inches from her face. The metal covering slid open and light from the hallway flooded into the room. Jacey held her breath as her heart pounded wildly and attempted not to gasp. She didn't know who it was, nor did she want to find out. She heard a series of beeps alongside the doorknob. There was an electronic click and the door handle vibrated in her hands. Jacey gasped softly. The footfalls walked away from her door. She waited what seemed a lifetime until the footfalls faded away then turned the doorknob. The door wouldn't open! She jerked on it several times then collapsed against it. A million thoughts on how to handle her situation raced through her head, but only one seemed logical. Jacey pounded on the door and screamed hysterically.

Chapter Twelve

*J*acey woke in the creepy institution bedroom to an electronic humming sound. Her eyes opened from where she sat, fully dressed and huddled in the corner by the door. The door opened. She nervously sprang to her feet and clutched her shoe in a deadly fashion. Maxwell stepped into the room with a look of concern then jumped when he saw her standing in the corner with her shoe.

"What happened?" he demanded. "Why was your door locked from the outside?"

Jacey sighed with relief, closed her eyes, and threw her arms around his neck. She clung to him and buried her face into his white, lab coat. His arms uncertainly tightened around her waist, but his concern was evident.

"Are you alright?" he asked then looked around the room for signs of trouble.

She trembled against him as tears filled her eyes. "I--I don't know. Someone locked me in." She sniffed. "I was so afraid they'd come back."

Maxwell gently rubbed her shoulder reassuringly. "But who would do that?"

She sniffed and lifted her head to meet his eyes. A look of fear suddenly swept over her. "The girls! Where are they?"

Maxwell searched her eyes. "I--I don't know. On this wing somewhere."

Jacey pulled away from him and ran into the corridor. "We have to find them."

Maxwell ran after her.

"Monique! Coleen!" She ran along several corridors until she didn't know where she was. "Monique! Coleen!"

There was pounding from one of the rooms just a couple of doors down the hall. Jacey ran toward the room with Maxwell on her heels. She attempted to open the door while both girls screamed hysterically.

"Let us out," they cried out.

Maxwell moved Jacey aside and pressed a series of numbers into the panel near the door. There was the familiar electronic hum, and he was able to open the door. Both girls ran from the room and hugged Jacey.

"We heard you calling, but the door was locked," Monique proclaimed.

There was a thump on the door next to theirs. "Uh, hello," came Professor's monotone voice from the room next to theirs. "I seem to be locked in here. Could someone let me out?"

Maxwell hurried to Professor's door and unlocked it with the same code. He opened the door to reveal Professor standing in the doorway with his arms folded across his chest and a stern look upon his face.

"Oh, ha--ha, very funny," he growled. "Don't you ever do that again."

"It wasn't me," Maxwell protested.

"It's always the quiet ones," Professor snapped and left the room.

†

Everyone had gathered within the massive kitchen. They had cups of coffee before them while most sat at the large table. Doc scratched his gray beard and shook his head while pacing before Jacey, who remained huddled over her cup of tea. Monique and Coleen seemed even less interested in their hot chocolate.

"I don't understand why someone would lock you in those rooms." He looked at Timon and raised his brows. "Anyone want to own up to this prank?"

Timon appeared horrified or possibly insulted. "I wouldn't do something like that," he protested. "Not to the ladies. Professor, maybe, but certainly not them."

Doc frowned and looked around. "What are the chances someone slipped into the building last night?"

Maxwell shook his head and appeared bewildered. "For what possible reason? Nothing in here would be of any value to someone from town. Particularly nothing in the west wing."

"Someone may have been trying to scare you," Jacey announced. "I wouldn't put it past some people in town."

Angela clucked her tongue with disgust and sneered. "How pathetic."

"She could be right," Doc replied.

"A few people were giving us the hairy eyeball in the diner yesterday," Timon remarked. "With the looks we were getting, I certainly wouldn't trust them."

"The front door remained unlocked all night," Maxwell said with a defeated sigh. "I just never thought to lock it."

"From now on, that door is locked and the gates will be closed after everyone's inside," Doc said firmly. "No more sleeping in the patients' wing either."

"Guess it wouldn't do any good to call the police on the matter," Brian said with a sigh.

"We could inform them," Jacey suggested. "But there's nothing they can do about it."

"Probably just stir the town more," Professor said lowly. His eyes widened dramatically as he raised his voice to a high shrill and waved his hands. "Oh, it's the curse! Shut the building down! Burn the scientists!"

"You're right," Doc said. "It'd do little good to notify the police presently. Keeping the building locked should keep the trespassers out."

They began to disperse from the huge kitchen. Jacey finally stood and sighed deeply.

"Come on, girls, we have horses to feed," she announced softly while frowning.

Maxwell studied her from where he stood at the counter alongside Professor while finishing his tea. Brian approached Jacey and smiled sympathetically.

"How's your friend doing?" he asked gently.

"He was his usual self by late evening and insisted we leave," she replied.

Brian looked at Maxwell, who promptly crossed the kitchen and left. He looked back at Jacey and smiled pleasantly.

"Glad to hear," Brian announced. "So how about dinner tonight? You pick the restaurant."

Jacey forced a smile but really wasn't in the mood. "Thank you, Brian, but I'm not leaving Monique and Coleen alone again. Last night was enough to frighten me for a while," she announced. "But if you want, the four of us could go somewhere."

Brian appeared to consider her remark and managed a smile. "I'm not sure I could entertain three ladies at once. What do teenage girls like to do?"

"I'd say most teenagers like to hang out at malls, but Monique and Coleen like to ride."

"Ride? Ride what?"

Jacey laughed at his question. "Horses, silly."

A look of concern swept over his face. "Horses? I haven't ridden in twenty years."

Professor slowly inched his way closer to them. "Did you, uh, mention horseback riding?"

Jacey looked at Professor and offered a smile. "Yes, I was just telling Brian about how Monique and Coleen love horses."

He put a hand to his chest and blinked dramatically. "I love horseback riding. If there's a stable nearby, I'd be glad to take them."

"They have their own horses at my farm," Jacey replied.

Brian scratched his temple with a frown. He was obviously losing interest in the conversation.

Professor held up two fingers. "Just two horses?" he asked then smiled deviously and raised a third finger. "Or three?"

Jacey laughed gently at his childlike behavior. "Including mine, there are ten."

Professor's eyes widened with excitement. "Ten? We could all go riding," he suddenly announced cheerfully. "You haven't seen anything until you've seen a genius on horseback. It's a laughable sight."

"I don't know, Professor," Brian muttered lowly.

"Don't be such a wuss. It'll be great fun. We can gallop across fields," he announced while riding his invisible horse, "splash through streams--"

"Fall off," Brian added.

"Timon will go," Professor remarked simply. "He's not afraid to try something new. Has to be more fun than wearing out yet another tiresome pickup line."

Brian sneered and threatened to kill Professor with one look. She couldn't believe Brian didn't know she saw through him all on her own. She didn't need anyone telling her the sort of man Brian was.

Professor clasped his hands together and pleaded with Jacey. "Please, please take me riding with you. I won't even sue when I fall off."

Jacey laughed. "Sounds like fun. I'll leave directions with you. Gather those who want to go riding and come to my place around noon."

"Oh, oh, you've got it," Professor chirped. "I want the biggest horse you have," he laughed. "So my feet won't drag." He then wagged his finger sternly at her. "No ponies, no, no."

Chapter Thirteen

$\mathcal{I}$t was a beautiful, warm sunny afternoon. Several horses were tired to the long, thick hitching rail in front of the barn at the McMurray farm. Monique and Coleen helped brush the horses. Jacey saddled her gray horse while the girls chatted excitedly about their afternoon riding adventure.

"So who's coming?" Monique finally asked.

"I don't know. Maybe just Professor," Jacey replied simply. She felt it best to brush the other horses in preparation for a larger number.

"I like Professor," Coleen chirped happily. "He's cute in his own, strange way. You should marry Professor."

Jacey laughed at how easy Coleen made it sound. If life and love only worked that way, it wouldn't be nearly so stressful. The girl was in for a rude awakening.

"I don't like Brian," Monique announced firmly then sneered a look of distaste. "He was really angry about your date being canceled."

Jacey's brows raised and she turned to face both girls. "He was, was he?"

Both nodded.

"Timon scolded him and pulled him from the room," Coleen informed her. "I think they got into a fight. Professor took us to his room for the movies." She appeared to consider. "I think Professor was angry too."

"Professor seems like a very nice guy," Jacey remarked then laughed. "He certainly likes horses. Any man who likes horses can't be all that bad."

Monique placed the saddle pad on her horse and leaned on the horse's neck to look at Jacey. "How old do you suppose Professor is?"

"Uh, thirty-two, I think he said," Jacey replied simply.

"A little too old for me, I suppose," Monique said with a sad sigh.

Jacey laughed softly. "He's practically too old for me," she remarked. "Ten years older."

"Ten years isn't bad," Coleen said.

"Jameson's ten years older than me," Jacey said simply. "And we saw nothing eye to eye." She hesitated then added, "Older men have *certain* expectations."

"So do teenage boys," Coleen replied dryly.

Jacey sharply eyed the teenage girl and wondered if they were talking about the same thing. She hoped they weren't, but there was no telling, and she wasn't about to ask. The luxury van drove slowly down the dirt driveway and approached the barn. When it stopped, all six scientists got out and approached them. Professor had brand new cowboy boots, designer jeans, and a new cowboy hat on his head. Jacey held back her laugh. Both girls snickered. The only one Jacey was really surprised to see was Angela. She couldn't imagine her coming along willingly. The woman wore dress slacks, dress boots, and a white, button blouse. The others wore old jeans, old shirts, and sneakers. Timon was the exception. He dressed like a biker in leather with a bandana over his head. Angela eyed the horses and shook her head while pointing. Her upper lip curled snobbishly.

"We're riding on them?" she demanded from Maxwell. "They're so big."

Timon excitedly jogged toward the barn and the horses. "I call dibs on the big, black one!"

Coleen sharply eyed him and clung to her horse's head. "He's taken," she said firmly.

Jacey chuckled softly. "Never get between a girl and her horse," she teased. "You can have any of the six on the far end."

"What's wrong with the others?" Timon asked as he approached Jacey while indicating the horses in the pasture.

"Too young," she explained. "They're still in training. I also need to place you according to your past riding experience. Some are more devilish than others."

"Ooh, ooh, I want a devilish one," Professor called after her and hurried to join them.

Once all the horses were saddled, Jacey and the girls helped the scientists mount. Angela didn't stop complaining from the moment she sat on the horse. As they rode away from the barn, Maxwell brought up the rear with Angela. Monique and Coleen rode in the front with Professor and Doc, while Jacey stayed in the middle between Timon and Brian. She looked back every couple of minutes to ensure that Maxwell and Angela were still with them. They rode nearly an hour through the woods and fields.

"We're going to be so sore tomorrow," Timon announced and stretched slightly in the saddle.

"Tomorrow," Angela remarked from several feet behind. "I'm sore already."

"You should be grateful, Angela," Brian announced with a soft chuckle. "Riding is a great butt conditioner." He looked behind Jacey and leered lustfully at her backside. "Jacey's proof of that."

Jacey eyed him and attempted a humored smile, but he wasn't winning any points with her. "You're such a dog, Brian," she remarked. "Has anyone ever told you that?"

Brian chuckled lowly in his throat. "Any position works for me."

Jacey rolled her eyes and shook her head.

"We're thinking about having him fixed," Timon added while grinning.

They approached the tall, steel fence surrounding the institution, though the building could barely be seen from the back of the estate. The four in the front stopped and stared at the back gate. Jacey rode up to them. Doc pointed at the open chain dangling on the gate.

"I wonder how long that's been open," Doc remarked.

Jacey stared at the cut chain. It looked freshly cut. "I'm sure it wasn't like that the other day."

"I remember it was locked," Coleen reported.

"Maybe we should go inside," Doc suggested.

Monique rode to the gate, leaned down, lifted the bar, and pushed the gate open. Everyone rode in behind her. They rode at a trot across the flat, lush grounds. Monique and Coleen picked up the pace. Professor loped after them, screaming like a psychotic cowboy. As they approached the front of the institution, they could see the police blazer parked before the main entrance. Doc looked with great interest at the institution and then Deputy Jameson standing before the front door. Jameson appeared startled by their presence, being they came from the back.

"Is there something wrong, officer?" Doc asked.

Jameson stepped off the elegant porch and approached them on their horses. "I'm not sure. Are you Dr. Zellner, the person in charge here?"

Doc nodded.

"I received an anonymous phone call just a few minutes ago urging me to investigate the institution," he announced. "Last night, Roseanne Pierce, Dr. Talbert's nurse, was abducted from her home. At least, it appears that way. Some of her things were gone through, and no one has seen her."

"And you suspect she might be within the institution?" Doc asked and seemed curious.

"Would you object if I had a look around?" Jameson asked simply.

Doc shook his head. "No, of course I don't mind. I'll show you around personally." He dismounted with some effort and handed the reins to Monique.

"Why don't we tie the horses and get a drink inside?" Professor suggested.

They all agreed. Jacey, Monique, and Coleen tied the horses to the porch. Jacey tied the last horse to the side of the porch and saw a shadow move within the caretaker's workshop.

"Are you coming?" Monique called to her.

Jacey looked at both girls and nodded, although she was clearly distracted by what she'd seen. "You go ahead. I'll be along in a couple of minutes."

Both girls hurried into the house. Jacey stared at the old, rusted door to the caretaker's workshop and eyed the broken windowpane. She cautiously walked around the side of the huge building and approached the workshop. She heard a metallic clang from the addition. The door was partially opened and old ivy vines had been displaced. She tilted her head to the side and slowly approached the door. Jacey gently pushed it open while standing back. The workshop was filthy and covered in cobwebs and old, rusted tools. She pushed the door further, stepped just inside the doorway, and slowly entered the workshop. The door shut behind her. Jacey jumped and spun around with a startled scream. Asher casually leaned against the back wall next to the old lawn mowers. Jacey's mouth opened with some surprise. She looked back at the door then to Asher. He smiled delicately and leaned on his cane as he straightened.

"I suppose you're wondering what I'm doing hiding in the caretaker's workshop," he said with some humor.

"That's just one of several questions," she remarked then cocked her head slightly to the side and squinted. "Why are you hiding in here?"

"I'd really prefer to explain it to you later. I'm sort of in a spot here, and I need an exit."

"No kidding!" She once more looked toward the door then took two steps toward him. "If Jameson sees you leaving here, he'll think you were up to something."

"I'm aware of that, Jacey," he replied casually. "But I think it would be worse if I was found here, don't you?" His look conveyed he *was* up to something. "Will you help me?"

Jacey remained silent a moment then nodded mechanically. "Yes, of course. What would you like me to do?"

"Keep the others busy while I borrow your horse and slip out the back gate," he said simply.

She stared into his blue eyes then nodded.

"I'll release your horse within the grounds and collect my jeep on the other side of the woods," he informed her.

"Give me a few minutes to locate them," she said gently then left the workshop.

Jacey nervously hurried around the institution and entered through the double doors. She could hear voices from the kitchen. Jacey looked around the lounge. She climbed on top of the sofa and began to scream. In a matter of minutes, everyone was within the lounge, staring at her.

"What is it?" Jameson cried out with concern and looked around the room.

She pointed across the room toward the bookcase. "It was a snake," she proclaimed. "It went over there. I think it was poisonous!"

Angela let out a startled cry, jumped on top of the coffee table, and looked around nervously. One of the horses neighed excitably from outside. Monique and Coleen both looked toward the window and were about to check on the horses. Jacey had to stop their prying eyes.

"There it is!" she screamed while again pointing across the room.

Everyone looked in the direction she pointed. Angela screamed hysterically, even though there was nothing to see. Timon jumped on the sofa beside Jacey. She eyed him with surprise. He forced a tiny smile.

"I, uh, don't like snakes," he replied timidly.

Jameson and Professor looked around the room for several minutes. When they were satisfied it wasn't coming out from wherever it had slithered, they urged everyone off the furniture. Monique looked out the window.

"One of the horses got loose," she said with a sigh then left the lounge to collect it.

Jacey sighed with relief. Asher had managed to slip away unnoticed. Despite her relief, she intended to have a lengthy discussion with him about his nasty habit of showing up when things looked bad for him.

Chapter Fourteen

It was late afternoon. Monique and Coleen rode their horses around the training ring and playfully jumped their horses over short jumps. They looked in the direction of the porch several times and appeared interested in Jacey's business. Asher sat on the porch near Jacey while sipping his brandy and stared at his crossed, propped feet on the porch railing across from where he sat. Jacey watched him in silence for a long moment. He obviously knew she was waiting for an explanation, but he never just came out with it. She was always forced to ask him point blank.

"Do you intend to tell me what you were doing at the institution earlier today?" Jacey finally asked while glaring at him as she sat sideways in her chair.

Asher stared into his brandy glass, sighed, and took another swallow before responding. "Early this morning I received a phone call. The voice on the line told me to meet them at the institution at one. It was concerning Katie's death." He turned his head to look at her. "Of course, I'm the skeptic, but I couldn't resist the offer. Just to outwit my mysterious caller, I purposely showed up half an hour late. I arrived on the grounds from the back and saw Deputy Jameson pull up looking all-official. Apparently I wasn't the only one invited to the institution."

"But for what reason?" Jacey asked. "Jameson didn't find anything there. Other than the fact that you were trespassing, what difference would it have made that you were there? Why would someone go to all that trouble?"

"I don't know," he said with a sigh. "Someone's up to something foul. Maybe there was something to be found and our deputy just wasn't clever enough to find it. I'm a little concerned about Roseanne's sudden disappearance as well. I can't help but wonder if it's tied in somehow."

"You had a small argument with Roseanne last night," Jacey reminded. "Maybe she's playing you for a fool and staged the entire thing."

Asher shook his head without looking at her and appeared concerned. "I don't think so. I fear Roseanne fell victim to something last night."

"You think someone may have killed her?" Jacey suddenly asked and felt alarm sweeping through her. It just didn't seem possible, and she wondered if Asher was being overdramatic. However, it wasn't like him. "But for what reason?"

"I couldn't even guess," he replied softly.

"Well, tell me about the voice on the phone? Was it male or female? Who do you think it could have been?"

"The voice sounded male, but I can't be sure. It was whispered in such a manner that it could have been a female lowering her voice." He then looked at Jacey. "It could have been Jill for all I know. She hates me with a passion. Of course, so does most of the town."

Jacey slipped into thought while staring out toward the two girls in the riding ring. Monique stood before her paint horse and made him rear up on his hind legs. The horse towered over the girl with his front hooves thrashing in the air. He landed softly and collected the treat she held in her hand. That girl was a handful. She wanted to scold her, but she had been just as bad when she was her age. Besides, she had more important things on her mind.

She looked back at Asher and shook her head. "None of this makes any sense."

"Of course it doesn't, but I'm sure it will soon enough." He placed his feet on the porch and leaned forward. "I need to ask you for another favor."

"What sort of favor?" she asked with some concern. His idea of a favor was most times troubling and borderline illegal.

"I need to get into the institution and have a look around, but I need to be invited."

Jacey's eyes widened with horror. "Are you out of your mind? If anything happens, whoever lured you there might continue with their plan."

"Returning to that place won't exactly be easy for me either," he announced boldly. "But I need to check on a couple of theories. I can sense something very bad is about to happen, and I'd like to prevent it."

Jacey's eyes were wide with fear. "Then I suggest you keep away from there," she announced firmly. "This isn't you fight, Asher. It would probably be best if you looked up an old friend and stayed away for a week or so."

He chuckled softly as his smile mocked her. "Are you suggesting I secure an alibi?"

Her brows raised in response. "It wouldn't be a bad idea. What if someone has killed Roseanne?" she demanded. "You know you'll be the first person they question."

"Yes," he replied with a wry smile and seemed a little too proud of his reputation. "My legacy continues."

"Not just that, but she was at your house the night she disappeared. Dr. Talbert and Maxwell witnessed the hatred between the two of you. It just looks bad."

"Yes, I see your point." He looked out to the training ring and watched the girls perform. "Tomorrow's the town fair. Are you taking the girls?"

She was perfectly aware he was once again changing the subject, but she was too tired to argue the current subject anyway. "They heard about the horse fun show and insisted we go," Jacey said and forced a tiny smile. "Their rooms are wallpapered with ribbons. I fear to say it, but they both ride better than I do."

Asher laughed softly. "And how are you and your young scientist getting along?"

"Brian?" she asked while raising a curious brow. "He's nothing to brag about. He'll eventually get bored and move on."

Asher tilted his head and appeared bewildered. "Brian? I was referring to our young Dr. Alvord."

Jacey was slightly surprised then smiled with some embarrassment. "Oh, Maxwell, well, he's already seeing someone. She's more his type anyway. I'm not exactly intellectually compatible with him."

Asher appeared disappointed and almost offended. "My darling," he announced simply while smiling wryly. "You don't have to battle wits with a man in order for him to want you. Even men of great intelligence yearn for women of endless beauty." His irritation with her comment seemed to escalate. "And I certainly hope you're not implying you're beneath any man just because he has fancy, little degrees."

She leaned forward, smiled slyly, and placed her hand on his. "He already has someone--give it up."

He lifted her hand and kissed the back of it warmly. His smile indicated there was no chance of that. "Not until I've found someone suitable to replace me." Asher laughed softly and stood. "I'd best be going. I'll talk to you tomorrow."

He set his glass on the small table. Asher walked with use of his cane down the steps and toward his jeep. Jacey watched him disappear into his jeep then drive along the old mining road, which was a more direct route to his isolated home. She had a bad feeling. Asher involving himself in anything surrounding the institution frightened her. She wished, just once, he'd be less curious and practice a little self-preservation. Perhaps, in his warped mind, investigating the uncertain was his idea of self-preservation. Why did men have to be so complicated?

†

*T*he small, sterile examination room was dimly lit by a single lightbulb in a surgical ceiling fixture containing several burnt bulbs. Roseanne, still in her nightgown, lie on the metal surgical table. Her body and white nightgown were soaked in sweat and her own urine. Her wrists and ankles were strapped to the table with leather, buckle-style restraints. She struggled in vain against the restraints. Her wrists and ankles were bruised and bloody from over twenty-four hours of struggling to free herself. She had duct tape over her mouth to prevent her from screaming. Despite her obvious exhaustion and injuries beneath the straps, she continued to fight her restraints. She lie motionless a moment while breathing heavily. Roseanne attempted to scream out with frustration and thrashed wildly against her restraints. A metallic ping was heard as her left arm pulled away from the surgical table. She stared at her free, left arm with the restraint still tight around her wrist. She appeared almost stunned then overwhelmingly relieved. Roseanne immediately pulled the tape from her mouth, gasped only a moment, and then worked on unbuckling the restraint from her right wrist. Within seconds, she was sitting up on the table and releasing her restrained ankles. She jumped off the table and nearly collapsed from an entire day of lying still on her back. She clutched the table for support and looked around the small, surgical room. There was a door to the front and one to the back. She hurried to the one toward the front, paused before it, and uncertainly turned the knob. To her surprise, it opened!

Roseanne, in her bare feet, slipped out of the room into what could only be described as a basement. She looked at the odd staircase before her. There was nothing else. Just the small, narrow stone steps. She uncertainly hurried up the nearly dark steps and paused before a strange looking door. She slowly opened the door and peered through the opening. She stared at the basement before her. The area she was within was massive and contained old furniture and various other useless items left in storage from the old institution. Most were covered in dust and thick cobwebs. She uncertainly shut the door behind her and looked back at it. It was actually a secret passageway. The door blended in with the wall. She hurried across the room to an opening. The next room over was more of the same. The basement was a maze! She heard movement, which resembled the sound of someone walking on metal stairs. Roseanne ducked into another storage area and hid behind an old stack of mattresses. She could see the shadow of someone walking past. When she heard the passageway door open and close, she ran out from behind the mattresses and hurried in the direction of possible stairs.

She ran up the metal fire stairs, knowing it would only be a matter of minutes before her abductor discovered she was gone. She ran through the doorway on the first floor and suddenly stopped. Roseanne stared at the familiar first floor hallway of the west wing. Although not the wing she worked in, being it burned to the ground ten years ago, both wings were setup exactly the same. Despite the eeriness of her location, it was familiar! She heard thundering footfalls on the basement stairs. Her abductor must have gotten to the sub-basement faster than she thought. Roseanne ran down the dirty hallway in her bare feet and entered the first doorway she found. She entered the massive, tiled shower room with rows of tile shower stalls with flimsy shower curtains covering the openings. The shower room smelled strong of mildew, possibly due to the dripping water that echoed throughout the room. There was no telling how long the water had been dripping.

Roseanne ducked into one of the damp shower stalls and pulled the curtain partially closed. She sat on the floor, hugged her knees to her chest, and remained quiet and motionless. If her abductor assumed she ran, he might bypass searching the floor for her and head outside. Keeping hidden and quiet seemed her best option. She rested her head on her knees and listened to the sound of the dripping water. Her eyes slowly closed. An hour later, Roseanne suddenly jerked awake and uncertainly looked around from where she still sat within the tile shower stall behind the plastic curtain. The sound of the dripping water continued. She looked under the plastic curtain and saw the shimmer of light. She appeared curious and slowly pulled the curtain back from where she sat and peered across the shower room. Judging by the small amount of light filtering through the grimy small window near the ceiling, it was nearly sunup. The window had bars outside, so there was no chance escaping that way. She again sat against the shower stall wall and stared at the ceiling. She knew she had been in the shower room for an hour or longer. With morning rapidly approaching, she stood a better chance of getting help.

She gathered up her courage and slowly stood within the shower stall. Voices could be heard in the hallway just outside the shower room. Roseanne became alert then alarmed. As she listened to the jovial voices, it was evident they were the scientists occupying the institution. It was almost impossible that they would have been involved in her abduction, which meant they were the good guys! Roseanne appeared almost relieved and attempted to hold back her sobs of joy. She pulled open the curtain. Light glistened off the scalpel a split second before it slashed firmly across her throat. Roseanne gasped and clutched her bleeding throat. There wasn't even time to scream. She attempted to clutch the wall as she felt her body sink. She slid down the wall to the tile shower floor in a sitting position and stared up at her attacker. As blood drenched her body, she no longer moved. Her dead eyes remained opened and fixated as if staring at her assailant. The shower room was again silent except for the relentless dripping of water.

Chapter Fifteen

Friday, 6:00 P.M.

The once quiet streets of Stony Ridge were now alive with people from all over the county. All the streets had been blocked off to accommodate the weekend event. Vendors lined the streets with their games and stands of greasy, overpriced food. Monique and Coleen pranced excitedly alongside Jacey, proudly carrying their ribbons from the horse show. Both girls chattered continuously between themselves, recapping the entire horse show. Jacey was glad she hadn't entered the fun show. They would have shown her up as they had everyone else.

"Have you decided what you want for dinner yet?" Jacey asked with curiosity.

"Pizza," Monique chanted.

"Hamburgers," Coleen said.

Jacey gave them each some money. "If I let you on your own for a couple of hours, do you promise to eat something other than ice cream and cotton candy?"

"Yes, of course. There's always French fries and funnel cake," Monique teased. "We can play some games too."

Jacey rolled her eyes and attempted to hide her smile. "I'd like to use the library computer and type that article for Shelly. I'm sure you'll find something more exciting to do here."

"Yeah, we certainly don't want to go to the library," Coleen replied.

Monique then pointed up the street just past Town Square and appeared excited. "Look, it's Professor!"

Both girls waved their ribbons and ran for Professor, who was tall enough that he was easily noticed in a crowd. Jacey followed obediently. The scientists had a stand along the street with a fossil exhibit, rocks, dinosaur bones, and the solar system. Timon even had his telescope set up. Maxwell appeared to be the only one missing from the group. Even Angela was present, though she appeared bored. Doc saw them and approached the inside of their stand.

"Do you like our little exhibit?" Doc asked. "I thought joining the festivities would be to our benefit."

Jacey nodded with a soft laugh. "When did you put all this together?"

"This morning," Doc replied. "We noticed the banner across the street yesterday afternoon."

Timon inched his way closer like a cat stalking a mouse and smiled at Jacey. "Hey, Jacey," he chirped.

Both girls flocked around Professor and showed him their ribbons. He seemed impressed with their wins.

"Had I known you were in the show, I would've slipped away from the exhibit to watch it," Professor announced cheerfully to both girls.

"Would you like it if I won you a teddy bear?" Timon asked Jacey with a childlike smile.

Brian practically jumped the table, nearly dumping the fossils, placed his arm around Jacey, and smirked at Timon.

"If it's a teddy bear she wants, I'd have better luck winning it than you."

Monique and Coleen bounced around Professor like lovesick schoolgirls. "Come on, Professor. You can hang out with us tonight."

"Sounds like fun," Professor announced cheerfully as they pulled him away from the stand.

Maxwell returned carrying a box of drinks and snacks for the entire group. Timon and Brian nearly tackled him for the goodies he carried. Sheriff Monroe approached the scientists' stand, eyed their exhibits, and gave a general nod.

"How's our town been treating you?" Sheriff Monroe asked pleasantly.

"Mostly everyone has been friendly," Doc announced with a hint of reserve.

Monroe snorted a soft laugh with apparent understanding. "It's okay, we share the same headache," he replied. "I'm sorry if my deputy caused you any grief with yesterday's search of the institution. It was bound to happen eventually. We're trying to keep our headache from turning into a migraine."

"I'm sure it'll die down," Doc replied while maintaining his good humor. "We're not building monsters in the basement."

"Speak for yourself," Timon teased and immediately received several annoyed looks. He rolled his eyes. "No sense of humor."

"If there's any trouble," Monroe announced, "just give us a shout. We'll handle Jill and her followers."

"Thank you, Sheriff," Doc announced.

Sheriff Monroe grinned at Jacey, gave her a polite nod, and continued his patrol of the fair.

Doc looked at the others and appeared more cheerful than he had. "Why don't the rest of you go out and enjoy yourselves at the fair," he announced. "I'll take care of the exhibit. I want to watch the unveiling of the new town statue at dusk anyway." He nodded toward the large, canvas-covered statue practically in front of their stand.

"Thanks, Doc," Brian announced cheerfully then looked at Jacey. "I'll escort Jacey."

Timon clung to her right arm and glared at Brian. "Why don't you go join the rest of the pigs at the farm exhibit," Timon snorted. "I saw Jacey first."

"I saw her first--the day we arrived in town," Brian snapped. "Find your own date."

"Now you two just behave," Doc said firmly. "If you don't stop fighting over the young lady, I'll take her away; then neither of you will have her."

Jacey laughed softly to Doc's scolding remarks. Both men became sheepish.

"Honestly," Jacey announced with an embarrassed smile, "I have some research to do at the library."

"And miss the town fair?" Timon gasped playfully then smiled. "At least allow me to buy you a snow cone."

Jacey could hear part of the conversation between Maxwell and Angela at the stand just behind her.

"Are you sure you wouldn't like to walk around the fair?" Maxwell asked Angela. "We could play some carnival games and win cheap prizes."

"Quite childish, don't you think?" Angela snapped coldly with obvious disinterest in the entire spectacle.

Jacey half turned and noted the embarrassed look on Maxwell's face and the way Angela was glaring at her. Jacey then realized that

Angela was actually upset by the way Timon and Brian were fussing over her.

"Come on, Jacey," Brian whined with a teasing smile and practically pulled her into his arms. "Let's go play some games and have some fun."

Jacey was slightly surprised by Brain's embrace. She gently pulled away from him and backed up several steps. She attempted to smile, though she was losing patience with him.

"I really need to finish that article for the paper," Jacey announced firmly. "It's due Monday morning." Jacey backed up another step and bumped into Maxwell. She spun nervously and forced a tiny smile. "Oh, I'm sorry."

"I'll help you with your research," Maxwell said softly. He then forced a tiny smile. "Research is my life."

Jacey looked at Maxwell with some surprise and smiled more naturally. "You'll help me?"

He nodded. Angela's eyes narrowed sharply.

"Thank you, Maxwell. I'd really appreciate any help you could offer."

Angela linked onto Maxwell's arm, apparently surprising him, and smiled sweetly. "I'd like to visit this library myself."

"Libraries?" Brian scoffed with a frown. "I'd rather play with fire ants. You three enjoy yourselves." He playfully smacked Timon on the chest. "Let's see who can be the first to dunk the mayor."

Timon eagerly left with him.

Chapter Sixteen

*T*he archives was located in the basement of the library. Despite the extensive lights, the basement remained dingy in appearance. There were aisles of bookshelves containing old books, magazines, and racks of newspapers. An older desktop computer was located in the back of the archives surrounded by bookshelves. Jacey sat behind the computer as she looked up several articles and printed the ones that interested her while Maxwell and Angela wandered around the shelves of old newspapers.

"Most libraries won't allow you in their archives," Maxwell remarked to Jacey from several aisles away.

"As a part-time employee," she announced simply, "I'm entitled to full access of their property."

The two scientists returned to the cluttered room she occupied. Jacey removed several folded papers from her pocket and straightened them out on the table. Angela peered over her shoulder and burst out laughing.

"Are those your notes?" Angela asked with a smile that mocked her.

Jacey turned back to the computer and avoided looking at the snobbish woman she'd come to loathe. "I never said I was very organized," she muttered and began her healthy dislike for the woman all over again. She wondered if Angela just felt she was beneath her, or did it have something to do with the other scientists taking an interest in her. Maybe it was just Maxwell's attention that bothered her.

"I guess not," Angela laughed.

Maxwell removed the papers from the printer and scanned through the printed articles from archived newspapers. "All this happened in this town?"

"In a matter of three days," Jacey replied without looking at him. "This town took a bad situation and made it into something even worse."

"Persecution of the innocent, curses, and legends back from the dead," Maxwell commented with a soft snort. "I heard Asher speak of his turmoil."

Jacey sighed gently. "He would know too. He was a victim ten years ago and every day since."

Maxwell removed a hi-lighter from the desk and began hi-lighting parts of the article.

"I don't suppose there are any science magazines in this place," Angela huffed while folding her arms across her chest as she looked around.

"The next room over," Jacey replied dryly without looking at the woman.

Angela walked away without further comment. Maxwell sat on the edge of the desk and sifted through the small stack of papers. He hi-lighted several more items.

"Do you believe your friend killed Hal Burgess?" Maxwell asked softly and interrupted the silence.

Jacey stopped typing and looked at Maxwell with surprise. "I certainly don't," she remarked curtly.

"I didn't mean to offend you," he said gently.

She sighed softly and looked back at the computer. "None taken," she said sadly. "I'm just getting a little tired of listening to people put Asher down."

"And not being able to defend him," Maxwell stated gently. "I've gathered that you try to keep your friendship with him a secret."

"It's his request," she said timidly and frowned while staring at the computer monitor. "He doesn't want the town to alienate me as well."

"Maybe he just needs to make some new friends," Maxwell said simply. "Tomorrow night is the formal party at the institution. It's supposed to be celebrating the new foundation, but they're generally for public relations and grants. I'm sure Brian's already invited you, but I thought that maybe you'd like to bring Asher. He'd probably enjoy socializing with that crowd. He seemed to enjoy scientific talk the other night."

Jacey spun in her chair and looked at him with surprise. "Do you mean it?" she asked excitedly. Her enthusiasm didn't even have anything to do with Asher's request to be invited to the institution. "I'm sure he'd love the opportunity to talk with people who don't know or care about his reputation here in town." She couldn't contain her smile. She was suddenly very happy. "He'll be thrilled to hear. He can be my date."

Maxwell smiled lightly and held back his chuckle. "I think Brian might object to that."

Jacey casually stood from her chair and sat on the desk near him. "Brian never mentioned the party," she replied simply. "He never asked me to go with him; therefore he has nothing to say about it."

Maxwell appeared surprised and gently tilted his head. "I really thought Brian had asked you already." He then smiled lightly and stood. "It probably just slipped his mind. He never remembers the formal parties. They're usually rather boring."

"It doesn't matter," Jacey said cheerfully as she stood. "I'm just thrilled that you thought to invite Asher." She threw her arms around his neck and hugged him happily. "You really are a wonderful man."

Maxwell uncertainly returned the embrace. She slowly pulled away, placed a hand on his face, and smiled happily.

"If there's ever anything I can do for you, don't hesitate to ask."

Maxwell stared into her eyes. Neither said a word. Jacey's bright smile became light and shy as she stared into his dark eyes. She gently bit her lower lip and ran her hand along his face before allowing it to drop to his shoulder. Maxwell smiled with apparent embarrassment.

"You could save me a dance," he said softly and touched her hand that still rested on his shoulder.

Her body shuddered from the sensation of his fingers running down her bare arm. Jacey felt her cheeks become hot and red. She allowed her gaze to stray to his mouth then quickly returned her eyes to his. Maxwell held his breath then gently touched her cheek with the back on his fingers. It was an intense moment. He slowly lowered his mouth to hers. Her heart pounded with anticipation.

"Maxwell," came a bored female voice from the next room.

They jumped apart seconds before Angela entered the archives. She folded her arms across her chest and leaned in the doorway with a look that easily conveyed her emotions.

"Maxwell, I'm bored and hungry," Angela retorted. "Let's go for something to eat."

Maxwell breathed rapidly and a broad, nervous smile crossed his face. "Yes, of course." He turned to Jacey with an embarrassed smile. "I'll, uh, get these papers back to you tomorrow night. I'm sure I can find more information for you on my computer as well."

Angela groaned impatiently. "Come on, Maxwell. Before I die of boredom."

Maxwell hurried across the room and joined Angela. They could be heard walking up the stairs.

"Honestly, there's nothing above a fourth grade reading level in this ancient library," Angela could be heard commenting as they vanished up the steps.

Jacey slowly sank back onto the desktop and stared after him until he was gone. A strange smile crossed her face. She wasn't sure what it was about him, but he certainly had her attention. Sadly, he already had Angela in his life. She heard someone on the basement stairs and immediately sprang to her feet. She sort of hoped it was Maxwell returning--without Angela. She attempted to act casual as she caught a glimpse of someone entering the area she occupied. Her heart sank when she saw Deputy Jameson. He appeared surprised to see her and offered a charming smile.

"I was wondering who was down here," he announced. "I saw those two scientists leaving and wasn't sure what to think."

Jacey flopped into the rickety, old chair behind the computer and returned to her article. "No, it's just me," she announced. "They were helping with some research for my article on the institution."

He rolled his eyes and groaned. "Hasn't there been enough articles on that rattrap the last decade?" Jameson sat on the edge of the desk and again smiled. "Why don't you do an article on the talented and handsome officers of the Stony Ridge police department?"

Jacey attempted to hold back her laugh. He never gave up. "I think Brenda *did* that already."

He suddenly appeared uncomfortable and straightened where he sat on the desk. "You do realize you'd already dumped me when Brenda and I went out."

"Yes, I'm aware of that," Jacey replied and tried to concentrate on her article, although his hovering made that difficult.

"So what's the problem?" he asked while leaning closer to her from where he sat on the desk.

She glanced at him and knew he was talking about them getting back together, but he was always so vague, he made it difficult for her to turn him down.

"There's no problem," she replied and returned to the computer.

His closeness was starting to bother her now. They got along better being friends, but there were times he just liked to double-check that she still wanted it that way. Jameson smiled and finally stood.

"I'd better patrol the fair before Monroe checks up on me," he replied. "See you later."

Jacey finally looked at him and offered a polite smile. She looked away to avoid watching him leave. As if on cue, he looked back before disappearing out of her view. If he even thought she was looking at him, he'd take it as a sign of her interest in him and possibly step up his 'wooing'. At times, she felt bad that she didn't feel the same for him as he felt for her, but then she'd remember his possessive, controlling behavior and the guilt would vanish. It was sad too. Jameson was exactly what she was looking for in a man. Handsome country cop, cowboy appeal, and horse lover to boot. She just couldn't get past his smothering personality.

†

*T*he streets of the fair were alive with activity early that evening. Monique and Coleen each carried large stuffed horses Professor had won for them. All three ate ice cream cones as they walked the slightly crowded streets. Professor looked more like a big kid now than a respected and highly intelligent scholar.

"This is the most fun I've had at a town fair," Coleen chirped. "We got to win ribbons with the horses, play games, eat junk food for supper, and spend the evening with Professor."

Monique raised her stuffed horse. "And don't forget Professor winning us these stuffed animals."

"Here, here," Coleen chanted and they clicked ice cream cones together as if they were wineglasses.

"It's been fun for me too," Professor announced cheerfully. "I didn't realize how much fun I'd been missing all these years. My work became my hobby, but I forgot there was an entire world full of simple pleasures--like having an ice cream cone."

"You need to come out riding with us again," Monique suggested.

"Oh, I'd love too," Professor announced cheerfully. "If we lose the stiffs, maybe this time we can gallop a little."

"You've got it," Coleen said with a laugh. "We'll race you on that big stretch of dirt road."

Brian and Timon joined them while carrying large plastic cups of beer. Both men appeared to be enjoying themselves as well. Brian had a small teddy bear, and Timon proudly carried a goldfish in a plastic bag.

"Quarter drafts," Timon said with a chuckle. "I could get used to these fairs."

"They make up for it on all those games you lost," Brian teased cheerfully.

Timon petted Monique's stuffed horse. "Nice horsy. How'd you win it?"

"Professor won them for us," Monique said excitedly.

"Darts," Professor said and made a throwing motion. "I'm really good at darts."

"It doesn't matter how good you are," Brian snorted. "They're fixed with weights."

"Not anymore," Professor said with a sly smile.

Timon laughed heartily. Jill lunged before them and startled all five. Timon clung to his goldfish to protect it. She glared evilly.

"It's because of you our town will suffer the curse," she announced boldly. "You've poisoned this town with your presence. You'll see! You'll see when people die!"

Timon looked at his watch then back at Jill. "Aren't you late for a witch burning somewhere?"

Jill pointed a warning finger at him. He again clutched his goldfish bag. "You'll see! I promise!"

"You're the only curse on this town," Brian announced with raised brows. "Get a life, lady."

All five walked past her without further comment. None were concerned with what had just happened.

"So," Professor announced to his fellow scientists while grinning slyly, "which of you idiots is taking Jacey to the formal tomorrow night?"

Timon and Brian looked at Professor with some surprise. "Formal? What formal?" Timon asked.

"That's next week, isn't it?" Brian asked with a look of surprise on his face.

Professor chuckled lowly in his throat while grinning. "Uh, no, that's tomorrow night."

Both men looked at each other then turned and ran down the crowded street. Professor seemed to take some perverse pleasure in watching them trip over each other to find Jacey first.

†

$\mathcal{I}$t was nearly dusk. Monique, Coleen, and Professor joined Doc, Maxwell, and Angela by the stand for the unveiling of the new statue. Brian and Timon soon returned as well. Monique and Coleen became bored during Mayor Norad's speech and swatted each other with their stuffed horses. Brenda approached the scientists' stand, posed almost seductively, and smiled sweetly at them. Brian and Timon were immediately taken by her beauty.

"I heard you'd arrived a week early," Brenda announced with plump lips brightly glossed with red lipstick. With her milky complexion and raven black hair, her lips practically jumped off her face.

Brian and Timon fumbled over each other to greet her with grins and extended hands. She politely shook their hands.

"I'm Brenda Heinz," she announced. "Journalist for our local paper."

"Oh," Professor announced cheerfully from alongside Monique and Coleen. "We met your colleague the other day."

"Colleague?" she said while snorting a laugh. "You mean Jacey? I'd hardly call her a colleague. She cleans up around the press and occasionally writes a blurb here and there."

Monique and Coleen glared at the woman and immediately took a step forward about to speak. Professor casually placed his hand over both their mouths with his arms wrapped around their heads to hold them back and silence them.

"I was hoping I could do an interview with you regarding your plans for the institution," she announced sweetly.

Brian and Timon both raised their hands to volunteer. Brenda grinned her approval. Howard Norad finally finished his speech. Brenda removed her cell phone and took video of the unveiling. Everyone looked toward the covered statue as Howard removed the canvas. Roseanne lie dead and bloodied while draped in the statue's arms. Her head hung back to reveal the deep gash across her throat, and her eyes and mouth remained opened with a fixated look of horror. Several cameras had flashed then instantaneous stopped as the crowd gasped aloud. Several women screamed. The mayor stared at the dead women, unable to speak. Sheriff Monroe and Deputy Jameson ran onto the platform to cover the body quickly. Brenda clutched her cell phone and pushed her way through the crowd. She'd gotten her story!

Jill could be heard shouting above the crowd. "It's the curse. They've returned to punish us!"

†

*J*acey finished typing her rough draft on the computer and sat back while it printed. She could hear a commotion from the crowd outside and assumed they were upset about something in the mayor's speech, since she hadn't heard any clapping. A floorboard suddenly creaked from upstairs, startling her. It had been unusually quiet in the library due to the fair outside. Jacey stood and walked toward the stairs. She listened a moment then, when she heard nothing; she went back to the printer and removed her papers. She typed five separate stories with different themes about the institution. She heard another creak from upstairs followed by thundering footfalls on the steps. Monique and Coleen ran down the stairs with Professor, Timon, and Brian close behind. Both girls hugged Jacey.

"Oh, Jacey," they cried out while clinging to her. "It was horrible!"

Chapter Seventeen

*J*acey slowly hung up the kitchen phone and looked at both girls with concern. "Considering what happened in town tonight," Jacey announced, "I think we'd better double check that all the windows and doors are locked."

Monique's mouth opened with a strange look as she stared at Jacey. "What was that phone call about?" she asked with the concern evident on her face.

"What has you upset?" Coleen asked.

Jacey shook her head and bolted the kitchen door. "Nothing's wrong. Brian insisted on staying the night so we wouldn't be alone."

"Is there something you're not telling us?" Coleen asked with a slight tilt of her head.

Jacey gently bit her lower lip then sighed. "It has nothing to do with us," she replied timidly then fidgeted. "It's just, well, Professor found a watch on the stairwell of the west wing. Dr. Talbert confirmed it belonged to Roseanne."

Both girls' mouths dropped open.

"But Jameson searched the institution just yesterday," Coleen protested softly. "If she was there, he would've found her, right?"

Monique's eyes widened. "She was abducted on the same night we were locked in our rooms on the west wing," Monique announced with a faint breath.

"I have my doubts about the thoroughness of Jameson's search," Jacey said with insecurity and rubbed her chilled arms. "It only took him twenty minutes to look around the entire institution, when it took us almost an hour to walk the building, and we didn't even go into the basement."

"So you think whoever locked us in our rooms, did it so we wouldn't see what they were doing?" Monique suddenly asked and appeared alarmed.

"It's possible," Jacey said. She forced a tiny smile and attempted to reassure them. "But Brian's on his way here, so we'll be fine. Let's check those windows and doors."

Once the house was secure, the girls approached the shelf filled with DVD's and searched for a movie for the evening. Jacey stood alongside the large bay window and stared down the dirt road. It had been nearly an hour since Brian called, and there was still no sign of him. She didn't know where he could be.

"I don't think we should watch any horror movies tonight," Coleen said nervously. "We've had enough horror for one day."

"I'll say," Monique huffed.

Jacey moved away from the window, allowing the curtain to fall back into place, and walked toward the kitchen. "Brian should've been here by now. I'd better call and see if he's on his way."

Both girls followed her into the kitchen.

"Maybe Professor could come instead," Monique suggested.

Jacey found the institution phone number on a piece of paper on the counter and dialed it. The phone rang several times before finally being answered.

"Timon's house of insanity," Timon announced from the other end. "How may I service you?"

"Timon, it's Jacey," she said into the phone while feeling tense.

"Hey, Jacey," he squawked enthusiastically from the other end. "Are you and the rug rats doing okay?"

"Yes, we're fine," she replied and felt her mood lighten. "I was just wondering if Brian had left yet."

"Yeah, he left right after he hung up with you," Timon replied then sounded alarmed. "Isn't he there?"

"No, he's not here."

"Should I come and get you? I can be there in ten minutes," Timon informed her from the other end.

Jacey forced a tiny smile. "No, you don't have to come and get us, we'll be fine," she replied. "I'm just worried about Brian, that's all. Just let me know if you hear from him."

"Will do," Timon replied.

Jacey hung up the phone and frowned, concerning both girls. "He left right after I spoke to him," she informed them then shook her head. "I don't like this."

"Do you think someone's kidnapped him?" Monique asked then gasped and placed her hand to her throat as her eyes widened. "Or *killed* him?"

"Stop it," Jacey scolded and attempted to reign in Monique's overactive imagination, although after seeing Roseanne murdered like that, she probably had reason for her thinking. "Let's not get ourselves worked up, okay?"

Both girls nodded but the stress was evident on their youthful faces. Jacey drew a deep breath, approached the gun cabinet within the living room, and removed a small revolver.

"I'll keep this nearby just in case," Jacey announced gently and placed the gun down the back of her pants.

More than half an hour had passed. Jacey sat on the arm of the chair and remained edgy throughout the first half of the movie, although the girls seemed to watch the television intently. Jacey finally sat in her chair and attempted to focus on the movie. Monique looked at the side window and stared through the separation in the curtains. Her expression suddenly dropped.

"Jacey," Monique announced and nervously scrambled into a sitting position. "There's someone at the window."

Jacey appeared alerted and slowly straightened.

"Maybe it's Brian," Coleen suggested and sat up as well.

"Just to be safe," Jacey said as she stared at the window. "Wait for me upstairs."

Both girls sprang to their feet and hurried up the stairs. Jacey removed the revolver from the back of her pants, hurried toward the kitchen, and paused in the archway. She stared at the kitchen window, listened a moment, and then looked at the door. She heard the porch creak, as it had so many times in the past--always for no reason. There were no other sounds, except for the wind chimes. Jacey sighed and relaxed. It was windy, which sometimes caused the porch to creak and branches to bend past the windows. She shook her head with a tiny smile.

"It's just the wind," she muttered softly.

The kitchen doorknob jiggled. Jacey jumped with a gasp and stared at the door with wide eyes. She flattened herself against the wall, clung to her handgun, and peeked toward the mostly glass door. She could hear a distinct footfall on the porch. A shadow moved past the door. Jacey let out a slight scream and darted up the stairs. She ran into her mother's bedroom with the girls and slammed the door behind her. She locked it and breathed heavily. Monique stared at her with wide eyes. Coleen stood alongside the bed and hung up the phone on the nightstand.

"The dispatcher's contacting Jameson right away," Coleen announced.

Jacey knew the girls were probably just as frightened as she was, but she needed to keep them calm. She placed the revolver down the back of her pants to give the illusion that she wasn't frightened for their sake.

"We'll just wait here until Deputy Jameson arrives," Jacey informed them and raked trembling fingers through her hair.

There was the faint sound of glass shattering from downstairs in the kitchen. Jacey backed away from the bedroom door and stared at it as if it was about to explode. She looked back at the girls, who now stood on the opposite side of the bed with the same look of horror. Jacey hurried to the far side of the bed with them and now removed her revolver. Monique looked out the large window next to her. Headlights appeared at the top of the long driveway. She looked back at Jacey.

"Jacey," Monique cried softly and pointed out the window. "Jameson's coming!"

Jacey hurried to the window and saw the large, white vehicle with bright headlights in the darkness. She looked at the porch roof then the large, oak tree near her bedroom window just a couple of feet away.

"Wait here," she announced and again placed the gun down the back of her pants.

Jacey quietly opened the screen and climbed out the window and onto the porch roof. She carefully walked across the roof, attempting to be as quiet as possible. Monique and Coleen leapt out the window and ran for her.

"Don't leave us alone in there," Monique whispered.

Jacey motioned them to the tree. Both girls climbed into the tree with Jacey behind them. All three began climbing down the branches as the vehicle got closer. Jacey lost her footing and tumbled from the tree to the ground below. She landed on her backside and hit her head. She cringed and looked toward the rapidly approaching headlights. The vehicle was almost on top of her. It skidded to a halt. Something moved within the woods near the house. Both girls screamed and pointed toward the woods. The van doors opened and both Professor and Maxwell jumped out and ran to Jacey's side. Maxwell knelt beside her and helped her to her knees.

"Are you alright?" Maxwell asked.

Professor ran to the tree and assisted both girls to the ground. They hugged Professor gratefully. Jacey placed a hand to her spinning head and looked around with some disorientation. She then looked at Maxwell and clutched his arm for support. He gently helped her to her feet. Monique and Coleen were screaming and pointing into the woods. They were talking so excitedly, their words barely made sense. Professor stared into the woods a moment, squinted, and then shook his head.

"I don't see anyone," he said then motioned them toward the van. "Come on; let's get you out of here."

Professor loaded both girls into the van then returned to Maxwell and Jacey. Jacey was now on her feet, although she was weighing heavily in Maxwell's arms. She couldn't get herself together enough to stand on her own.

"Is she okay?" she heard Professor ask Maxwell.

"A little dazed, I'd say," Maxwell remarked gently. "Let's get her back to the institution."

Professor saw the revolver lying on the ground beneath where Jacey had fallen. He uncertainly picked up the gun by the barrel with his fingertips, eyed it, and raised his brows.

"Welcome to the sticks, Professor," he muttered softly and carried it with him as if it would explode.

Jacey exhaled deeply, leaned on Maxwell, and shut her eyes. When she opened her eyes, they were already driving up the dirt lane. Both girls were chattering nervously. Jacey held her pounding head then looked out the window and saw headlights coming at them. Colored lights flashed on the vehicle's roof. Jacey slowly turned her head and looked at Maxwell, who held her. He was talking to her, but she didn't understand his words. She rested her head on his shoulder and shut her eyes to the barely audible conversation.

†

O‌nce in the institution lounge, Doc and Timon fussed over Jacey where she sat on the old, worn sofa despite her insistence that she was fine. As she held ice to her head, she couldn't understand their continuous questions on how she felt. Sheriff Monroe sat on the coffee table across from Jacey and studied her a long moment in silence. She was so busy telling the guys she was okay that she hadn't even noticed Sheriff Monroe quietly sitting before her. She wasn't sure how long he'd been sitting there, although she really wasn't sure how she even got to the institution. It was hard to concentrate with the walls breathing as they were.

"You didn't actually see anyone?" Monroe finally asked.

Jacey slowly shook her head. "I was so startled by someone at the door that I ran upstairs to the girls," she informed him. "It wasn't until I was upstairs that we heard the glass on the door breaking." She gave him an odd look. "You know, Timon, I don't think Sheriff Monroe would appreciate you wearing his uniform."

Monroe studied her and raised a curious brow. He glanced at Doc in silent question.

Doc shrugged. "She called me dad twice."

Monroe gently cleared his throat and focused his attention on Jacey. "Well, Deputy Jameson tells me nothing was taken that he could tell," he informed her. "Your friends' arrival may have scared him off." He studied her a long moment and eyed the ice pack she held to her head. "Are you sure you don't want me to call Dr. Talbert to have a look at you?"

Jacey snorted a laugh and glanced around the room. "I'm already up to my elbows in doctors, Uncle Russell. I don't think there's room for one more."

"At least your sense of humor is still intact," he replied and offered a tiny grin. "Jameson is going to patrol your place a while longer, and we're having someone board up that broken window on the door for you. I don't think you should return home tonight."

"Under the circumstances," Doc announced firmly, "I think she should remain here overnight for observation. I'll have Professor lock the gates behind you. She'll be safe here."

Monroe smiled and nodded.

✝

$\mathcal{I}$t was only a few minutes after Sheriff Monroe left when Professor returned from locking the main gate and the doors. He entered the lounge where Jacey and the girls were beginning to relax after their scare. Brian seemed to be the only one missing. Jacey couldn't even remember if she had seen him since she arrived. Everything was fuzzy in her mind. Oddly enough, the only thing she seemed to notice was the pleasant smell of Maxwell's aftershave lingering on her shirt. She barely remembered how it even got there.

"We're secure," Professor announced firmly. "No one's getting in here tonight."

Jacey lifted her head and her mouth opened slightly. She wanted to speak but her head was pounding now, leaving her feeling dizzy and oddly confused. A moment passed, and she finally remembered what she wanted to say.

"Where's Brian? Has anyone seen him?" she asked nervously, only now remembering he'd never shown.

All four men stared at her with the same blank expression. Professor finally smiled and gently scratched his temple.

"Well, you know, Brian," Professor said mildly. "He probably stopped somewhere and lost track of time. I wouldn't worry too much." He then clapped his hands together, startling everyone, and looked at Monique and Coleen. "How'd you girls like to come to the kitchen for some ice cream?"

Both girls gladly joined Professor.

Jacey sighed while clutching her head. "I suppose I've watched too many horror movies, but I'm just worried that something happened to him. I mean," she said and inhaled deeply, again smelling Maxwell's wonderful scent on her, "he was coming to the house, never showed, and then we're attacked. It's just *odd*."

Timon walked to the window and looked out. "There he is," he said then sighed. "I suppose I should unlock the gate for him."

"He has a key," Doc said lowly. "I'll arrange rooms for our guests."

Jacey watched Doc straighten and leave the lounge. She caught the look Timon and Maxwell exchanged. Neither man said a word. Maxwell joined Jacey on the sofa and checked the bump on her head. She glanced at him briefly and marveled at his bedside manner. Maybe it was just the concussion or that marvelous smell, but he suddenly seemed amazingly handsome at that moment. He returned the ice pack to her head and offered a tiny smile.

"Someone's going to have one hell of a hangover tomorrow," he teased.

Jacey stared at him and grinned at how cute he was. "You smell good," she announced, surprising him.

Timon stood by the large window and slowly turned his head to stare at her. His mouth opened slightly from the comment. Maxwell smiled, snorted a laugh, and turned away with embarrassment.

"I guess Doc gave you the good painkillers," Maxwell teased.

Timon snickered softly. The front door was unlocked and opened. Brian hurried into the room, looked around, and paused when he saw Jacey.

"There you are," he exclaimed. "I went to your house. The glass on the door was broken. What happened?"

Timon walked toward Brian with a cold look on his face. His eyes were narrow and harsh. "Very rude of you not to phone and tell us where you were," he snorted. "We thought you were dead." His harsh voice indicated there was something more than concern behind his comment.

Brian appeared a bit puzzled. "I was talking with Deputy Jameson about the murder of that woman. We talked a little longer than I anticipated."

Jacey's disorientation was lifting and something didn't make sense. "Deputy Jameson? Were you with him the entire evening?"

"Until half an hour ago. That's when I went to your house," he replied. "That's why I was late. Are you sure you're okay?"

Jacey's eyes narrowed to his lie. "Yeah, everything's fine," she scoffed. "I just had some trouble with a break-in."

She knew Jameson had been at her house earlier, so Brian couldn't have been with him. Both Maxwell and Timon listened to the conversation but didn't comment. Maxwell appeared uncomfortable then stood and approached Doc's medical kit. He returned items to the kit but appeared to listen with interest to the ensuing conversation.

"At least you're alright," Brian announced in a soothing tone and appeared sympathetic. "I was worried when I saw the kitchen door and found no one home." He approached the sofa and sat extremely close to her. "I'm glad you're okay. I would've felt terrible if something happened to you."

Timon grunted lowly. "I need a drink."

He left the room as Angela entered with coffee for everyone. Jacey stood with some dizziness and attempted to put some distance between her and Brian. Maxwell saw her sway and twitched as if debating whether or not to rush to her side.

"I've had a trying day followed by an appalling evening," Jacey remarked lowly. "I think I'd like to just get some sleep."

Brian sprang to his feet to assist her. Jacey ignored him, held her head, and stumbled toward Maxwell.

"Would you mind walking me to my room?" she asked gently.

Angela's eyes narrowed at Maxwell and snorted her disapproval.

"Of course," Maxwell announced with a tiny smile, apparently not noticing the look he received from Angela.

As she clung to his arm, he walked with her from the room and guided her toward the stairs. Jacey walked up the stairs while clinging to Maxwell then finally looked at him. Oddly enough, she didn't remember how she ended up walking with him or where they were even going.

"Why did you and Professor come to my house tonight?" she asked.

"When you called and said Brian didn't show, we thought we should come for you," Maxwell gently informed her, although he seemed to be leaving something out of his story. "We were concerned about leaving the three of you alone after what happened in town. It seems we had good reason to be worried."

She sighed and stared down the long hallway on the second floor. She marveled at how big her house suddenly seemed. "I find it odd someone would try to rob the house while we were awake. We had half the lights on."

"Perhaps someone is upset that you're writing that article for the paper," he announced. "Roseanne's death has the town in a tizzy."

"Brenda's working on an article too, so I've heard," Jacey replied. "No one's gone after her."

"Forgive me, but that woman has a little too much air in her head to write a meaningful story," Maxwell announced then immediately silenced.

Jacey looked at him and appeared surprised. "You met Brenda? When?"

Maxwell fidgeted and appeared uncomfortable. He attempted a smile. "Well, she, uh, sort of stopped by this evening."

Jacey rolled her eyes. "Oh, so that's why no one was worried about Brian. He made a little side trip to do an interview with Brenda, huh?" She snorted a laugh. "Or just *do* Brenda?"

Maxwell fidgeted.

"You don't have to spare my feelings about Brian," she informed him. "He pursued me; not the other way around. I have zero interest in him."

Maxwell glanced at her, offered a tiny smile, and shrugged. "In that case, he's a whore."

She suddenly eyed him and had to keep from laughing. "Wow, that's pretty bold coming from you. A little out of character."

"Considering your memory loss, you probably won't remember this conversation in the morning. I can afford to be bold."

"Oh? Well, in that case," she announced with a tiny grin. "I'm a virgin."

Maxwell stared at her with some surprise and tilted his head. A tiny smile crossed his face while hiding his humor. "I think you completely misunderstood the concept of *your* memory loss."

Chapter Eighteen

*P*rofessor drove Jacey and the girls back to her house early the next morning. It was already planned that he would come that afternoon to go riding with them before the party. During their drive, Professor invited Monique and Coleen to the institution gala. They just smiled but didn't respond. That they didn't jump at the chance to attend the party at Professor's request was almost odd, in Jacey's opinion. As the white van drove along the dirt road and away from the house, both girls looked at Jacey.

"I think I speak for both Coleen and myself when I say you're not getting us to wear dresses," Monique announced firmly. "Not for a party and not even for Professor."

Coleen nodded in agreement.

Jacey finally understood their reluctance to attend the party. She managed a smile and laughed softly. "I understand. I'm not much for dresses myself. I certainly wasn't at your age." She considered her options then inhaled deeply and sighed. "I suppose I'll have to borrow a dress from Shelly." She looked back at the girls. "I'm not leaving you alone tonight. I'll see if Shelly will stay with you until I return."

Both girls frowned their disapproval. "We don't need a baby-sitter," Coleen whined.

"Yeah, we can take care of ourselves for one evening," Monique agreed. "Jameson said the break-in was probably just an isolated incident."

Jacey rolled her eyes and groaned, not wanting to be reminded. "I still don't want to leave you alone--especially here."

Monique wrinkled her nose. "Do we have to go to Shelly's apartment above the press? There's nothing to do there."

"Maybe Jameson could stay with us," Coleen suggested.

"Yeah, I bet he likes watching movies and eating junk food," Monique announced. "Wouldn't need more protection than a country cop."

"Unfortunately, Jameson's on duty until eight o'clock, and then he's going to the institution to patrol the area," Jacey said simply. "Word has it that Jill is forming a protest."

"How special," Monique muttered under her breath.

"Why don't you two feed the horses, and I'll call Shelly about the dress and her coming to stay with you," Jacey suggested. "We'll go to town this afternoon for lunch before your ride. I don't think the fair was canceled, so you can play some more games while I take care of things with Shelly."

Both girls nodded.

"Just as long as we're back before two o'clock for our ride with Professor," Monique announced.

"We'll be back in time," Jacey assured them. "I wouldn't want to keep you girls from your *date*."

Both girls snickered in response.

✝

*I*t was late morning. Jacey entered her mother's bedroom and poked through the assortment of dresses in the closet. As she suspected, her mother didn't have anything she would consider wearing. She picked up the phone on the bedside table and called Shelly. She looked out the window from her mother's bedroom to the barn where the girls were washing their horses.

"Shelly?" she announced into the phone. "Hey, it's Jacey."

"Jacey," Shelly chirped back through the phone. "Do you have my article?"

"Yeah, I'm going to drop it off this afternoon," she announced then hesitated. "I was hoping you had a dress I could borrow for the party tonight."

There was an odd silence from the other end. "Uh, yeah," Shelly announced. "I have plenty of dresses, but I'm not sure any will actually fit you."

"I think we're around the same size," Jacey informed her. "I'm sure something will fit."

"Yes, I'm sure they'll fit," Shelly replied from the other end. "But you might be popping out a little more than you'd like."

Jacey was silent and uncertainly looked down at her chest. She groaned softly. Shelly was barely an 'A' cup and Jacey was a solid 'C' cup.

"I'm sure you have something I can wear."

"You're welcome to stop by and look," she replied. "I hope you're planning on getting some good stories at that party. I didn't realize you were invited."

"It was last minute," Jacey informed her. "Speaking of that, I was hoping you could entertain the girls while I'm out tonight."

"Sure," Shelly replied and a deep sigh was heard from the other end. "It's not as if I was invited to the party."

"I heard they're boring anyway," Jacey remarked. "I'll drop by in an hour."

After Jacey hung up the phone with Shelly, she heard movement from downstairs. She again looked out the window and saw the girls still running the hose over their horses. Jacey slowly stood from where she sat on the bed and walked toward the bedroom door. There was another, more distinct sound. It sounded as if it came from the kitchen. Jacey held her breath as her heart pounded roughly. She looked around the bedroom and hurried to the closet. The shotgun had long since been removed and placed in the gun cabinet--another one of Uncle Russell's brilliant ideas. Put the guns in the locked cabinet. Never mind if you need one when you're upstairs. Jacey snatched a baseball bat from the corner of the closet. She hurried toward the bedroom door, slipped into the hallway, and quietly crept down the stairs. She carefully avoided the two steps that usually creaked and approached the kitchen. Jacey heard the distinct sound of a knife being removed from the knife block. She clutched the bat in sweaty hands and held her breath. She slowly looked around the corner and into the kitchen. Jameson cut his sandwich at the kitchen counter. She released her breath, rolled her eyes, and muttered softly to herself. She stepped into the archway as he turned around. Jameson jumped and nearly dropped his sandwich from the plate. He let out a startled gasp then relaxed and groaned.

"Don't ever sneak up on a man with a gun," he announced firmly.

She realized he hadn't even made a motion for his gun. She doubted if Jameson had ever drawn his weapon in his nine years as a deputy. Usually nothing ever happened in their little town. Although there was that one time--

"After last night, I'd think you'd announce yourself before prowling around my kitchen," she remarked sternly.

"Oh," he said then smirked sympathetically. "I wasn't thinking. You're out of mayo." Jameson sat at the table and ate his dry sandwich. "Besides, I thought you were in the barn with the girls."

Jacey leaned against the counter. "No, I had other things to do. I still need to find a dress for tonight," she informed him while frowning. "I'd really hate to buy one for just one night."

Jameson stared at her with some confusion then tilted his head. "You're going to the institution party?"

"Yes, Maxwell suggested I attend and--" she stopped herself and considered not mentioning Asher. She didn't feel like getting into another debate about Asher. "--and I thought it was a good idea. I thought I could write an article on it."

"Maybe you could have, but Brenda's attending that party tonight, from what I'm to understand," he informed her. "She's not going to give up that story without a fight."

Jacey tilted her head with a curious look. "I wonder why Shelly didn't tell me Brenda was going."

"Probably because she wants to be able to choose her story," Jameson said while snorting a laugh. "Say what you will, but Shelly's interest in friendship ends when it comes to money."

Jacey smiled wryly. "Maybe I'll just have a good time instead," she replied.

Jameson laughed in a way that mocked her. "You? Somehow I can't imagine you enjoying yourself at some formal affair with a bunch of scientists, doctors, and politicians."

She shrugged with a knowing smile. "It all depends on the company you keep."

His brow raised sharply. "Oh, are we anticipating a certain scientist's attention?"

"Maybe," she replied and remembered her promise to dance with Maxwell.

It was going to be a great evening for her just to see Asher enjoying himself, but Jameson would learn of Asher's invitation soon enough. She felt they were getting off subject.

"So have they found the guy who murdered Roseanne?" she asked, swiftly changing the subject.

"Well," he said with a depressed sigh, "we're checking a couple of possibilities, but there's nothing to really go on. Just about everyone in this town is in bed by midnight," he announced. "No one saw Roseanne being abducted. There weren't any fingerprints in her apartment, well, other than those you'd expect to find. Nothing really around the scene of the crime either. The area had been so trampled throughout the day by fairgoers that we couldn't really find anything useful." He considered something and appeared more enthusiastic. "But we do have an approximate time of death. She was murdered early yesterday morning. Considering the coroner's comments on her time of death and the time at which the vendors were setting up, we estimate she was murdered sometime between five and six Friday morning." He sighed deeply, finished his sandwich, and wiped his mouth with a napkin. "According to the coroner, she was killed with a scalpel. Her throat had been slit and there was a symbol carved into her body."

Jacey's head tilted, and her eyes narrowed. "The same as the murders ten years ago. Hal Burgess?" she questioned. "But that's impossible. If he's even alive, there's no way he'd return to this town just to murder Roseanne."

Jameson shrugged. "I'm with you on that. I'm still convinced Asher did him in anyway, which makes me wonder if someone had an ax to grind with Roseanne, or if someone was just trying to make a point."

"If she wasn't killed until early Friday, where was she all day Thursday?" Jacey asked.

"I think she was hidden within the institution," he said with a deep sigh. "If I'd only searched more thoroughly, maybe I would've found her before any of this happened."

Jacey gently rubbed her chilled shoulders. The thought was horrifying that they may have been able to prevent a murder and that she was so close to witnessing something. "What about the killer?" she asked. "Does everyone just assume it was Asher, or is there some actual police work involved?"

Jameson glared at her and frowned his disapproval. "We're taking this very seriously, Jacey. We're not going to arrest someone according to the popular opinion poll."

Jacey lowered her head. "I'm sorry," she said softly. "I didn't mean to offend you. I'm just worried about the accusations. You know how this town thinks."

"Yes," he replied then stood. "I may have my opinion of what happened to Hal Burgess, but I don't intend to let that dictate how we proceed with our investigation. Besides, Asher has Monroe on his side. He'll see that justice is served."

"And besides," Jacey continued as if she hadn't heard a word he'd said. "Asher couldn't possibly have abducted Roseanne on Thursday night. He could barely even walk, let alone carry a woman from her apartment."

"Yes, Dr. Talbert informed us it would've been difficult for Asher to have overpowered her," Jameson replied simply. "Her ex-husband was with a girlfriend an entire state away at the time." He placed his dirty plate in the sink and probably didn't even consider washing it himself. "Dr. Talbert was at young widow Glease's from early Thursday evening until Friday morning the day Roseanne was killed, and her best friend had been out of town all week with her husband. The only one left would be her sister, who lives several hours away. She was at home with her husband and never left the house." He inhaled deeply. "Once we eliminate those closest to her, it could have been anyone for any reason. Roseanne was a bit flirtatious. There could've been a man in a bar not from around here. Some one-night stand. Perhaps even one of Dr. Talbert's patients."

"Or someone who knew Roseanne lived alone and would be a good target to make their point, possibly framing Asher at the same time."

"There's no evidence that anyone's attempting to frame Asher," Jameson said firmly.

Jacey was still considering the phone call Asher received, which would have put him in the institution at the same time Jameson received his anonymous phone call to search the place. If he had discovered Asher there, uninvited, he probably would have searched the place with great care and would have found Roseanne. Asher would have been arrested, but Roseanne may have been found alive. She hated even thinking about it.

"Have you checked Jill's alibi?" Jacey asked as she leaned against the sink near him. "She has mental problems in her family, and she's willing to go to any length to keep the place closed. I think she's capable of killing to get her way."

"She doesn't have an alibi. We already checked on her for that very reason," he announced. "We're smarter than we look." He flashed a smirk. "At the time of the abduction and the murder, she was by herself, sleeping both times, like myself and a majority of the town."

Jacey nodded. "That includes me too."

It seemed more plausible than ever that they were locked in those rooms to prevent them from seeing Roseanne's abductor carrying her to some secluded location within the institution. The thought frightened Jacey. Perhaps last night's break-in was actually Roseanne's killer tying up loose ends. If he suspected they saw something--? Jacey suddenly shuddered. She didn't even want to think such things.

Chapter Nineteen

$\mathcal{T}$he fair was less crowded despite it being a Saturday. Attendance would spike toward late afternoon. By evening, it would be crowded once again. Most of the afternoon patrons were from neighboring towns. Jacey walked with Monique and Coleen through town, being most of the roads were blocked off for the fair. As they approached Town Square, they noticed the scientists' stand was gone. There were broken eggs lying in the area where the stand had been, telling Jacey they were needlessly attacked by Jill's disciples. It was going to be a tough road ahead convincing people that the new institution would help their town while Jill was promoting fear and anger. Monique and Coleen looked at the broken eggs then each other and frowned.

"Those poor guys," Coleen said sadly. "They're just trying to feel welcomed, and this town is treating them so badly."

Jacey frowned and shook her head. "Sometimes I think Asher has the right idea by avoiding this place. I never knew quiet people could be so cruel."

"And the guys at the institution are really nice," Monique added. "Well, except for Angela. She's a bitch."

Jacey glared at Monique.

Monique smiled with a tiny laugh. "Oops."

Jacey glanced at her watch and sighed. "Okay. Let's meet back here around one. That should give you plenty of time to meet Professor for your ride."

Both girls nodded. Jacey gave them some money then walked across the closed off street to the press. Monique and Coleen immediately headed for the nearest hamburger stand. They each got a hamburger and shared some fries. While sitting on a bench in the center of town, Monique pointed to an alleyway.

"Doesn't that go past the murdered woman's apartment?" Monique asked.

Coleen shrugged. "I don't know. Jameson said something about the alley near the press."

Monique slowly stood and strained to look down the alley in the distance.

"If you're so curious," Coleen announced, "we could take a walk that way."

Monique nodded. Both girls ate their food while walking along the blocked roads in town. They passed the new statue with its bright, yellow police line around it.

Coleen shivered. "Gives me the creeps," she said softly then ate a fry.

"Do you think Jill did it?" Monique asked curiously. "Or Asher?"

"I don't know," Coleen replied and stared at the statue as they passed. "Someone wants to shut down the institution, that's for sure."

"Or at least make it look that way," Monique informed her. "Maybe someone just hated Roseanne, and they're using the institution as an excuse."

Coleen chuckled softly. "You sound like a detective in a novel."

They approached the alley as they finished their hamburgers, tossing their garbage into a nearby garbage container.

"I think Jill's batty enough to kill," Monique replied.

"But would she?" Coleen asked with a curious stare. "She's put the fear of a curse into a lot of people. Someone may have killed Roseanne out of fear."

"True," Monique replied.

They walked down the alley and saw a car near the gates to a ground floor apartment. They approached the black station wagon with its back door opened and several boxes piled within it. Both casually peered inside one of the boxes and noticed some medical books. They heard sound from the back gate to the apartment. Dr.

Talbert approached them while carrying a box filled with personal items possibly belonging to Roseanne.

"Afternoon, girls," he said with a pleasant smile.

"Whatcha doing, Dr. Talbert?" Coleen asked while glancing at the box with a curious look.

He appeared saddened then sighed. "Putting Roseanne's belongings into storage until her sister can get here to sort through them," he informed her. "Her sister didn't want to pay an extra month's rent on the apartment, and the landlord isn't very understanding."

"Wants to rent it out right away, huh?" Monique asked with a raised brow.

Dr. Talbert snorted a laugh and placed the box in the back of the station wagon. "Something like that, I suppose." He leaned on the side of the car and eyed them. "How'd you two like to make ten dollars each?"

They looked at each other and then at Dr. Talbert. "We could use money for fair games," Monique replied. "What do you need?"

"There's at least twenty more boxes inside the apartment and I need to drop these off at my garage," he informed them. "I'll never get them all loaded myself before my next appointment. I didn't anticipate it taking this long." He studied both girls. "If you could seal some boxes and pack the rest of her books while I drop off these, I'd be grateful."

"We can do that," Coleen chirped happily.

Monique smiled slyly. "Yeah, we'd be happy to help."

"Great. I'll be back in fifteen minutes," he said. "I have to get my appointments finished early. I have a party to go to at the institution."

"Oh, Jacey's going there tonight too," Coleen said.

"And several very prominent people," Dr. Talbert added.

"Yeah, naturally we were invited, but we'd have to wear dresses," Monique replied while making a face.

"Oh, the horror," Dr. Talbert teased then grinned. "It's an important evening for me. I want to open a clinic in the next county. Support from some of the attendees would be a great help."

"We'll have everything packed before you return," Monique assured him and rocked on the balls of her feet while grinning.

They watched him drive away then hurried into the apartment with a mischievous agenda. The apartment was mostly cleared and more than twenty boxes were piled throughout the kitchen. The girls poked and sifted through the open boxes.

"What are we looking for?" Coleen asked.

"Anything that could point to her killer," Monique informed her while poking through her own box. "We'd be in luck if she'd kept a diary or something."

Coleen laughed softly. "That doesn't happen in real life--just in the mystery novels. Besides, wouldn't the police have confiscated anything of real use?"

"Don't ruin my fun," Monique remarked while opening a fancy little bag that resembled a clutch purse. She looked quizzically inside then suddenly gasped and tossed the bag to the floor. "Oh, shit!"

Coleen saw the horrified look on her friend's face then eyed the bag lying on the floor. "What is it?" she suddenly cried out. "Is it a severed finger?"

Monique remained frozen and shook her head. Her eyes remained wide and fixated on the bag. "I think," she gasped, "I think it was a man's--you know."

Coleen was now shocked. "It's a severed penis?"

"I think so!"

Both stared at the bag a moment and appeared uncertain what to do. Coleen removed a spatula from her box, bravely took a step closer to the bag, and slowly opened it with the spatula. She suddenly gasped then hesitated and stared a moment longer. She uncertainly tilted her head and poked inside the bag.

"It's fake," Coleen informed her friend then straightened.

Both made faces and exchanged looks.

"Who'd want something like that?" Monique suddenly asked.

"I don't know," Coleen replied while shaking her head. "Seems a little twisted to me."

Monique cringed and carefully picked up the bag with the tips of her fingers and dropped it into the box. She appeared sickened and shut the box.

"We'll ask Jacey about it later," Monique replied then looked at her friend with all seriousness. "We better be careful. There's no telling what other gross things we might find."

Coleen nodded with the same concerned look. After ten minutes of useless searching through boxes, they entered the living room and frantically packed books from the bookcase into an empty box. The bookcase was all that needed to be packed. As Coleen removed the last book, an envelope slipped out and fell to the floor. She picked it up and appeared curious. Monique saw her with the envelope and approached.

"What is it?" Monique asked.

"I'm not sure. It's sealed, but there's no address on it," Coleen replied.

Monique removed the envelope from her and held it to the light from the window. Coleen glanced at the front cover of the book she held.

"Sins of a Nurse," Coleen said then giggled. "I wonder if it's a dirty love letter."

"We're about to find out," Monique remarked and opened it. She removed the copied note in cutout newspaper letters. Monique read, "I know what you did. If you don't want the police to find out, place ten thousand dollars in a brown paper bag in the barrel of the cannon Friday at midnight."

Both girls looked at each other. Coleen flipped through the book. In the very center of the book, there were three instant photos and a small drawing on a scrap piece of paper. It looked like a drawing of the institution. Both studied it carefully.

"It's the institution," Monique announced.

Coleen squinted. "How can you tell?"

"All the rooms are setup like at the institution," she announced. "Where else in this town is there a building with that many rooms?"

"If it is, it's just the main building. But according to this, there's another room somewhere in the basement," Coleen replied. "We were never shown the basement."

"Maybe they're hiding something."

Coleen glared at Monique. "Who? Professor? You can't be serious."

"You never know," Monique announced with distrust. "I think we should investigate the basement."

Coleen's eyes widened. "Are you kidding?"

"No, I'm always serious," Monique replied simply. She then studied the photos of a hospital surgical room. "Wonder what these have to do with anything?"

"Probably just photos she stuck in the book," Coleen said and carelessly tossed them into the box on top of the books.

A car was heard just outside the apartment. Monique stuck the envelope and paper into her back pocket. Dr. Talbert walked into the apartment and approached them in the living room while wearing a pleased smile.

"Looks like you girls have been busy," he announced and eyed the box containing books. "You can take the lighter ones. I'll take the heavier ones."

Coleen attempted to lift the box containing the books and immediately groaned. Dr. Talbert chuckled and easily picked up the box.

"There are lighter ones in the kitchen," he announced then left with the box of books.

Both girls entered the kitchen and searched for lighter boxes to carry.

"Maybe we should've kept those photos," Monique remarked while appearing deep in thought. "They might mean something."

"We can still pull them out," Coleen announced.

Monique nodded. Each girl grabbed a box and hurried out after Dr. Talbert. Dr. Talbert shoved the box of books toward the front of the cargo area and headed back into the house for more. Monique crawled into the back of the station wagon, placed their boxes next to the box of books, and grabbed the photos. She closed the box's flaps then crawled back out. She grinned, pleased with herself.

"Got them."

She placed them in her other back pocket then returned to the apartment with Coleen.

✝

*S*helly walked down the back stairs into the press with Jacey in tow. Jacey couldn't believe how many beautiful dresses Shelly owned and not one would keep her breasts contained. She didn't realize either how small Shelly's bust was or how big her own breasts really were. Either way, it was disheartening. She still had nothing to wear for the party. She didn't feel things could get any worse. As they crossed the press, Jacey saw Brenda casually leaning on the front desk while scanning a paper in her hand. Jacey suddenly frowned. She was wrong; things just got worse. Brenda saw them approaching and immediately grinned deviously. Oddly enough, Shelly frowned in unison with Jacey. It was becoming obvious that Shelly no longer cared for her lead reporter either.

"I have that article for you," Brenda announced cheerfully to Shelly while seductively waving the paper.

Shelly smirked and took the paper from her. She set it down without even reading it. "I'm sure it's great."

"Naturally," Brenda remarked while casting a glance at Jacey. "I had a front row seat for the unveiling of Roseanne's murder." Her eyes swept over Jacey and almost mocked her. "Where were you when the second biggest story in this town broke?"

She glared at Brenda, held back her comment, and then looked at Shelly. "I'll talk to you later."

Jacey walked across the press and headed out the front door. She stepped onto the porch with a depressed sigh and looked around the now congested streets. Monique and Coleen were nowhere to be found. She looked at her watch and frowned. It was nearly one o'clock. She walked across the street to the general store. All five women from Jill's group stood outside the store and leered at something with great interest. Their mouths were in motion, though Jacey wasn't close enough to hear about what they were gossiping. She was sure she didn't care either. She looked toward the police station down the street, where their attention seemed to be focused, and saw Asher just outside Town Hall. Asher almost never came to town. Something must have happened! She was suddenly concerned and hurried along the sidewalk toward the building. At the same time, the five gossiping women approached through the crowd and the rows of vendors. Asher walked down the steps of the building while being escorted by Sheriff Monroe. The chatter could be heard from more than just Jill's group. Asher paused on the bottom step of the building near the sidewalk and observed the small crowd.

"My adoring public," he announced with a mocking smile and gave his best royal queen wave above his head.

"Okay, break it up," Monroe announced firmly while walking down the last step and forced the crowd to disperse.

Asher walked behind Monroe and paused when he saw Jacey. A slight smile crossed his face. He raised his finger to his brow and gave her a tiny, secret wave then continued toward the police car. Jacey ran for him. Monroe turned and put his hand up for her to stay back. Jacey instinctively stopped.

"It's okay," Asher said softly to Monroe. He then turned toward her, smiled, and casually looked around the crowd that still remained present but from farther away. "Everything's okay," he said softly so no one would hear. "I'll call you when I get home."

Asher attempted to turn toward the police car when Jacey grabbed his arm. Locals were heard gasping. He turned to face her with some surprise.

"I don't care if everyone knows we're friends," Jacey said firmly. "What's going on? Why are you here?"

Asher shifted uncomfortably, looked around at the people staring at them while whispering, and then looked back at Jacey. "Someone broke into my house. I came home and found the glass on the sunroom door broken. Nothing seemed to be missing, but I thought I should report it anyway."

"Why the escort?" she asked with some concern.

Asher nodded toward Monroe, who now yelled at the collection of people. "He feared I might be mobbed. These people think I've killed Roseanne. It's as if we're living in the Dark Ages all over again. I'm surprised they aren't carrying torches and pitchforks."

Jacey wondered why someone would break into Asher's home. Most people in town feared him too much to even drive past his house, let alone attempt to enter it. She wondered if there was a more sinister reason. She was almost convinced someone was attempting to frame him.

"Maybe you should keep watch for things *added* to your house rather than things removed," she said softly under her breath.

Asher's head cocked slightly and his brows raised. "You are a clever girl," he said with an odd smile across his face. His look told her he'd already thought of that. "I'll call you later to discuss when I should pick you up."

Jacey suddenly frowned. "At the last minute," she pouted. "I still don't have anything to wear. I'll probably have to wear one of my mother's flapper dresses."

Asher stared at her a moment then smiled warmly. "Come to my house. I think you'll like what I have for you."

Jacey nodded with some confusion. "Okay. I'll stop by when Professor comes out to ride with the girls."

Asher smiled warmly at her then walked with Monroe to his awaiting police cruiser. Derek Falcone suddenly appeared alongside Jacey, startling her. His stare was creepy.

"Interesting company you've been keeping," he announced sternly. "Better watch yourself. Some men kill the women they love."

She gave him a quick once over, not about to be intimidated by a short-order cook. "Is that a threat or a confession?" Jacey asked while casually tilting her head. She wondered why she couldn't have been as confrontational with Brenda.

"You think you know that man?" Derek demanded. "You don't know anything about him. No one does."

"Go away," she scoffed and turned to leave.

Derek suddenly grabbed her arm, startling her. She glared at him with surprise. His look was mildly psychotic. "You're going to regret knowing him."

She attempted to pull her arm free, but he wouldn't release it while staring into her eyes. His wrist was suddenly grabbed and his arm was twisted behind his back. Asher slammed Derek over the hood of a nearby car with a loud crack, causing the crowd of mostly locals to gasp. Asher leaned over Derek where he held him pinned face first over the car hood and spoke low in his ear.

"Fucking touch her again, and I'll--"

"Asher," Jacey scolded softly.

Asher didn't move or take his eyes off Derek only inches from his face. He suddenly sneered, released him, and took a step back. Everyone was staring at him. Asher briefly glanced at the crowd and smiled deviously.

"Is everyone happy now?" he casually announced while making eye contact with several people, including Jill.

The locals immediately scattered, including Jill and her followers. Derek cast a glare at Asher then hurried along the blocked off street. Asher frowned and looked at Jacey, who stared at him with a disapproving glare.

"Please don't look at me like that, my dear," he replied while offering a tiny smile. "Once a wolf; always a wolf."

Sheriff Monroe stood several feet away, glared at Asher, and folded his arms across his chest. Asher glanced back at Monroe then looked at Jacey.

"I guess that's my cue to leave," Asher announced. "I should go while he's still asking nicely." He appeared oddly timid. "Are we still on for tonight?"

Jacey groaned softly and shook her head. "Of course," she replied with defeat in her voice. "Go on; go home."

Asher smiled at her then joined Monroe near the police cruiser. She watched him climb into the passenger side of the police car. Monroe drove him along the busy, blocked streets to the area outside town where Asher must've parked. Jacey stared a moment longer and smiled secretly to herself. It must've been one hell of a sight. She wished she could've seen him parade along the street in his usual arrogant manner, giving the hens something to cluck about. Jill hadn't seen Asher in years, so it must've been a real treat for her. Monique and Coleen hurried through the crowd from the direction of the cannon in the center of town and ran for Jacey.

"Did we miss something?" Monique quickly asked.

"What's everyone staring at?" Coleen chirped.

Chapter Twenty

*J*acey followed Asher along the hallway in his house and into his bedroom. It was after 2:00 P.M., and she had left Monique and Coleen in Professor's hands for their afternoon ride. As he approached the closet, she stopped within the doorway and looked around. She'd never actually been in his bedroom before. It was decorated tastefully with antique furniture made of rich wood and surprisingly colorful material in varying shades of burgundy and gold. The room's close resemblance to a castle chamber was startling. Asher removed a dress and turned to face her. She stared at the expensive, elegant black evening dress Asher held proudly while grinning. Jacey met his smile and appeared astonished. The dress must have cost a fortune. She suddenly felt subconscious.

"Are you sure you don't mind if I borrow it?" Jacey asked timidly.

"Mind?" Asher chuckled softly in his throat. "I want you to wear it. It was Katie's favorite dress." He smiled with some embarrassment. "Well, perhaps it was my favorite dress, and she just wore it to appease me. You'd better try it on. We haven't long before we should be leaving for the party."

Jacey nodded, took the dress, and watched as Asher quietly slipped from the bedroom. She changed into the dress and looked at herself in the full-length mirror. It fit almost perfectly. It was an off the shoulder evening gown with a revealing neckline and a back that plunged daringly low. There was a slit up the left side that nearly reached the top of her thigh. It was extravagant and sexy to say the least. She could see why Asher loved when Katie wore it. She pulled her auburn hair from her shoulders and wondered how it would look pinned up for a formal occasion. Her eyes then strayed to a photo on the dresser in the far corner of the room. It was of Katie in the same evening dress Jacey wore. She approached the photo and studied it a long moment. She'd never realized it, but there was a resemblance between her and Katie, although Katie was a true redhead. She lifted the picture and stared at it. There was a soft tap on the door. Jacey replaced the picture and turned toward the door.

"Come in," she announced simply.

Asher opened the bedroom door. He suddenly stopped and stared at her for a long moment without a word. He looked almost as if he'd seen a ghost. For a moment, Jacey was concerned by his silence.

He suddenly smiled and appeared pleased. "You look absolutely beautiful."

Jacey smiled and felt the color rush to her cheeks. "Do you think so?"

He chuckled lowly. "I'm going to have my hands full keeping Dr. Alvord from seducing you away from me."

She immediately tensed and attempted not to smile. "Will you stop with Maxwell? He's not interested in me, and he's seeing someone."

"He'll be interested tonight, I assure you," Asher said with a sly look in his eyes. "Oh," he injected sharply. "I almost forgot; I have the perfect jewelry to go with that dress."

He crossed the room to the dresser and opened the top drawer. Asher removed two velvet boxes from the drawer, carelessly dropping a folded slip of paper to the floor. Jacey approached him and studied the boxes with great interest. He opened one to reveal a diamond and ruby pendant necklace with matching earrings. He proudly handed them to her.

"Katie had always wanted these," he said gently with a tiny smile. "She had so much jewelry." He handed her the earrings and assisted her with the necklace. They were truly elegant and obviously very expensive. Jacey put the earrings on and turned to face him with a smile. He then opened the second box and removed a diamond tennis bracelet.

"And this will complete the set."

She stared at the brilliant, shining diamond bracelet with awe. "Might be a little much," Jacey said with a tiny laugh.

He placed the bracelet around her wrist and smiled deviously. "You're going to look like royalty among peasants," he announced cheerfully and held her hand to stare at the sparkling bracelet around her wrist. His eyes then lifted to meet hers. "You'd get more use out of these than the dresser," he said warmly. His look turned more serious. "I think you should keep them."

Her mouth opened slightly with surprise at the offer. She didn't want to take Katie's jewelry. It didn't seem right. "Asher, I couldn't--"

"But I insist," he announced cheerfully. "They're doing me no good, and I'm sure Katie would've wanted them to go to someone special to me."

Jacey stared into his blue eyes and couldn't help but smile. She sometimes wondered if Asher loved her too much. And sometimes she didn't care. She'd lost her father many years ago, and Asher was the only one who could compare.

She nodded with a warm smile. "If it makes you happy, I'll keep them."

"It would." He released her hand and turned serious. "I don't mean to rush you, but I have to pick up my tuxedo at the dry cleaners in the city. I'm going to be late as it is," he informed her. "Perhaps we could meet at the institution, so I won't have to stop back this way."

"Sure," she replied. "That's fine. Maybe I'll have my hair done." She was humored at herself. "I may as well go all the way."

"You do that," he said with a soft laugh. "I'll be there with my cane to fight off all the young men." He hesitated only a moment to look over her in the dress then smiled. "I'm going to head out right away. Lock up when you leave."

Once Asher left the room, Jacey changed back into her everyday clothing. She noticed the stray piece of paper on the floor. She picked it up and glanced at it, hoping it wasn't his drycleaner slip. Her head tilted and a strange feeling swept over her. It was a bill for the jewelry. A very expensive bill with yesterday's date on it! She heard Asher's jeep drive away. Jacey ran her fingers through her hair while staring at the jewelry receipt. Why had he lied? She uncertainly folded the receipt and stuck it in the nearby drawer. Jacey glanced at the diamond tennis bracelet around her wrist and sank into thought. Perhaps she was over thinking it. Asher was, at times, extremely generous with his wealth, and she'd turned down many offers of money in the past. It was possibly just his way of giving her something without protest. She decided to just forget about it and allow him his fun.

†

*J*acey's jeep pulled up to the institution a little after 6:00 P.M. for the exclusive party. Jacey hated being late, but it took longer at the hairdresser than she'd anticipated. She was also surprised at how many women in town were attending and decided to get their hair done at the last minute. She was actually lucky they had the time to take her in on such short notice. Jacey stepped out of her jeep and accepted the ticket from the young valet. The young man's gaze swept over her in the expensive, black evening dress. He attempted to conceal his grin but failed. She felt a little self-conscious, not used to wearing dresses or high heels. She felt uneasy as she walked to the entrance of the institution. Her auburn hair was up in a French twist with a stray lock hanging just over her brow. Her make-up had been carefully applied by the beautician in town, using the 'less is more' technique. She was elegance from the top of her head to her black, strapless heels.

Despite her appearance, she felt out of place. She wished Asher had been able to accompany her. She knew she'd feel secure on his arm. He had attended many formal parties with Katie, according to his stories, and she was positive he knew the ropes. Jacey looked back to the front gate where Jill and her four coconspirators protested with cardboard signs. They looked completely idiotic marching before the shut gates while security closely watched. Jacey took a deep breath as the hired butler answered the door and welcomed her inside. As she entered, Doc was waiting in the foyer with his arms outstretched.

"Jacey," he announced cheerfully and clasped both her hands. His eyes swept over her. "You look absolutely beautiful." He looked past her, appeared bewildered, and then met her gaze. "Where's Professor? I thought he'd be with you?"

"They weren't back yet when I got home, but a woman I know is waiting for them at my place," Jacey informed him. "I could call and find out if they've returned yet."

Doc shook his head with a deep sigh. "Professor always finds an excuse to be late for these gatherings. He's not much for business parties."

Jacey just smiled. The way she was feeling right now, she could understand.

"Weren't you bringing a friend?"

"Yes, but he had to run to the cleaners for his suit," she replied with a warm smile. "I'm sure he'll be along shortly. I doubt he'd miss an opportunity to hobnob with intelligent people."

Doc nodded with a look of concern. "I hope he won't be too late," he informed her. "I ordered the gates locked at seven o'clock due to that wretched woman from your town. I don't want her offending any of my guests. They're quite important to our facility." He then smiled proudly and held out his arm. "Allow me to escort you to the party."

Jacey linked onto his arm and walked toward the banquet room at the end of the hall. She was mildly surprised to see the crowd of people attending the party. Despite her appearance, she felt even more out of place than before. After a quick glance around the room, she saw Mayor Howard Norad, Dr. Talbert, Brenda Heinz, Derek Falcone, and Sheriff Monroe. It wasn't surprising that she didn't see the mayor's wife attending. She was practically one of Jill's disciples and probably refused to attend on principle alone. Seeing Sheriff Monroe made her feel a little more at ease. She was certain the sheriff was feeling just as out of place as she was feeling, if not more so. She'd never even seen the sheriff in a tie, let alone a tuxedo. Brenda looked stunning in a daring red dress with plenty of leg and cleavage showing. Jacey considered some trashy comments to describe Brenda's dress, but quickly realized her dress was just as revealing. As she looked down, she was almost shocked at her own exposed cleavage. She didn't realize her boobs were that big! She gave the dress a gentle tug to cover some cleavage to no avail. Timon approached them looking fine in his modern tuxedo with a glass of brandy in his hand. His mouth opened, as he looked Jacey up and down twice.

"Well, well," he said with a slight gasp then looked back into her eyes while attempting to behave and grinned. "You look *fabulous*."

Brian approached from the left and grinned at the attractive woman linked onto Doc's arm. "Introduce me to your lovely guest," he announced then finally looked at her face and realized it was Jacey. His mouth suddenly opened with surprise. "Jacey," he gasped then grinned.

"For just one evening, won't you two try to behave like gentlemen," Doc said firmly.

Brenda was suddenly standing alongside them. She linked onto Brian's arm and purposely brushed her cleavage against his arm. She succeeded in catching his attention.

"Hey, Brian," she said sweetly while flirting at him with her eyes.

He checked her out and grinned his approval. "Brenda," Brian announced. "You look stunning."

"Thanks," she replied then eyed Jacey while raising a cocky brow. "I didn't realize you were coming tonight, Jacey." Her eyes strayed to the expensive, diamond tennis bracelet. It apparently caught her eye. She had a hard time looking away from it.

As Jacey stared at Brenda, she thought of the perfect comeback. She was about ready to clobber her with her best sarcastic remark when Brenda added to her own comment.

"Did you bring a date?" Brenda asked.

Jacey suddenly fumbled and wasn't sure how to respond. She hadn't actually thought about what she would tell others about Asher attending with her. Angela and Maxwell joined them and it was no longer necessary to respond to Brenda. Angela wore a sparkling evening dress that was both elegant and subtle. She smiled in her typical, mocking manner while looking over Jacey.

"If I hadn't seen it for myself, I never would've believed it," Angela remarked with a tiny, humored laugh. "A bit revealing though."

Jacey suddenly realized she had entered the bowels of hell! Brenda and Angela together spelled disaster for her! She needed to be rescued.

Timon linked onto Jacey's free arm and defensively raised his brows. "I like revealing."

Not exactly the rescue that she'd hoped, but she'd take it.

"I might remind you two, Jacey already has a date for tonight, and he'll be along shortly," Doc announced firmly.

Jacey hoped he would too. She also hoped she wouldn't have to get into that conversation just now.

As if on cue, Doc once again saved her. "Now run along and promote our facility," he ordered firmly, successfully chasing away Timon and Brian with Brenda in tow. He released Jacey's arm and patted it affectionately. "I'll leave you in Angela's care." Doc then looked at Maxwell. "Maxwell, I want to introduce you to the mayor."

Maxwell excused himself, smiled warmly at Jacey as he passed, and followed Doc across the crowded room. When Jacey looked back at Angela, she had her arms folded across her chest and a scowl on her face while watching Timon and Brian leave.

"They act as if they've never seen a woman before," Angela muttered then eyed Jacey and raised a skeptical brow. "Should we get some drinks?"

Angela didn't wait for a response. She walked away from Jacey and across the room toward the bar. Jacey rolled her eyes and followed her. Derek glared at Jacey as she passed. She caught his stare and promptly ignored him. She wondered how he managed to get an invitation when so many others in town didn't. Derek was about to be in for the surprise of his life when he discovered Asher was attending.

Chapter Twenty-one

*P*rofessor galloped his large horse behind both girls on their horses. He appeared to be enjoying their gallop on the long, flat stretch of dirt road. Both girls slowed, finally allowing Professor to catch up. All three laughed.

"I think you cheated," Professor informed both girls. "You were already running on 'go'."

"Monique always cheats," Coleen informed him while casting a sly look at her blonde friend.

"I don't cheat," Monique protested while patting her horse's neck. "Storm Cloud is just very competitive."

"Storm Cloud cheats too," Coleen quipped.

"Yeah?" Monique snipped. "Well Thunder was the one leading the way that got us lost. Now Professor's going to be late for the party. It's already six-thirty. The party started half an hour ago."

"Professor isn't complaining," Professor muttered. "I intend to be bored out of my mind the rest of the evening anyway. Doc will give me an earful though."

"It won't be much longer," Monique promised. "It's a short ride to the mining road. That'll get us to Jacey's place in half an hour if we book it."

"I don't mind booking it either," Professor teased then gave Monique a curious look. "I noticed you don't kick your horse to make him run. Why is that?"

Monique smiled and shrugged. "He's a smart horse," she announced proudly. "A gentle squeeze is all he needs. I actually think he's ticklish."

"Ticklish?" Coleen scoffed. "Try vindictive. I kicked him once and he threw me."

"He's not vindictive; he's ticklish," Monique grumbled. "At least he's not spoiled like Thunder."

Before Coleen could continue the argument, Professor interrupted them. "Okay," he announced playing peacekeeper. "You're both very attached to your horses. I get it. Let's not fight about it."

They entered the woods and rode along an old road through the wooded hillside. Monique and Coleen exchanged looks then glanced at Professor while silently questioning each other. Coleen nodded. Monique removed the folded paper from her pocket, held her horse back, and rode alongside Professor while Coleen led. She handed him the paper.

"We found this when we were helping Dr. Talbert pack up the dead woman's belongings," Monique gently informed him.

Professor studied the paper with newspaper cutouts on it then looked at both girls.

"Is this some sort of joke?" he asked sternly.

"No," Monique replied. "I believe it's called blackmail."

Professor looked back at the paper with his mouth hanging open. "This can't be good," he said under his breath then looked back at them. "Does anyone else know you've found this?"

Both shook their heads.

"We're usually pretty sneaky," Coleen informed him simply. "Do you think someone was blackmailing Roseanne, or the other way around?"

Professor shook his head. "I don't know what to make of it. I'm not very good at this sort of thing," he informed them. "I think you should tell the police about this. It may help with their murder investigation."

"We thought about that," Monique announced then sighed. "But we're not sure how to explain where we got it."

"Truth is always best," Professor said. "I don't believe lying ever solved anything."

"Sometimes telling the truth can be deadly too," Coleen muttered softly.

Professor eyed her.

"We even checked the cannon," Monique announced. "But there wasn't any money in it. She could have been blackmailing someone, and they killed her because of it." She then removed the drawing from her back pocket and handed it to Professor. "Do you recognize this place?"

Professor studied the crude drawing then nodded. "Sure, it's the institution."

Monique then pointed to the bottom corner. "What do you make of this area?"

He stared a moment longer then shook his head. "Looks like an addition to the basement. Maybe someone had plans for the institution before we moved in."

"But does this area even exist?" Monique pressed.

"I've been in the basement maybe four times," he replied simply. "I don't know where this room is." Professor returned the paper to Monique.

Both girls stopped their horses and glanced across the woods with bewildered looks. Professor stopped his horse as well and attempted to see what had them befuddled.

"Huh," Monique muttered. "We took the wrong path." She nodded up a steep incline. "The old mining road is up there. This road takes us back to the main road. That'll put us miles out of our way."

"Can you handle a steep incline?" Coleen asked Professor.

"I can manage," he replied.

They approached a steep path on the hillside, which led to the old, mining road. Turning right onto the road led to Asher's house, which was a ten to twenty minute ride. Turning to the left would take them back to Jacey's house, which was a good thirty-minute ride at a fast gate.

"You need to get a running start and hold onto the horse's mane," Monique instructed.

"And lean forward *real* far," Coleen added.

They rode up the hill one at a time. Monique went first, sending her paint gelding into a gallop up the steep path, knocking stones and kicking dirt to the bottom. Professor watched with his mouth hanging open. Once she'd reached the top, Coleen galloped up the path on her black horse.

"I don't like this," Professor muttered lowly. He leaned forward and patted the horse's neck. "Are you ready? That's a good horsy."

Once Coleen reached the top, it was his turn. He took a deep breath and raced toward the slope. The horse tackled the steep path and began to slow halfway up. The horse suddenly bolted with a spurt of energy. Professor toppled off the horse and rolled down the hill with amazing speed. Both girls screamed then yelled to him. The horse reached the top of the slope and trotted along the dirt road. Monique raced her horse down the slope, leaning back so far her head almost touched the horse's rump. The horse skidded most of the way then jumped the last couple of feet. Monique sprang off her horse and ran to Professor, who lie motionless in a ditch with his leg pinned under a fallen tree alongside the dirt road.

"Professor," she cried out, though she didn't touch him.

He moaned and looked at her. "That stupid horse," he muttered lowly. He cried out in pain. "Oh, oh, my leg!" He half sat up and touched his pinned leg.

Monique sprang to her feet and attempted to move the tree. It wouldn't budge. He stared at her as she attempted to move the excessively large tree.

"It's, uh, a little too heavy for you," Professor casually pointed out.

Monique appeared defeated and looked at Professor with concern. "Is your leg broke?" she asked nervously.

"It hurts," he replied, "but I can move my foot. Maybe you should get some help."

She nodded. "Asher's house is just ten minutes from here. If we can get some rope, we can pull the tree from your leg with our horses."

"Good idea," he said and cringed.

"Will you be okay?" she timidly asked. "Neither of us wants to go to Asher's house alone."

"I'll be fine. Just don't be too long," he informed her and attempted a smile.

She nodded, sprang onto her horse, and rode for the steep slope. Professor watched as she raced up the hill and shook his head with disbelief.

"They make it look so easy," he muttered.

†

*P*rofessor remained pinned beneath the tree and attempted to look casual while strumming his fingers on the trunk. The girls had been gone nearly fifteen minutes already. He looked around, appeared frustrated, and finally pushed on the log with his free foot. He yelped in pain.

"Bad idea--very bad idea."

A vehicle could be heard approaching on the road near where he was pinned. The jeep stopped a few feet away. As the driver got out, Professor strained to see him.

"Oh, thank God. Am I ever glad to see you," Professor chanted without actually *seeing* the approaching man.

Asher walked around the jeep and observed where Professor lie in the ditch. He looked at Professor calmly and without emotion.

"Are you hurt badly?"

"No," Professor replied with an embarrassed laugh. "More like stuck. The two girls I was riding with rode for help. I'm worried about them. They went to some guy's house, whom they suspected might be a killer."

Asher raised a curious, cold brow and looked at him cynically. "Oh? Do you think he's done away with them?" he asked as he limped along the area with his cane. He looked back at Professor quizzically. "Would they happen to be Jacey's young houseguests?"

Professor nodded vigorously. "I'm really worried about them," he informed Asher. "They've gotten themselves involved in something. They could be in serious danger."

Asher approached the tree and the man pinned beneath it. "What sort of danger?" he asked with a curious tilt of his head.

"They found a blackmail note," Professor informed him and motioned him closer to help. "Please, help me with this tree. I need to find them."

Asher's eyes narrowed in question. "Blackmail note? Now *that* is interesting."

Chapter Twenty-two

*M*onique and Coleen rode around the back of Asher's house at a trot and rounded the corner to the front. It had taken them fifteen minutes to reach Asher's house despite their fast gait. Both stopped when they saw Jameson's police blazer in the driveway.

"The police are here," Monique announced with surprise.

"Good," Coleen remarked. "I feel better now."

They dismounted their horses, tied them to the porch, and hurried to the front door. Both knocked on it with urgency. Only a minute passed before Jameson opened the door. He looked at them and appeared surprised or possibly concerned.

"Oh, Deputy Jameson," Monique cried. "Thank God we ran into you first. Professor's trapped under a tree in the woods. You have to help us. We don't know how badly he's hurt."

"A tree?" Jameson gasped. "Is he conscious?"

Both nodded.

"But his leg may be broke," Coleen announced.

"Then we'd better get to him," Jameson said. "Just give me two seconds here. And don't touch anything."

Both girls looked confused as Jameson darted back into the house. They stepped into the living room and looked around.

"What's going on?" Coleen asked.

"Where's Mr. Asher?" Monique asked curiously.

They watched Jameson gather plastic bags. One contained a scalpel with plant dirt on it. The other was a piece of paper.

"Good question," Jameson remarked lowly. "I'd like to know where he is myself."

"What happened?" Monique gasped as her eyes widened.

"Looks like we'll be arresting him for the murder of Roseanne," Jameson informed them.

Both girls gasped.

"You two lead the way to your friend. I'll follow with my truck," Jameson announced.

Coleen looked at Monique and appeared alarmed. "Didn't Jacey say Asher was going to the party with her tonight?"

Monique nodded. "Yes, you're right. She did."

Jameson's head tilted with apparent concern. "The institution?" He sank into thought then looked at them. "Sheriff Monroe is there already. I'll call a paramedic for your friend, but I have to get to the institution. There's no telling what Asher might do in his state of mind."

"State of mind?" Coleen gasped as her eyes widened.

Jameson nodded as he frowned. "Our theory is that Asher murdered his wife in a jealous fit of rage over an affair she'd been having, although we don't know the man's identity. I'm afraid Jacey might be his next victim."

"But he adores Jacey," Monique protested with a look of concern in her eyes.

"Exactly," Jameson snapped. "And she's interested in someone else."

"Do you suppose Roseanne was blackmailing Asher, and that's why he killed her?" Monique suddenly asked.

Jameson was momentarily stunned. "Blackmail? How did you know she was blackmailing him?"

Monique produced the letter. Jameson looked at it then looked at the paper in the plastic bag.

"A little more complicated than I'd feared," Jameson said softly. "Can I keep this as evidence?"

Monique nodded and appeared embarrassed. "Sorry we didn't give it to you sooner."

"Where did you get this?" he then asked.

"It must've fallen out of one of the boxes we helped Dr. Talbert carry from Roseanne's apartment," Monique replied.

"Show him the drawing," Coleen announced.

"Later," Monique informed her friend. "We have to get back to Professor." She looked at Jameson and his puzzled expression.

"What drawing? Does it have something to do with the murder?" he asked with concern.

"We'll show it to you later," Monique informed him. "You'll call the paramedics for Professor, right?"

He nodded. "Whatever evidence you girls have, I suggest you keep it to yourselves until I have a look at it."

They nodded.

†

*M*onique and Coleen galloped along the untraveled, dirt road and skidded to a stop near the steep path. It was now seven o'clock and thirty minutes had passed since Professor was trapped under the tree. They carefully rode down the path one at a time and approached the fallen tree. Both stared blankly. Professor was gone! They looked around with concern.

"Professor," both called nervously.

There was no response. They spun their horses around several times while looking around the surrounding woods.

"Where is he?" Monique demanded to know.

"He couldn't have gotten far," Coleen commented. "His leg was injured."

"We'll go back to Jacey's," Monique announced with wide, fearful eyes. "He'll probably return there for the van. You take the main road, and I'll take the mining road."

"The paramedics will be here soon. Shouldn't we wait?"

"I'm not waiting around," Monique practically shouted then galloped toward the slope and raced up it.

Coleen turned her horse in a circle then looked toward the dirt road that led to the main road. She took a deep breath then galloped in that direction. Monique rode along the old mining road. There was another path that led to the main road as well, but she rode in the direction of Jacey's farm. Within twenty minutes, she appeared on Jacey's property. She'd made good time, having galloped almost the entire way. She galloped alongside the fence and saw the white van was still parked before the house. Professor's horse grazed in the yard near the house. She pulled her horse to a sliding halt just near the house and practically dived off. Monique ran onto the porch and into the house.

"Professor," she called out as ran through the empty kitchen and into the living room. She looked around with some confusion. "Shelly?" There was no response.

Monique hurried back through the kitchen and looked out the crudely patched window on the door. Shelly's car and an unfamiliar motorcycle were parked in the driveway. Her brows knitted with confusion. There was a creak from upstairs. Monique's head snapped upward, and she stared at the ceiling a moment. She approached the stairs and cautiously walked up them. There was a loud clunk from one of the bedrooms. Monique stopped near the top of the stairs and held her breath while staring down the small hallway. She stepped into the hallway and crept along it, looking into the open bedroom to her right. She approached the closed bedroom door on her left. The door opened, and Shelly hustled into the hallway while buttoning her shirt. Monique jumped and let out a startled scream along with Shelly.

"Don't do that," Monique cried out.

"I wasn't expecting you to be sneaking around the hallway," Shelly replied.

"If you would've answered me, I wouldn't have been sneaking," Monique snapped back. "Did you see the man we went riding with? His horse is back, but he's not here."

Shelly nervously raked her fingers through her slightly mussed hair. "No, I haven't seen anyone since Jacey left. Where's Coleen?"

"She's coming back by the main road. We can't find Professor," she announced. "He was injured, but now he's missing. I'd better call the institution."

Shelly shook her head. "It's no use," she remarked. "I tried calling the institution, and I got an answering machine. I guess they're not answering the phone tonight."

"We have to search for Professor," Monique informed her. "Could you call the hospitals and see if someone took him there?"

Shelly nodded. "I suggest you stay put now. I don't want Jacey thinking I let you girls run all over the place."

"We will," Monique announced. "Just as soon as we find Professor." She turned and hurried down the stairs.

Monique ran through the kitchen and onto the porch. Coleen galloped along the dirt driveway and slowed as she neared the house.

"Is he here?" Coleen asked.

"No," Monique replied and ran to her horse. She mounted with ease. "I think we should take another look around the woods. Shelly's going to call the hospitals and see if someone picked him up along the road."

"Maybe Jameson found him and took him to the hospital," Coleen suggested. "It's going to be dark soon."

"I know," Monique said with concern. "So we'd better hurry. We can't call the institution. They must've turned the ringer off for the party. We'll have to ride out there and see if Professor called or turned up there. We'll call Shelly from the institution and let her know where we are."

"Jameson said he was going there too," Coleen remarked. "He was going to arrest Asher. You don't really think Asher would hurt Jacey, do you?"

"Certainly not at a party," Monique informed her. "Besides, I'm sure Jameson has him in custody already."

They galloped toward the barn and turned onto a path that would eventually lead them to the institution.

Chapter Twenty-three

*J*acey sipped her champagne and appeared bored while looking around the ballroom filled with well-dressed men and women of obvious wealth. It was now 7:30 P.M. Asher was almost ninety minutes late. It wasn't like him to be late for anything. She hoped he didn't run into traffic driving to the city for his tuxedo. She remained with Angela, who talked endlessly and mostly insulted Jacey and her town. It was almost torturous being stuck with the insufferable woman. She found herself daydreaming and watching others seemingly having a good time. Dr. Talbert looked proud as he escorted young widow Glease through the crowded room. He wasn't lying when he said she was the most attractive widow in town. Widow Glease was a thirty-something, strawberry blonde with the largest green eyes. The longer Jacey stared, the more she wondered if the young widow wore colored contacts. No one's eyes could be that shade of emerald green. Jacey suddenly realized Angela was still droning on about the dregs of Stony Ridge.

"I mean, it's nothing personal against you," Angela announced in a casual tone. "You can't help that you were raised in an intellectually inferior town." She then smiled with a look of pity. "I'd hate to see you embarrass yourself when everyone starts talking above you."

Jacey held the glass to her lips and glared at the woman before her. She contained her comment, sipped her champagne, and then lowered the glass while straightening proudly.

"I think I'll manage just fine. Fortunately for me, Brian and Timon are kind enough to help with the formalities of dealing with the snobs of society," she hissed and wondered if Angela got her subtle hint.

Angela cocked her head to one side. "I'd like to speak to you about that." She then smiled in a chastising manner. "Those two are only after one thing, Jacey, and it's certainly not your sense of humor."

Jacey's eyes narrowed as her hostility rose. She was about to let this woman have it, when Maxwell approached Angela from behind and smiled charmingly at both.

"How are you two getting along?" he asked pleasantly to either even though he mostly stared at Jacey.

Angela looked back at him and flashed a fake smile. "We're getting along just fine," she announced cheerfully. "Was the mayor impressed with you?"

"If I understood people, I'd be a psychiatrist," Maxwell replied with a timid smile. His eyes again strayed to Jacey, possibly noticing her cleavage, and then looked back at Angela. "If you don't mind, I'd like to introduce Jacey to some of our investors."

Angela flashed a humored smile. "Sure," she replied. "That should be entertaining."

Maxwell smiled at Jacey and extended his hand to her. Jacey held her breath, forced a smile, and accepted his hand. He led her across the room to a small group of men. Angela glided behind them with a sly grin plastered on her face. Jacey could hear her snickering the entire way. She was introduced to four of the men, who appeared pleased to meet her--or so they claimed. Their smiles appeared genuine enough. Mayor Howard Norad was with the four men. Jacey had very little interaction with the mayor of Stony Ridge over the years. She knew him by sight, but he didn't appear to recognize her. As he talked to her, she was certain he didn't know she was a resident of Stony Ridge. He treated her like one of the wealthy investor guests. It was almost laughable. The men asked Jacey about her occupation. She was slightly embarrassed to admit she wasn't a professional of any kind. They didn't seem to care and included her all the same. Their interest in her despite her non-professional status irritated Angela. The conversation strayed to investments and stocks, involving everyone except Jacey. She shifted nervously from foot to foot and wished she could crawl into the woodwork. Jacey had almost zero knowledge of stocks and investments, probably because she only made enough money between the library and press to clear expenses. She was horse broke. Caring for that many horses wasn't cheap and training them for resale was a long process with small rewards.

"Do you invest, Jacey?" Angela asked slyly in an obvious attempt to embarrass her.

Maxwell's eyes fixated on Angela and gave her a look of disapproval. Angela was getting some sick pleasure out of embarrassing her, and she would continue all evening if allowed. It became apparent to Jacey; she'd be leaving early. A hand touched Jacey's waist, startling her.

"Jacey's far too sensible to play that little game of Russian roulette," came Asher's calm voice.

Jacey looked at the man who stood beside her and smiled with relief. Asher had finally arrived, and she felt better already. The four investors laughed. Howard glared at Asher and frowned in response. Asher looked at Howard and smiled almost pleasantly, but it was obvious there was some animosity between them.

"Wish I hadn't gotten started myself," one man replied while shaking his head.

"And who are you, sir?" the second man asked.

"Allow me to introduce Konrad Asher," Maxwell announced with a broad smile.

He then introduced the other men to Asher, and they politely shook hands. Howard made a hasty departure during the introductions. Asher seemed to mold into one of the high society men, never forgetting his calm demeanor. His smile was confident yet defensive. Jacey marveled at the way Asher handled himself around perfect strangers. She'd never really seen that side of him. She'd heard about his charm before he became the infamous legend she'd come to know. His presence was commanding and yet endearing. He was a hit!

"Are you gentlemen from New York?" Asher questioned with a slightly raised brow.

One laughed. "Yes, how did you know?"

"Your suits are from La Mount," Asher explained. "I recognize the fabric and the style of buttons. A very exquisite tailor. I've had the pleasure of meeting him personally."

The men appeared to marvel at his associations. Brenda noticed Asher from across the room, and without warning, walked away from Brian to get closer to the infamous legend. Brian noticed her departure and hurried after her. Jacey noted Brenda's curiosity regarding Asher but refused to acknowledge her. Asher placed his arm securely around Jacey and smiled pleasantly at her.

"Have these men treated you well, my dear?" he asked.

Jacey nodded and hugged him for security. The look on Brenda's face was priceless. She obviously saw the interview of a lifetime for their little town and appeared jealous that it was one interview which Jacey would have exclusive rights.

"Returning to the institution must be difficult for you," Brenda said to Asher as she fished for a story. "What do you think of the changes?"

Asher glanced at Brenda, raised a sly brow, and smirked. "I don't have an opinion," he informed her then returned his attention to Jacey. "Remind me to give you those notes for my memoirs, darling. That book of ours isn't going to write itself."

Jacey stared into Asher's eyes and tried not to laugh. She put on her best serious face and nodded. "Of course. We can work on that this weekend."

Asher turned to the men surrounding him. "Jacey's a journalist for our local rag sheet," he boasted. "I'm sure she's going to have some brilliant articles on the institution's transformation and tonight's gala. You may want to be careful what you say around her, she's liable to print it."

The men laughed and suddenly focused their attention on Jacey. She had several questions about journalism thrown at her. Brenda sneered and walked away. Brian realized she'd walked away and hurried after her. As Jacey answered their questions without faltering, she secretly gloated over Brenda's sudden departure.

One of the men noticed Asher's cane. "What an exquisite walking stick," he marveled.

Asher held it up for the man to examine. "It was a gift from a fellow I'd assisted while overseas."

"It's a fabulous likeness to Duke Winslow's cane," the man remarked.

"It's not a replica, it's the real thing," Maxwell informed them.

Asher lowered the cane and smirked. "I don't believe I know any royalty."

"It's possible you don't," Maxwell replied simply. "I did some research on your cane. It has quite a history."

Asher stared at Maxwell a long moment. Neither man said a word, though Maxwell seemed pleased with himself. It seemed as if Asher wasn't interested in what Maxwell had discovered. He looked at Jacey and swiftly changed the subject.

"Would you care to dance?" he asked warmly.

"If your ankle's up to it," she replied.

He extended his cane to Maxwell. "Kindly hold this for me, so I may dance with the lovely young lady."

Asher's limp was better as they approached the dance floor for the slow song. Jacey could tell he was having some discomfort from the movement, but he smiled all the same. Derek glared at them as they passed. Asher either hadn't noticed or didn't care. Jacey stared back at Derek and cursed him with her eyes. Asher gently pulled her into his arms and slow danced with her.

"You look beautiful," Asher said with a dashing smile and held her near him for the slow song.

"You don't look half bad yourself," she teased warmly.

He laughed softly then appeared more serious. "Nervous?"

"A little," she said with a soft sigh then smiled lightly. "I feel better now that you're here. Between Angela and Brenda, I was being eaten alive. If I wouldn't have been dressed like such a lady, I probably would've knocked both on their asses."

Asher chuckled softly and gently brushed the stray lock of hair from her brow. "Don't give them a second thought. I'll take care of the shrews," he announced cheerfully. "You just enjoy yourself."

She sighed deeply. "That's difficult to do that when you don't understand what anyone's talking about."

"There's more than one way to answer a question," he casually replied. "If you think about it, you don't even have to give the right answer. Evasiveness can be your best friend. I should know."

"I'll try to remember that," she said and placed her head on his shoulder.

"It just occurred to me," he said firmly almost alarming her. She lifted her head and met his gaze. He smiled warmly. "We've never danced together before."

Jacey smiled and returned her head to his shoulder. "I haven't danced ever."

Asher laughed softly. "You're doing fine. In fact, I think you're ready to dance with our young Dr. Alvord."

Jacey lifted her head and looked into Asher's eyes. She smiled with some embarrassment. "Don't even think it," she scolded. "I don't need you throwing me at him. Angela has it out for me as it is."

Asher grinned then suddenly limped harshly and stopped dancing. Jacey took a step back and saw him clutch his leg and motion for Maxwell. Maxwell approached with his cane.

"Are you alright?" Maxwell asked with some concern.

"Yes, I'll be fine," Asher announced and took his cane. "You'd better finish this dance for me." With that, Asher dramatically limped away.

Jacey stared after him with her mouth hanging open. Oddly enough, his limp mysteriously got better as he disappeared into the crowd. She couldn't believe he played her like that! Jacey caught a glimpse of Angela in the crowd. She was staring at Jacey and Maxwell through piercing, squinted eyes. Jacey looked back at Maxwell and smiled with some embarrassment.

"It's not necessary to finish the dance," she replied.

"No, I don't mind," Maxwell said and smiled timidly. "You did promise me a dance, remember?"

Jacey blushed and nodded. "Yes, I did."

Maxwell appeared uncertain about moving closer to dance the slow song with her, but they were soon fumbling their way across the dance floor.

"I'm afraid I'm not very good," Maxwell announced with a tiny laugh.

"Me either," she replied. "I probably wouldn't have noticed if you hadn't mentioned it."

Both were silent a moment. Maxwell then spoke, almost startling her. "I found some information you might find useful for a future article. Remind me to fetch it from my room before you leave."

"Thanks, Maxwell," she replied. "I really appreciate all your help."

"It was nothing, really."

"I saw Brenda scouting out her next story," Jacey announced. "She's always one step ahead of me, I'm afraid."

"Don't fear yet, I also have some interesting information on some of the people in town," Maxwell remarked and grinned deviously. "I took the liberty of invading the government files. You'll have enough information to write a better article than your adversary, Brenda."

Jacey raised a curious brow with surprise. "You invaded top secret files?" She didn't know if she should be alarmed or proud of him.

He shrugged then grinned. "I do it quite a bit," Maxwell informed her. "It's not as if I have anything better to do with my spare time."

Jacey bumped into Dr. Talbert and young widow Glease. He spun her around with the enthusiasm of a young man. Dr. Talbert dipped the younger woman. Jacey smiled and shook her head while watching him.

"It's amazing he has that much energy," Jacey said to Maxwell.

Maxwell's gaze strayed along her dress, possibly admiring her cleavage. He then looked away with embarrassment. "I like your dress," he said gently. "It's very *flattering*."

Jacey smiled warmly with some embarrassment. It became obvious he had been looking at her cleavage. Oddly enough, she didn't mind. "Yes, I clean up nicely," she said with a soft laugh. "But at midnight I turn back into a tom girl."

His lips curved into a tiny smile, though he didn't look at her. "Doesn't change the woman underneath," he remarked gently then looked at her. "You're still beautiful."

She stared at him as the music stopped. She had no idea how to respond to his comment, although she wrestled with the idea of throwing her arms around him and kissing him. He stepped away from her, lifted her hand, and kissed it warmly.

"I'd better return you before Asher thrashes me with his golden cane," Maxwell announced while smiling warmly without releasing her hand and led her across the dance floor.

Asher had a group of men surrounding him while he talked about the government and political viewpoints. Jacey and Maxwell approached and listened quietly as the debate continued. No one seemed able to argue his points. They finally submitted and laughed at any small joke he made. He'd won them over. Jacey smiled warmly and glanced at Maxwell. Asher turned and looked at Jacey proudly. He held his hand out to her, which she accepted and moved to his side.

"Have you gentlemen met my common-law daughter?" he said cheerfully.

Several men laughed warmly. He introduced her to all the men he'd been entertaining and instinctively placed his arm around her waist.

One of the men checked her out and smiled deviously. "You're a lucky man to have such a beautiful lady by your side," he remarked, embarrassing Jacey.

"She's my world," Asher replied with a brilliant smile. "I don't know what I would've done without her."

"What do you do for a living?" another man asked. "Must be something political."

Asher chuckled with amusement and shook his head. "No, I'm afraid I'm too honest to get involved in that. Actually, I'm retired. I made my fortune early in life and took my leave as quickly as I could."

"What business were you in?" another asked.

Asher smiled wryly. "Sound investments--the usual gamble. It just happened that it worked in my favor."

Maxwell gently cleared his throat and smiled lightly. "Could I have a word with you in private, Asher?"

Asher looked at Maxwell, tilted his head with a look of confusion, then smiled and nodded. "Certainly."

Jacey watched both men walk several feet away to an area where they could talk privately. She ignored the conversation among the wealthy men and watched both Maxwell and Asher while they talked. Maxwell initially seemed to do all the talking while Asher listened. Asher finally smiled and shook his head. When Asher began to speak, Jacey wondered about their conversation. A couple of minutes passed before both men returned. Asher captured Jacey's arm near her elbow and smiled at the group.

"If you gentlemen will excuse us, we're going to have a look at the banquet," Asher said and guided Jacey away from the group. He appeared distracted now and even a little tense.

"Is everything okay?" she suddenly asked.

"Yes, yes," he replied without looking at her. He stopped her near the tables with trays of food on them and faced her. "There's something about me I must tell you; something I should've told you a long time ago." His eyes then strayed past her.

Jacey turned and looked in the direction he stared. Jameson, dressed out of place in his police uniform, pulled Sheriff Monroe aside and was speaking to him. Jacey looked back at Asher and tilted her head. He continued to watch the two men. He looked back at her and smiled lightly.

"I think there's going to be a small problem here tonight." His eyes searched hers. "Do you trust me, Jacey? And I don't mean sort of kind of, I mean do you trust me without question?"

Jacey stared at him a long moment with some concern and confusion to his question. "You mean do I believe you *didn't* kill Roseanne?"

Asher nodded slowly.

"Yes," she said without hesitation. "I'm convinced you had nothing to do with her death."

"I know I can depend on your help," he said simply. "You noticed Deputy Jameson's arrival?"

She nodded.

"He's here for me."

Her mouth opened slightly and with surprise. "What do you mean?"

"He's here to arrest me for the murder of Roseanne," Asher explained then looked around the room. "I don't have time to explain. I just need a chance to search the basement. That's where I was supposed to go the other day."

Jacey stared into his eyes then slowly nodded. "Okay, I'll buy you some time," she said softly. "Just be careful."

He smiled and winked at her. She watched him limp toward the kitchen just twenty feet away. Jacey turned in the crowd and rejoined Maxwell and the group of men. Derek glanced around the room then followed Asher into the kitchen.

"Where's Asher?" Maxwell asked with surprise and looked around.

Jacey smiled lightly and shrugged. "I'm not sure. He mentioned checking out the observatory," she announced. "I think he wanted to see the stars."

Maxwell laughed softly and shook his head. "He's something. Probably knows all the constellations as well. Can I get you something from the bar?"

"Yes, I could use a drink. Thank you," she replied with some tension.

"I'll be right back," Maxwell announced and left.

Chapter Twenty-four

*J*acey remained in the company of the group of men whom Asher had been socializing while waiting for Maxwell to return with drinks. Several men ventured off to mingle with others, but a few stayed behind and questioned her about Asher. Apparently, they were quite taken with him. Howard joined Jacey and the group of men she entertained in Asher's absence.

"I didn't know you were Russell McMurray's niece," Howard announced with some embarrassment to his earlier mix-up. "I don't know why I didn't recognize you."

"You know my Uncle Russell?" she asked. She never heard her uncle talking about the mayor before; at least not while using pleasant terms.

"Oh, yes," he replied. "We go way back. He helped campaign for my political run."

Jacey knew that was a lie. She distinctly remembered her uncle cursing and telling her mother he didn't want that son-of-a-bitch in office. She wondered why he'd even bring it up if he were uncertain of the details. It seemed odd.

"I didn't realize you were friends with Konrad Asher," Howard casually announced.

And there it was! He wasn't interested in striking a conversation with her; he wanted information on Asher.

"Best kept secret in Stony Ridge," she remarked but felt uncomfortable discussing her relationship with Asher to the mayor.

She knew he was the driving force behind placing blame on Kate for Hal Burgess' escape.

Sheriff Monroe, looking suave in his rented tuxedo, approached them and smiled pleasantly at Jacey.

"You look very lovely tonight, Jacey," Monroe announced.

She smiled her thanks, but she had a sneaky suspicion he didn't join them to admire her dress. Monroe turned to Howard and appeared moderately serious.

"Could I have a word with you, Mayor?" Monroe asked although his eyes demanded his presence.

"Certainly," he replied then looked at Jacey. "If you'll excuse us--"

Jacey nodded and watched them walk away while quietly talking. Jameson made his way through the crowd and approached her. He smiled as his eyes swept over her.

"Good evening, Jacey," he said warmly then cleared his throat and contained his smile. "You look, wow, fabulous."

"Thank you," she replied then swept a look over his uniform. "You, uh, look *official.*"

"Well, yeah, I'm sort of here on business," he replied. "If I wasn't, I'd certainly be asking you to dance."

"But since you are here on official business," she announced, "what can I do for you?"

Jameson fidgeted and attempted to keep the mood light. "I, uh, hear you came with Asher tonight."

"Yes, he was invited as well," she replied simply and played dumb. "Is everything under control?"

"Jill's still leading her group in protest outside the front gate, if that's what you mean. They're keeping the gates locked. The butler almost refused to admit me. I had to pull official business on him," he said with a tiny laugh. He once more became serious and curbed his smile. "Do you know where Asher is? I need to have a word with him. It's rather important."

Jacey stared into Jameson's eyes with a slightly frozen expression. "He had mentioned the observatory in the attic. I suppose he's still there." Her frozen look didn't change.

Jameson gave a warm nod and allowed his eyes to stray across her attire. "Thanks, Jacey. I'll talk to you later." Jameson disappeared back the way he came.

Jacey frowned. A champagne glass was extended before her. She looked at Maxwell and accepted the glass with a tiny smile. "Thank you."

He nodded after Jameson, who now left the room. "What was he looking for?"

Jacey slowly shook her head and stared at the doorway. "I don't know," she said softly. "I have a terrible feeling about tonight." Jacey turned and looked Maxwell in the eyes. "Could you show me the files you'd found?"

"What? Now?" he asked curiously with a strange look on his face. "Is something wrong?"

Jacey nodded mechanically.

"Doc's going to be cranky if I disappear too," he said gently. "Is it important?"

She searched his eyes. "Yes, it's very important."

Maxwell sighed and forced a tiny smile. "I suppose if we're not gone too long, he won't be too upset. I'd better tell him I'm leaving for a few minutes. Don't go away."

"I won't," she replied softly then watched him hurry through the crowd. Jacey was grabbed around the waist. She jumped with a slight gasp and looked at Timon, who laughed heartily.

"Didn't mean to frighten you," he teased with a wicked smile. "You're jumpy tonight."

She held up her glass and forced a smile. "It must be the champagne."

"Have a few more," Timon said. "You'll relax." He laughed again in his usual humorous manner.

Jacey studied Timon for a moment then smiled more naturally. By the color in his cheeks and the boyish smile he wore, she could tell he'd had enough to drink himself.

"Guess Brian's out of the picture now," Timon said while appearing pleased.

Jacey eyed him and tilted her head with confusion. "What do you mean?"

"He tossed you over for someone less moral," he said and raised his brows in lustful suggestion.

"My loss," Jacey replied humorously with a mocking smile.

"Yeah, some woman from town," he remarked. "That other reporter, Brenda."

Jacey rolled her eyes and tried to keep from laughing. "Yes, I figured Brenda would seize Brian with her low morals to get a good story. She conducts a lot of interviews between the sheets. They'll have a good time together."

"Guess my chances just increased greatly, huh?" Timon said with a laugh and a suggestive brow.

Jacey patted his puffy, red cheek with a delicate smile. "You're drunk."

He laughed and nodded. "Someone has to liven this party. Wanna dance?"

Jacey listened to the fast music then shook her head with a soft laugh. "No, thanks. I don't think I could keep up with you even if I tried. And in these shoes, I'd probably fall on my butt."

Angela paused alongside Timon and glared disapprovingly at him with her arms folded across her chest. "Will you stop throwing yourself at Jacey," she snapped. "You're making a spectacle of yourself."

Timon looked at Angela, mimicked her stance, and made a prudish face while bobbing his head back and force. "Lighten up, Angie. You're just jealous because she's turning every head in this place, including your wannabe boyfriend." He laughed at his own joke. "Poor Angie."

Her hateful glare didn't even appear to faze him in his intoxicated condition. Timon then chased after the waitress with a tray of hors d'oeuvres.

"Twit," Angela snarled lowly while watching his departure. She shifted her attention to Jacey and gave her the same, cold look she'd given Timon. "You just stay away from Maxwell. He may show some interest in you tonight, but by tomorrow, you'll be the same poor farm girl you were yesterday."

"Fuck off," Jacey muttered lowly with narrow eyes and a cold stare. She surprised herself. She had no idea where that came from. Possibly residue from Asher's charming personality.

Angela snorted lowly. "I should expect that sort of comment from someone of your upbringing."

"What's going on?" Maxwell asked and paused nearby. He looked at both women with a bewildered stare.

"Nothing," Angela replied while raising her head proudly and smiled brightly. She moved closer to Maxwell and placed her hand on his lower arm. "Let's dance."

Maxwell raised a curious brow. "You've never wanted to dance at one of these parties before."

"I do now," Angela announced warmly.

"You'll have to find Timon or Doc," Maxwell said simply. "I have a prior engagement with Jacey."

Angela's eyes narrowed spitefully. "With her?" she hissed then sneered. "Better keep the conversation simple. Or is it a non-verbal engagement?"

Maxwell's brow raised sharply. "I don't suppose that would be any of your business," he retorted coldly. "I don't need to answer to you or anyone else. You're not my mother, and you're certainly not my girlfriend."

Angela folded her arms across her chest and mocked him with her smile. "As if you didn't pursue me since we'd met," she snapped.

"I may have considered a relationship when I first met you, but since then I've seen you for the coldhearted bitch that you really are." His head sharply tilted. "Ever since we've arrived here, you've been playing some sort of game with me and abusing Jacey just because you see her as a threat. Allow me to set the records straight. I like Jacey," he snapped. "I like her a lot. She's interesting, and she treats me the way a man wants to be treated. Now, if you'll excuse me, I'd like to enjoy myself for a change." Maxwell extended his hand to Jacey.

Jacey smiled warmly and placed her hand in his. He led her from the room with several long, quick strides. In her high heels, she had a difficult time keeping up with him. He slowed his pace once they reached the nearly empty hallway, though he didn't release her hand.

"I'm sorry about that," he said gently and sighed. "I didn't mean to start that in front of you. I can't believe I actually said those things out loud."

Jacey laughed softly. "Believe me, I enjoyed it. That woman has been out to get me from the start."

"She has a need to control people," he explained then looked away with a frown. "I suppose she wanted to control me too. I've never been overly confident, and I was just happy to feel needed, whether it was real or not."

"I would think you're needed around here," she remarked. "Doc seems to depend upon you." He was obviously well-respected among his peers.

He smiled with some embarrassment. "That's a little different. I know where I stand professionally. It's not always enough," he said gently.

Jacey turned and walked sideways while studying him. "I need you. Does that count?" she asked with a grin.

Maxwell looked at her with some surprise then smiled. "You may be the only one who does," he said softly.

They found their way upstairs and entered Maxwell's room. It was a neat, well-kept room. He removed a folder with several papers from the top of his desk and stared at it with some confusion. He opened it and flipped through the papers.

"Is something wrong?" Jacey asked curiously.

He turned to face her. "Something's missing," he replied and looked around the room. "This wasn't where I had left it, and now there's a page missing."

"Was it anything important?" Jacey asked.

Maxwell shook his head and flipped through the pages again. "I'm not sure," he replied. "I had several pages in here. I didn't really study them." He then stopped and looked at Jacey. His eyes narrowed. "It was a page on Asher."

"Asher?" she said with surprise. "You were investigating Asher? Why?"

"I was investigating him, in a manner of speaking. I did some research on his cane and came up with some interesting discoveries," Maxwell informed her. "He was supposed to tell you after my talk with him. He promised he would."

Jacey felt her heart pound nervously. "He said he had to talk to me, but he was preoccupied about *something*," she said more softly.

Maxwell inhaled deeply and nodded. "It's only fair that he tell you himself." He handed her the folder.

"But who would take the paper?" she asked aloud although she was mostly talking to herself.

Maxwell raised a brow and shrugged. "Maybe Asher himself," he announced. "He wasn't very happy with me about my discoveries."

Jacey lowered the folder and frowned. "Maybe you should tell me."

"No," he replied. "I promised Asher I wouldn't. I should at least give him the chance to be honest with you."

She groaned and opened the folder. "You're just as bad as he is." Jacey heard someone walk past the partially opened door. She looked toward the hallway and sank into thought while closing the folder. She looked back at Maxwell. "Can we go to the observatory?"

"Sure," he replied. "Just not for too long. Doc wasn't very happy about my leaving."

Jacey cocked her head to one side. "What did you mean earlier when you said about you 'disappearing too'?"

He inhaled deeply then forced a tiny smile. "Brian ducked out with some woman he'd met earlier, and Professor conveniently eluded the party entirely."

"Yes, I've heard about Brian and Brenda," Jacey remarked while hiding her smile then studied Maxwell and appeared curious. "Professor never showed?"

Maxwell shook his head. "I assume he's with your two cousins watching horror movies at your house."

"I don't doubt it," Jacey said with a sigh.

Chapter Twenty-five

$\mathcal{I}$t was nearing eight o'clock that evening. Monique and Coleen ran their horses across the rapidly darkening field. They slowed their horses within the woods and soon approached the back gate to the institution. They'd made excellent time getting there. Both stopped their horses and stared with horror at the new padlock and chain wrapped around the gate.

"We'll have to go around to the front," Coleen said with a deep sigh.

Monique looked toward the thick woods surrounding the gate then the path that would take them into town. She looked back at Coleen. "That will take another twenty minutes to get through the woods. It's already dark." Monique dismounted her horse and approached the gate.

Coleen watched as her blonde friend removed something from her back pocket. It was a slim, silver object.

"What's that?" Coleen asked.

Monique flashed a smile and inserted the pick into the lock. "My father's official lock pick," she replied proudly.

Coleen's eyes widened. "You swiped that from your father? Stealing from a federal agent is a federal offense."

"I didn't steal it," she insisted. "I borrowed it." Monique gave a slight groan while working on the lock. "I intend to replace it.

174

Besides, do you honestly think my father's going to have me arrested?"

The lock sprang open. Monique removed the chain and opened the gate. She returned to her horse, jumped onto his back, and rode through the gate. Coleen instinctively followed. They trotted across the neatly mowed lawn with its tall weeds hovering above the fence. They dismounted near the porch and tied their horses to the rail. Both ran onto the porch. Jill and her small group of followers could be seen picketing the front gate. They now stopped and pointed at the two girls on the porch. Monique hurried to the door and rang the bell. The door opened a moment later. The hired butler stared at them.

"May I help you?" he asked coldly.

"We need to see Doc," Monique replied firmly.

"This isn't a hospital," he said lowly. "Do you have your invitation?"

"No, but my cousin--"

"Then I can't admit you," he replied and slammed the door before Monique could even protest.

Monique looked back at Coleen.

"Ring it again," Coleen remarked. "Demand to see Jacey."

Monique turned toward the door and rang the bell again. The door was thrown open.

"Either you leave, or I'll call the police and have you removed," he said firmly then slammed the door.

Monique turned and walked off the porch.

Coleen hurried after her. "What? We're leaving? Are you going to give him that satisfaction?"

"No," Monique snapped and walked past the horses. "I'm going in the back door."

"Through the kitchen?" Coleen asked.

Monique stopped by the caretaker's workshop and pointed. "No, this back door."

Jill and her picketers hurried along the fence while watching the girls. Monique and Coleen entered through the workshop. Coleen stopped within the dark, dirty shop and looked around. The rusted tools hung from the walls with large cobwebs as their shadows created an eerie backdrop.

"I don't think I like this idea. Let's try the kitchen," Coleen suggested.

"I'm sure there's someone there to stop us as well," Monique remarked. "We'll just slip in through the basement and take the elevator. We can find the party from there."

Coleen reluctantly followed into the dimly lit corridor that resembled a dungeon.

"Creepy," Coleen muttered lowly.

"Stop being such a wuss," Monique snapped. "We have to find Jacey and see if Professor is here."

"But what if they haven't heard from Professor?" Coleen asked. "Where could he possibly be? Surely he'd call here."

"I'm sure he's here," Monique said.

Just outside the institution grounds, Jill and her clan made their way through the thick woods along the fence and finally reached the open, back gate. Jill entered through the back gate with her sign firmly in her hands. The other women paused just outside the gate and looked inside the grounds with wide eyes. She looked back at them. They shook their heads and backed away from the open gate. Jill rolled her eyes and continued across the grounds.

✝

*D*erek crept along one of the many basement rooms and uncertainly looked around the vast area of junk. The room was filled with so many boxes and old furniture, it was almost impossible to see more than five feet ahead. He paused, looked around, and then listened to the unusual sounds within the basement. Someone was moving around, but it was impossible to tell if it was a person, a rat, or where the sound was even coming from. Ducts within the basement ceiling seemed to carry sound with a metallic echoing. As he looked around while scratching his head, it appeared almost certain he was lost. All the rooms looked alike. He continued through the maze of old furniture and entered a well-lit corridor. To the far end of the corridor was an elevator. He approached the elevator and pressed the button. Nothing happened. Derek looked to the opposite end of the hallway, appeared to contemplate his next move, and then uncertainly approached the room at the far end. He slowly entered the laundry room and looked around.

The laundry room was filled with both clean and dirty laundry. It was surprising the condition in which the institution had been left when they abandoned the building. Something moved within one of the laundry bins. Derek slowly approached the bin and uncertainly looked inside. The old, dirty sheets and towels moved. He jumped back with surprise, hesitated, and slowly lifted one of the towels. Several rats scurried over one another in an attempt to hide within the dirty, white sheets. Derek dropped the towel, jumped back, and then sighed with relief. A shadow loomed over Derek, alarming him. While attempting to turn, he was grabbed from behind. A hand in a latex glove slipped over his mouth, and he was harshly pulled against his assailant from behind. Derek attempted to cry out while struggling against his attacker. A scalpel suddenly appeared before his face and dragged firmly across his throat. He muffled a scream as blood gushed from the large, gaping gash. As he sank, his assailant shoved him into the laundry bin. Several rats squealed and scurried through the dirty laundry. Within seconds, the rats crawled across Derek's body and feasted on his rapidly spilling blood.

✝

*J*acey looked through the telescope within the attic observatory while Maxwell stood behind her and told her what she was viewing. She couldn't concentrate on what he told her about the stars. She was preoccupied with what Asher was up too. Maxwell adjusted the telescope over her shoulder. His body brushed against hers from behind, causing her to return to her present situation. She hadn't realized he'd been so close. His right hand adjusted the telescope as he looked through it just over her shoulder. The scent of his aftershave immediately aroused her senses. His left hand touched her waist so lightly, she almost hadn't noticed. She again felt his body gently press against hers from behind. Although seemingly innocent, it was possibly the most erotic moment of her life.

"Of course," he continued on the current subject, which she couldn't recall. "This telescope is insignificant compared to the one being delivered. You can see everything with that one." He was silent a moment. "I'm boring you," he said gently as his hand dropped from her waist.

Boring her? Was he that much of a genius that he didn't realize the sexual signals he was sending? She was starting to wonder if it was just her. Maybe he didn't mean anything by pressing his body against hers. She knew she had to say something that sounded somewhat intelligent. Jacey turned her head and looked back at Maxwell with a warm smile.

"No, you're not boring me," she said with some embarrassment while attempting to keep from blushing at his closeness. He wasn't boring her; she just didn't understand a word he was saying, and the closeness of his body wasn't helping her focus any either. She looked back through the telescope. "I enjoy your company. You're certainly nothing like Brian."

Maxwell chuckled in his throat while grinning. "I have years; he has miles."

Jacey looked back at him briefly and grinned. He seemed almost embarrassed and avoided looking at her. She focused her attention on the telescope, since it seemed he gained confidence while her back was turned.

"You're not like other women your age," he remarked almost softly then immediately fidgeted. "I mean, you seem more mature."

Jacey relaxed while looking through the telescope at the stars. "I suppose that has a lot to do with the company I keep." She found something of interest through the microscope. "Look, there's Jupiter," she said with a tiny laugh.

Maxwell once more leaned over her shoulder and looked through the telescope. "It's a nice, clear night," he replied. "You can see farther." His left hand again rested on her waist.

Jacey held her breath then seized the opportunity to welcome his closeness. She placed her hand over his but kept the conversation casual. She feared scaring him off.

"You'll have to invite me back when you get the big telescope," she said warmly without looking back at him. She stared at the stars but paid more attention to his hand on her waist and his body gently pressing against hers. Her heart was now beating rapidly.

"I'll probably have to fight Timon for that privilege," he teased with a tiny laugh.

Jacey gently caressed Maxwell's hand and slipped her fingers between his. He was still a moment then his right hand touched her hip. She could hear his breathing become slightly irregular and his body pressed more firmly against hers. She no longer looked through the telescope and welcomed the erotic feeling sweeping through her. In two weeks of dating Jameson, she never felt such arousal, which was probably why they never got beyond casual kissing. Although Maxwell had never even kissed her, she was already yearning for his body against hers. She'd never yearned before. It seemed improbable! He wasn't even a cowboy!

"I'll just have to stop by when he's not around," she said so softly it came out sounding like a sigh. Had she just flirted with him? She'd never before heard her voice sound like that.

His arms tightened around her waist in a warm embrace, indicating she had, indeed, flirted with him, and he was responding appropriately. "I'd like that," he replied in a whisper and brushed his lips along her neck.

Jacey closed her eyes and held her breath. His warm lips and breath on her neck was almost more than she could stand. Her body twitched in response. He gently cleared his throat and suddenly tensed, forcing her back into reality.

"We, uh, should probably return to the party. I seem to be misbehaving," he said with a nervous laugh.

Jacey gently caressed his hand on her abdomen and pressed her back against his body. "So what if you are?" she said softly.

He was unusually silent. "I don't want to give you the wrong impression," he said. "I don't want you to think I'm like Brian, but it's difficult to control myself when you're so warm and receptive." He fidgeted. "I really want a relationship with you."

He gently kissed her neck while breathing heavily. Jacey released a sharp breath and clutched his hand. Her heart pounded harshly in her chest. Maxwell became motionless then groaned.

"So much for dignity and grace," he said lowly with the sound of embarrassment.

Jacey turned in his arms, uncertainly placed her hands on his chest, and stared into his eyes. "I'd really like to get to know you, Maxwell."

Maxwell inhaled deeply; appearing almost relieved, and searched her eyes. "You would?"

She nodded.

He smiled timidly and looked down with embarrassment. "I guess there's something to be said for making a fool of oneself," he said with a soft chuckle. He then looked into her eyes. "Let's not go back to the party. Let's just stay here." His eyes then widened with concern. "I wasn't suggesting sex," he said defensively and became tense. "I just meant to spend time alone together."

Jacey smiled warmly and felt her cheeks blush. "I knew what you meant," she said gently. "I'd like that."

He appeared relieved and exhaled softly. "Why don't you wait here? I'll go downstairs and find a bottle of champagne."

She nodded.

He released her and backed away. "Promise you won't go anywhere?"

"I promise," she said with a tiny laugh.

Maxwell turned and hurried from the room with a lively gate. Jacey gently bit her lower lip while grinning then removed her hairpins, allowing her hair to fall to her shoulders. Jacey looked at the folder Maxwell had given her. She opened it and sifted through some of the papers. Jacey looked over the police report from the night of the fire and the murder of Kate Asher. It gave a detailed account of what had happened--even better than what the papers had said. She read the papers and scanned Asher's statement from his hospital bed. He'd arrived at the institution at 11:30 and had been in the second floor lounge until 11:45 when he reported hearing someone in the hallway. He left the lounge to see what had happened. He heard the page for security and moments later a fire call, which prompted him to return to the first floor to find Kate. The smoke became thicker. When he reached the first floor, there was a blaze at the end of the hall. There were nurses, orderlies, and patients coming from rooms everywhere. He found Kate murdered in the archives on the first floor a little after midnight. He had passed out from the smoke and firefighter's rescued him.

Jameson's version was similar but from a different point of view. He made rounds, securing the second floor, and ran into Kate on the first floor around 11:35. She said she was going to the archives. He went for coffee then went to patrol the first floor at about 11:50. He entered the archives to check on Kate and found her murdered. Hal Burgess attacked him and escaped. He immediately phoned Dr. Talbert, who instructed him to make a security call and locate the patient. He made the fire call at midnight. Roseanne told the same story as well. Kate left the nurse's station at 11:20 for her last rounds, which was fifteen minutes later than usual for Kate. At 11:30, Asher arrived, talked to Roseanne, and went for a cigarette in the lounge. At 11:55, Roseanne entered the second floor lounge with coffee for Asher, but he wasn't there. She heard the fire call and ran from the room.

Dr. Talbert had been in his office most of the evening. He received a phone call from Jameson at 11:50 and told him to call for a security check. He heard a noise in the hall and discovered the second floor linen closet had been set on fire. He attempted to put out the flames. He battled the fire until he heard the fire call on both levels then immediately began evacuating patients. Jacey lowered the papers and sighed sadly. She knew it must have been hell on Asher that night as well as those who attempted to rescue patients. Jacey paused and lifted the papers once more. She scanned several lines. Her eyes narrowed.

"You lied," she whispered softly while staring at the papers. "But why?" Jacey remained deep in thought a moment. Her eyes widened. She tossed the papers down and ran from the room.

†

*B*renda giggled as she walked down the narrow steps beyond the hidden doorway into the secret sub-basement with Brian just behind her. She entered the brightly lit surgical room and stared at the medical equipment on a rolling table used for surgery. It was the same room as in the pictures Monique found.

"What is this place?" she asked and looked back at Brian.

"Looks like an operating room to me," he replied simply then laughed. "Secluded though. Like a secret lab."

Brenda shook her head while grinning. "Must be, considering it was hidden within the wall. What do you suppose they did here?" she asked. She removed her cell phone without Brian's knowledge and took a picture when he wasn't looking.

"Probably conducted experiments on the mental patients," Brian teased while running his finger along the surgical table. "Who knows? Doc never told us about this room. I'm assuming he didn't even know about it when he bought the place. Maybe they gave electric shock treatments here or did their lobotomies," he teased with a soft laugh.

"That's gross," Brenda replied firmly. She continued to look around the sterile equipment in plastic covers and the shiny, metal examination table with its leather restraints.

"I thought if Doc didn't know about this room, I'd clean it up, put in some furniture, and make it my secret room." He laughed. "It'd give me someplace to hide where the others couldn't find me."

Brenda ran her finger over the examination table then looked at the door on the opposite wall. "Where does that go?"

"A secret morgue," he said with a chuckle. "Want to see it?"

Brenda cringed. "No, thanks."

Brian placed his arms around her waist and pulled her close. "How'd you like to be tied down on my table while I give you a full body exam?"

She giggled and clung to his neck. "Sounds kinky." She glanced at the leather wrist and ankle straps attached to the table then looked back at him. "But I think you'd better put a blanket down. Looks kind of cold."

Brian glanced at the table and smiled. "You're probably right. No point in torturing you while I'm torturing you. I think there are some blankets in storage in the basement upstairs. I'll be right back." Brian kissed her quickly then hurried from the room.

Brenda immediately removed her cell phone and photographed every corner of the room. The room was very quiet. Sounds from the party couldn't be heard within the basement or the secret room in the sub-basement. Brenda stared at the door to the morgue for a long moment. She approached the door, hesitated, and then opened it slowly. The room was completely dark. She felt the inner wall and turned on the lights. The room became bright. Brenda jumped to the sight of a sheet-covered gurney along the left side of the room. Four morgue freezer doors encompassed the back wall. There was a small, old elevator to the right. Brenda took more pictures with her cell phone and grinned with a slight grimace. She was obviously pleased with her discovery. She slowly walked into the room and looked at the freezer doors. She appeared to consider opening them, grinned slyly, and reached for the first door. Brenda pulled on the lever. There was a loud, vacuum sound, followed by a cloud of cold, foul smelling air. Derek Falcone lie on the tray with a blood-soaked sheet wrapped around his body. His eyes were rolled back, and his mouth hung open. Brenda screamed, slammed the freezer door, and jumped back with a horrified look on her face. She stared at the closed door as the cold air dissipated and held her chest a moment. She glanced at her cell phone then looked back at the freezer door. Brenda took a deep breath and again opened the door to reveal Derek on the slab. Her cell phone trembled in her hand as she took several pictures. The fear was evident in her eyes, but she wasn't about to give up this amazing opportunity. She took a deep breath and uncertainly pulled the sheet from his body. His throat had been slit so deep, he was nearly decapitated.

The gruesomeness of his injuries was evident by the wideness of her eyes as she stared with horror. She nervously took several pictures, making certain to get close-ups of the graphic wound. As Brenda continued to take pictures with her cell phone, a shadow loomed over her. She suddenly hesitated and uncertainly looked behind her, undoubtedly expecting to see Brian. Her startled look immediately turned to horror. She was suddenly shoved backward against the metal freezer doors by a hand in a bloodstained surgical glove. She fought the hand that pinned her to the freezer by her throat as a stained scalpel appeared in the attacker's other hand. She stared at the scalpel, gasped with horror, and attempted to scream as it plunged into the side of her neck. Her cell phone dropped from her hand. She struggled only a moment as the blood erupted from the wound on her neck. The scalpel was dragged hard and deep across her throat as her thrashing slowed. The gloved hand released her, and she immediately sank to the floor.

Chapter Twenty-six

*M*onique and Coleen wandered around the maze of old mattresses and furniture in the main basement. The basement was an assortment of large rooms with doorways leading to other rooms. One could easily get lost for hours. Each room appeared to look alike with its piled junk and cobwebs.

"This place gives me the creeps," Coleen said while looking around. "There must be stairs somewhere."

Monique looked around then suddenly felt her wrist. "Damn it, I lost my bracelet." She looked around the dark floor. It could be anywhere. "That was my good luck bracelet too." She then looked across the room and pointed. "There's the elevator."

Both girls hurried toward the elevator and pushed the button. They waited several minutes but the elevator never came. They finally realized the button didn't light either.

"Let's go back," Coleen suggested. "We'll demand to see Jacey or Doc."

"We could, if I knew which way was back," Monique replied. "I don't know where we are."

"We're below the lounge," Coleen replied. "That's where the elevator is on the first floor. I remember that." She then frowned. "I think I remember Timon saying the elevator didn't work."

"There has to be a stairway somewhere," Monique remarked with a defeated sigh.

They continued to walk through the basement. Coleen stopped Monique and nodded toward a door.

"Maybe that's a way out," Coleen suggested.

They hurried toward the door. On the frosted glass window was the word, 'morgue'. Monique looked at Coleen.

"That's a way out alright," Monique muttered and walked away.

Coleen opened the door and turned on the light. Monique returned and looked into the room over her shoulder. There were six freezers built into the back wall and several gurneys lined the wall to the right. An old privacy screen was against the left wall.

"Creepy," Coleen breathed.

"They're empty," Monique said lowly. "Don't be such a baby."

Coleen looked at her blonde friend. "Oh? And how do you know they didn't forget someone when they left? Jacey said they shut the place down in a hurry."

"I think they'd know if they'd misplaced a corpse," Monique remarked lowly.

"I've heard of hospitals losing bodies before," Coleen replied. "It could happen."

Monique stared at the privacy screen against the wall. She walked toward it and pushed it aside to reveal a small freight elevator.

"Coleen, over here," Monique called out.

Coleen approached as Monique pressed the button. The doors opened. The small elevator was only halfway to their floor and halfway below their floor. Both looked at each other.

"I think Doc was taken for a ride on this place," Coleen remarked.

"Just get in," Monique announced with a groan.

Coleen took a deep breath then sat on the floor and slid in through the small opening to the elevator. Monique followed. They stood in the small elevator that was barely big enough to fit an orderly and a stretcher. Monique was about to press the unmarked button when Coleen stopped her and pointed down to the opening near their feet. There was light coming from the opening below.

"What do you suppose is down there?" Coleen asked.

Monique shrugged. "We're in the basement already. There shouldn't be anything below us."

"I'm telling you there is. I can see a light," Coleen informed her.

Monique lowered herself to her hands and knees and looked through the narrow opening below them. There was a metal gate just below and a light shinned through. Monique straightened on her knees and looked at Coleen.

"It appears to be a room. If there's a light on, that must mean someone is down there," Monique informed her. "Should we try down?"

Coleen nodded. Monique stood and pressed the bottom, unmarked button. There was a grinding sound but nothing happened. She sighed and extended her hand to the narrow opening at the bottom on the elevator.

"After you," Monique said.

Coleen chuckled with a nervous smile. "No, after you."

Monique again lowered herself, pulled open the gate with some effort, and slid her legs though the opening while on her belly. The opening was almost too narrow for her to fit. She held on to the elevator floor with her elbows and attempted to look behind her to see where she'd land. She couldn't see anything past her own dangling legs. She pushed herself out and caught the elevator with her hands then dropped to the floor. Monique caught her balance and looked into the open elevator shaft before her. Fortunately, it would only have been a five-foot drop down had she missed the floor. Monique turned around and almost collided with Brian. Monique screamed. She clutched her chest and stared at him while he studied the opening from which she'd appeared.

"Monique," Coleen cried out from the elevator while attempting to peer through the opening. "What's wrong? Are you okay?"

"You scared me," Monique gasped.

Monique then looked around the room. They were in the sub-basement morgue where Brian had left Brenda. All four freezer doors were closed, and there wasn't a trace of blood to be found along the floor.

"Another morgue!" Monique cried out with horror.

"What are you doing?" Brian asked with surprise. He looked up to the opening as Coleen peered out.

Coleen saw him looking at her and screamed with surprise.

"Where did you come from? I thought you were staying at Jacey's," Brian remarked then looked back at the opening. "Come down from there before you get hurt."

Coleen slid through the opening as Brian assisted her down.

"It's really a long story," Monique said with an embarrassed smile. "Is Professor here?"

Brian released Coleen and looked back at Monique with apparent confusion. "I thought he was with you at Jacey's," he remarked. "When he didn't show for the party, we assumed he made an escape."

Both girls stared at him with concern on their faces. "That's part of the long story," Monique told him. "He fell off his horse. We went for help, but when we returned, he was gone. The van was still at Jacey's house, but he wasn't there either."

"We should probably call Shelly and see if he was taken to the nearest hospital," Coleen suggested.

Monique nodded.

Brian stared at them with his mouth hanging open and appeared concerned. "How bad was he hurt?"

"Not too bad," Coleen informed him. "But he was pinned under a tree. He may have broken his leg."

"We can't imagine him walking far on his own," Monique explained.

Brian nodded. "We'd better find out what happened to him," he announced then tilted his head and appeared curious. "You didn't happen to see a woman with black hair wearing a red dress, did you?"

Both shook their heads. "No, why?" Coleen asked.

"She was here a minute ago," he explained. "When I came back, she was gone."

Coleen's eyes widened. "Just like Professor!"

"Don't get hysterical on me," Brian remarked simply. "I'm sure she had second thoughts and went back to the party." He motioned for them to follow. "I'll take you back upstairs."

Monique and Coleen followed him from the morgue to the surgical lab. A close-up of one of the morgue doors revealed blood dripping from the opening into a small puddle on the floor. None had noticed. As they entered the surgical room, Monique stopped and looked around with apparent surprise.

"Coleen," she gasped and removed the photos from her back pocket. "Look, it's the room."

Coleen compared the pictures to the room with which they stood. Brian approached.

"What's wrong?" he asked with a curious tilt of his head.

Monique showed him the photos. "We found these."

Brian shrugged. "So? They're pictures of this room. Not a big deal." He turned and walked toward the stairs.

"You don't understand," Monique chirped. He paused and turned around. "These were found at the murdered woman's apartment along with a blackmail note."

Brian's look became serious. "Let's find Doc," he said firmly. "I'm not so sure I want to be down here anymore."

Both girls nodded in agreement. They hurried through the surgical lab, up the secret staircase, and to the secret entrance within the basement. Brian pushed on the door. When it didn't open, he pushed harder. He inhaled deeply and spun on the narrow steps to face both girls.

"I don't like this," he said softly then motioned them back down to the lab. "I've been down here several times, and that door has never gotten stuck."

Monique and Coleen hurried down the stairs with Brian practically pushing them.

"Where does that elevator go?" he asked as he hurried past them.

"Up to the main basement. There's another, much bigger morgue," Coleen informed him as they entered the sub-basement morgue.

The lights flickered and went out. Both girls screamed in response. All three fell silent.

"There's, uh, a flashlight on the wall near one of those machines in the other room," Brian said with a soft gasp.

"What are the chances the lights just happened to go out?" Monique asked softly.

The room was pitch black and didn't allow them to see anything, including one another.

"Let's not panic," Brian said firmly, though his voice conveyed fear. "You two stay here. I'll go find the flashlight."

"No way," both cried out and grabbed his arms.

"You're not going anywhere without us," Monique gasped. "You'll disappear too!"

Chapter Twenty-seven

*J*ameson spun around in the darkness of the basement and shined his large flashlight in several directions. He saw his own shadow and jumped. Jameson sighed with relief and relaxed. There was a dull clunk from somewhere nearby.

"Asher?" he asked softly and looked past the mounds of old furnishings. He inhaled deeply and slowly removed his gun from its holster. "This is no time to play games."

Jameson remained still a moment then moved against the wall and walked in the direction of the sound. He approached the opening to another room and paused alongside the doorway. He inhaled deeply, clutched his gun in his sweaty palm, and then jumped into the darkness of the room. There was a loud thud, followed by Jameson's gasp, and then a thump. The flashlight struck the floor and rolled out the doorway.

†

*T*here was a dull, electric hum as several red lights came on. Jill looked around the darkened basement barely lit by red lights. The emergency generator had automatically kicked on. Jill groaned and set her sign against a mattress. She looked around the cluttered storage area.

"Where am I?" she moaned softly.

She walked along the narrow path between mattresses and boxes. There was a sound further ahead. A shadow passed along the wall in the next room. The light was bright, indicating a flashlight. Jill slowly approached the room and noticed the old stairs before the room. She continued toward the opening and strained to peer into the laundry room without being seen. She saw Asher shutting one fuse box then opening another. Jill's eyes widened and she held back her gasp. She turned and hurried away. There was movement from behind her. Jill looked back. There was no one there. She crawled behind some mattresses and remained still and silent. She could hear someone walk in the opposite direction, but she still refused to move. She waited another few minutes. Nothing moved except a mouse that ran past her feet where she was huddled. Jill watched the mouse without a sound, though her eyes were wide. She looked out from behind the mattress. Nothing moved in the red glow of the emergency lights. She slowly crawled out from behind the mattress on her hands and knees. Her hand touched something hard and smooth. She looked at the black, dress shoes. Jill's mouth opened as she slowly looked up. An ax, held in black gloved hands, was coiled back. She attempted to scream as the ax blade came at her face. Blood spattered the mattress behind her, and the sound of her head was heard rolling across the stone floor. Jill's headless body collapsed to the floor just near the black, dress shoes. Blood spilled across the floor in a small flood.

†

*J*acey stood in the basement corridor and looked around the dimly lit area. The red, emergency lights created an eerie setting. She nervously looked around and listened to movement. It was more than likely just a mouse. She began to walk slowly along the corridor that led to a room. The room appeared darker than the corridor. She paused outside the archway and looked inside the room. She had no choice but to enter. She didn't understand why the basement was designed with so many passageways and rooms. Her only guess was they had intended to use it for therapy and group sessions. She suspected they had changed their minds when they realized the patients brought in were more violent than they had originally anticipated. Jacey stepped on something. She paused and looked down to her feet. She picked up a Monique's braided bracelet and stared at it. Jacey looked around with horror in her eyes.

"Monique," she gasped softly. She spun around with concern. "That can't be. They wouldn't be here--" She inhaled deeply. "Damn it." Jacey hurried across the room. "Monique? Coleen?"

✝

Asher stood over a laundry bin within the laundry room. He held a blood-soaked towel then tossed it into the bin with a few other bloodied towels. Jacey's voice was heard echoing through the vents.

"Monique! Coleen!" her voice echoed.

Asher heard her voice and suddenly looked around. His mouth curved into a scowl. "No, Jacey," he muttered. "Why did you have to come down here?"

He hurried from the laundry room.

✝

Brian held the gurney still while Monique climbed on top of it and pulled herself through the small opening into the raised elevator. She lay on the floor of the elevator and accepted the flashlight from Brian. Coleen climbed on top of the gurney and climbed through as well. Monique helped pull her the rest of the way. Both looked back at Brian. He climbed on top of the gurney and looked at the opening. He shook his head.

"I won't fit," he announced.

"Come on," Monique firmly insisted. "Give it a try, Brian. You can do it."

Brian attempted to move through the opening but couldn't get more than his head through. "I won't fit," he said once more. "You two go for help. I don't know if the lock is stuck, or if there's a more serious problem. Under no circumstances are you to come back on your own. Do you understand?"

"What if there's someone in there with you?" Monique gasped. "We can't just leave you."

"I locked the morgue door. I'll be fine," Brian informed them. "There are two sets of stairs in the basement. If you're where I think you are, you'll never find the main one in the darkness. There are stairs leading to the west wing if you just keep right. There's a long corridor once you pass the room with shelves in it. If you go straight, you'll end up in the gardener's workshop. Make a left before the workshop. There are stairs there."

190

Coleen glared at Monique. "Hear that? There are stairs by the workshop."

Monique looked away with disgust. "Stop being petty."

"Fight about it later," Brian growled. There was the sound of someone within the surgical lab just outside the sub-basement morgue. Brian stared at the morgue door then looked back into the elevator opening. "Go on. Get someone back here right away."

Both girls nodded in response. They scrambled to their feet and climbed through the opening above them to the main morgue in the basement. Monique helped Coleen to her feet then shined the light around the small room. The light revealed droplets of blood on the floor. Coleen grabbed Monique's arm and pointed at the blood.

"Look," Coleen gasped with the horror evident in her eyes. "That wasn't there before."

Monique followed the droplets of blood with her flashlight. There was blood up the side of the freezers and stopped at the first door. Both held their breath. Monique slowly shook her head.

"I'm not about to look in there," she whispered with a shiver in her voice.

Coleen grabbed her arm and pulled her toward the door. "Come on. Let's get out of here!"

They ran for the basement morgue door, carefully stepping around the trial of blood droplets, and threw open the door. Asher stood in the doorway. Both girls screamed. Coleen slammed the door shut, and both threw their bodies against it.

"Open this door," Asher cried out as he firmly pounded on it.

"We're dead," Monique gasped softly.

When they didn't comply, the door was thrust open, tossing both girls partially across the room. Monique clutched the flashlight and held it above her head, prepared to strike.

"What are you doing down here?" he demanded in a harsh tone. "You can't be down here."

Coleen nervously looked down at the blood on the floor then back at Asher. His eyes strayed to the blood as well. He shined his flashlight across the morgue and up the wall to the first freezer. Asher took a step toward them and the freezer.

"Stay back," Monique cried out and clutched the flashlight.

Asher paused and stared at her with a look of surprise. "What's with you two? I'm not the enemy here. Now stop this behavior."

Jameson fell into the doorway with his gun drawn. He had a cut on his temple, which bled freely. "That's far enough, Asher," Jameson growled lowly while nearly out of breath. "You just get away from those girls."

Asher became still. His expression stiffened. He didn't turn around nor say a word.

"Against the wall--hands where I can see them." Jameson's hand seemed to tremble slightly on the gun.

Asher's expression remained stiff. He obediently did as he was told, placing his hands against the wall, with his cane still clutched in his hand.

"Drop the cane," Jameson ordered.

Asher complied.

Jameson looked at the girls while breathing heavily. "Are you okay?"

Both girls sighed and nodded. Monique finally lowered her flashlight. Jameson removed his handcuffs and approached Asher. He attached the cuffs to Asher's wrist and a nearby pipe. Jameson backed away and stared at the blood on the floor. He walked past the girls to the freezer, took a deep breath, and opened it. A cloud of cold air escaped then cleared. Monique nervously looked away and caught a glimpse of Asher. His head rested against the wall. His eyes were pinched shut as if he were in pain. Monique looked back at Jameson. Jill's head was displayed proudly on the slab facing the open, freezer door. The look of horror was frozen on her face. Jameson appeared horrified and jumped back a step. Monique and Coleen screamed at the gruesome sight.

"My God, it's Jill," he gasped softly.

Monique looked back at Asher. His head lifted, and he looked to the freezer with surprise and yet relief. Monique's eyes narrowed in confusion.

"Where's Jacey?" Asher demanded. "I heard her down here."

"Don't you worry about Jacey," Jameson snapped. "She's not your concern."

"Find her," Asher growled lowly with narrow, evil eyes.

"Brian's trapped downstairs," Coleen told Jameson while avoiding looking at Jill's severed head. "We have to get him out."

Jameson shut the freezer door and looked at Coleen. "Downstairs? We are downstairs."

Monique shook her head. "No, there's a basement below this basement. A sub-basement. We'll show you."

He slowly nodded. "Okay. We'd better hurry."

Coleen motioned for him to follow her. Monique paused and looked back at Asher. Asher stared back at her.

"If you care about your cousin, you'll find her," Asher said softly with raised brows. "Find her and bring her to me."

Monique hurried from the room.

Chapter Twenty-eight

$\mathcal{D}$oc ushered the last of the guests out the front doors of the dimly lit institution. "Sorry about the inconvenience," he announced politely. "We'll try again some other time."

Timon closed the door and glared at Doc, Angela, and Maxwell. "No one's seen either of them," Timon remarked firmly.

Angela folded her arms across her chest and shook her head. "Brian's just doing his usual thing," she remarked simply. "As for Jacey, well, she probably left to avoid hurting Maxwell's feelings."

Maxwell glared at Angela. "She wouldn't have run out," he snapped coldly. "The papers I'd gathered for her were scattered all over the floor. Something happened to her."

Mayor Norad came out of one of the offices and approached the small group of four. "I spoke with Jameson on the hand radio just moments ago. He's in the basement. He'll keep a look out for Jacey and Brian."

"What's he doing in the basement?" Doc asked curiously.

Mayor Norad inhaled deeply. "He's searching for Konrad Asher. He found evidence to link him to the murder of Roseanne. Sheriff Monroe is checking the upper floors of the main building, and Dr. Talbert went to look around the west wing."

"Evidence?" Maxwell asked with a curious tilt of his head. "What sort of evidence?"

"They found the murder weapon in his home earlier today," Howard replied. "More than that, I'm not at liberty to say."

"I wouldn't rely on any evidence found in Asher's home, Mayor," Maxwell remarked. "Asher said someone had broken into his house. The murder weapon could've easily been planted there to frame him."

Everyone stared at Maxwell.

"I hope you're not suggesting corruption of our police department," Howard said loudly with his eyes wide.

"No, of course not," Maxwell replied. He then looked at Doc. "I need to find Jacey. Excuse me."

He began to walk away when Howard called after him. "The police can handle this, Dr. Alvord. It would be best if you just remained here and allowed them to do their job."

Maxwell turned and stared at the mayor. "I've waited long enough already. I'm going to find Jacey." Maxwell turned and continued down the corridor.

Timon ran after him. "Maxwell, wait! I'm coming with you."

✝

*J*acey moaned with frustration as she looked around the filthy caretaker's workshop. She looked through the open outside door and saw the two horses tied not far from the workshop. She shook her head with disappointment.

"I can't believe them," she muttered lowly.

Jacey looked around the dimly lit room filled with tools and gardening equipment. She approached the back wall and removed an old, rusted sling blade from above the tool bench. She drew a deep breath, looked around nervously, and carried it with her into the corridor. She wasn't going to admit that she was paranoid, but she knew it didn't hurt to be prepared. As she looked at the rusted sling blade in her hand, she wondered if she'd been hanging out with Asher too long. Had he made her cynical and distrusting? Or just scary prepared?

✝

*C*oleen led Jameson to the hidden, secret passageway door within the basement. It was right where Brian said it would be, almost hidden in plain sight.

"It's just through there," Coleen said. "There are stairs that lead to a sub-basement of sorts. There's a surgical room of some sort and a small morgue. We left Brian in the morgue."

Jameson moved her aside and clutched his gun nervously. "Okay, you two stay back." He opened the unlocked door and looked down the dimly lit stairs into the darkness.

Both girls were alarmed.

"That door was locked," Coleen quickly informed him.

Monique clutched Coleen's arm and pointed to a dark stain on Jameson's tan pants near his nightstick. Coleen tilted her head and raised her brows in silent question. Monique gently touched the bottom of the nightstick without Jameson's knowledge. There was blood on her finger. Coleen stared at the blood. Monique pulled Coleen away from the small stairway as Jameson descended down the steps.

"What's wrong with you?" Coleen asked softly. "It's just blood from Jill. He touched her body. He's going to have blood on him. He also has a cut on his head." Coleen followed Monique and looked around the more familiar rooms. "Where are we going?"

"To talk to Asher," Monique replied.

"What?" Coleen gasped. "Are you out of your mind? I'm more worried about Brian. What if Asher killed him?"

"I'm afraid Brian's dead already," Monique said stiffly. "The door to the secret passageway had been locked, but now it's not."

Both girls entered the basement morgue and saw the handcuff dangling from the pipe. Asher was gone! Both looked around nervously.

"I don't like this," Coleen whispered.

"Me either," Monique said softly.

"Let's go back upstairs and find the others," Coleen said. "We need to find Maxwell and Timon."

"Brian said the stairs were this way," Monique said and pointed to the right.

They hurried from the morgue in the direction of the gardener's workshop. After several minutes, they found the corridor. The stairs were right where Brian said they would be. They hurried up them.

†

*M*axwell paced the small area in the laundry room while Timon poked around the fuse boxes located along the back wall. Maxwell exhaled deeply and appeared impatient.

"Have you figured it out yet?"

"I think so," Timon announced. The lights went out completely. "Oops," he said softly. "It's okay. I can fix it."

He suddenly cried out in pain. The red lights came back on. Timon clutched his bleeding forearm. Maxwell hurried to his side and examined the bleeding cut.

"Looks pretty deep," Maxwell said. "You'd better go upstairs and let Doc have a look at it."

Timon slowly nodded then looked back at Maxwell. "Are you staying down here by yourself?"

"Just long enough to find Jacey," he replied. "I'll be back in a few minutes."

Timon looked around the room and grabbed a pillowcase from the nearby linen rack. He wrapped it around his arm and tied it. "You look for her. I'll get the lights on."

Maxwell nodded then hurried from the room.

✝

*J*acey walked cautiously along the corridor. The brief moment the lights went out was enough to frighten her. She clutched her sling blade and listened to several strange sounds. She swore she heard movement all around her. She paused before an entranceway to one of the many storage rooms in the maze like basement. She stared into the dark doorway. There was movement, she was almost positive. Jacey pinned herself to the wall near the doorway and listened more carefully. She could hear someone walking through the large room. She raised the sling blade and held her breath. Someone stepped into the doorway. The lights went out. When they came on, Jacey screamed, jumped back a step, and swung the blade. Maxwell ducked. The blade struck the inside of the doorway.

"Maxwell," Jacey gasped with surprise and dropped the rusted weapon. "Oh, my God! I'm so sorry."

Maxwell's eyes were wide. His body sagged as he exhaled and looked away while holding his chest. "You could've killed me," he gasped.

Jacey sprang into his arms. "I'm really sorry," she cried out softly and hugged him happily. "I'm so glad to see you." She pulled away just as his arms tightened. Her eyes were once more wide. "I have to find Monique and Coleen. They're here somewhere. Their horses are outside."

"They weren't upstairs that I'd noticed," Maxwell said and looked around the corridor. "I'll look for them just as soon as I get you upstairs, so I know you're safe."

Jacey backed away from Maxwell while he stood near the doorway. "We don't have that kind of time. There's no telling what happened to them." Jameson stepped into the doorway behind Maxwell. Jacey looked at him and sighed with relief. "Oh, Jameson. We could use your--"

Maxwell turned as if to look behind him. Jameson plunged a scalpel into Maxwell's shoulder, narrowly missing his back. Jacey screamed with shock and horror. Maxwell cried out, clutched his shoulder, and fell against the nearby wall. Jameson lunged for Maxwell. Jacey swooped down to the floor, snatched the sling blade, and swung it at Jameson. The blade tore into his upper arm then struck the wall and fell from her hands. Jameson cried out as he hit the doorway. He clutched his bleeding arm while reaching for his gun. Jacey looked at the discarded sling blade on the floor.

"Run," Maxwell cried out and kicked Jameson's leg out from underneath him.

Jameson hit the wall with his shoulder but didn't release the gun. Jacey screamed and bolted down the corridor and into another room. As she stepped into the dark room, she froze with terror. She'd just given Maxwell to Jameson! Why did she run? Just because he told her to? Her heart pounded with anticipation of hearing a gunshot. The gunshot rang out, but the bullet ricocheted off the wall near her head instead. He was shooting at her! She didn't know what happened to Maxwell, but now she had no choice but to run. Jacey screamed and ran deeper into the dark room.

✝

*M*onique and Coleen stopped in the familiar west wing corridor and looked around. Dr. Talbert was at the opposite end of the first floor hallway looking into rooms as he walked.

"Dr. Talbert," both cried out and ran along the hallway.

He spun with a look of surprise and waited for them. "What are you girls doing here?" he asked. "It's not safe here."

"There's a dead woman downstairs," Monique gasped. "Brian might be dead too."

Dr. Talbert appeared surprised. "We've got to call Monroe or Jameson," he announced sternly.

"No," Monique gasped and clutched his sleeve. "Jameson had blood on his nightstick. He might be involved."

"He was there at the time of the murder," Coleen added.

"Jameson?" Talbert gasped with wide eyes. "That's impossible. I've known Jameson for years. No, Asher's around here somewhere. There's evidence that links him to the murder of Roseanne. Jameson's here to arrest him."

Monique shook her head. "I saw the look on Asher's face when Jameson opened the freezer door. He was afraid it was Jacey in there. If he was the killer, he would've known it wasn't her."

"Jameson was the one who conveniently found the evidence at Asher's house," Coleen informed him. "We think he's trying to frame Asher."

Dr. Talbert stared at them with surprise and possible disbelief. "We should get you two safely back with the others," he said firmly. "We'll leave the detective work to the professionals." He guided them along the hall toward the first floor nurse's station. "Why would Jameson want to kill Roseanne?" Talbert finally asked as they neared the nurse's station.

"Blackmail," Monique replied simply and removed the photos from her back pocket.

"Blackmail?" he asked from behind them and attempted to look at the photos over her shoulder.

"Yeah, Roseanne must've known Jameson was involved in Mrs. Asher's death and tried to blackmail him," Monique continued.

"Apparently there was a secret lab--" Coleen added.

Asher suddenly jumped over the tall nursing station desk and tackled Talbert into the opposite wall. Both girls screamed as Asher knocked a gun from Talbert's hand and watched it slide across the floor. Asher held his cane to Talbert's throat. Talbert shoved Asher backward. Monique sprang out of his path as he fell against the tall counter with a loud crack. Talbert dove for the gun. Coleen screamed with fright and kicked it down the hall. Both girls ran after the swiftly gliding revolver. Talbert removed a scalpel from his pocket and slashed at Asher. Asher jumped and thrashed him on the shoulder with his cane. Talbert yelped and jumped back a step. Asher swung his cane like a escrima stick used for karate fighting. Talbert slashed through the air toward Asher's face. Asher slung his cane and struck Talbert several times, as he attempted to cut him with the scalpel. Monique picked up the gun. Both girls ran back to the fighting men.

"Who do I shoot?" Monique gasped nervously.

"Neither," Coleen exploded with horror.

Talbert slashed at Asher and cut his side. Asher spun into a roundhouse kick and knocked Talbert against the opposite wall. Talbert was slightly dazed. Asher clutched his cut side and looked at the blood. Talbert sprang back for Asher and slashed for his throat. Asher dove to the floor and kicked Talbert as he rolled across the floor. Dr. Talbert was thrown off balance. Asher sprang to his feet and pushed a button on the cane. A three-inch blade popped out the bottom. He jabbed the blade into Talbert's foot. Talbert cried out in pain, pulled the cane free, and held onto it while lunging for Asher's throat with the scalpel.

"No," Monique screamed and aimed the gun.

Asher pulled back on the top of the cane. It detached to reveal a twelve-inch, stiletto dagger. Asher blocked Talbert's right hand, thrust the dagger forward, and impaled Talbert through the midsection. Both girls screamed. Asher pulled the dagger free and watched Talbert fall to the floor. Asher breathed heavily for a minute or two. He turned and looked at Monique and Coleen. Both girls screamed and ran down the corridor. Asher looked back at Talbert and kicked the scalpel from his hand. He lowered himself to one knee. Talbert clutched his bleeding midsection and gasped in agony. Their eyes met.

"The intention was to frame me and torch the institution," Asher said calmly. "Why kill these innocent people?" Asher moved closer to Talbert and stared into his eyes. "Tell me, Doctor, who was giving the orders?"

Talbert breathed deep, shallow breaths as blood seeped out the corner of his mouth. "Howard," he gasped softly. "Howard Norad gave the order to kill Katie when she found the secret lab." He was silent a moment. "Jameson killed Katie then released Hal Burgess in the file room to frame him."

Asher was silent a moment then drew a deep breath. He exhaled with an odd relief. "Thank you, Dr. Talbert. You've given me closure," he said with little emotion as the doctor wheezed his last breath. His eyes turned hateful as he looked away from the dead man. "Now, it's time for revenge." He patted the dead doctor's shoulder, straightened, and casually walked down the corridor.

Chapter Twenty-nine

Jacey ran up the stairs to the west wing and bolted out the door and into the hallway on the first floor. She ran along the hallway and turned toward the main corridor, which would take her to the main building. She could hear Jameson in the stairway not far behind her. Jacey suddenly stopped and stared at Dr. Talbert lying on the floor in the hallway several yards ahead. She could see blood surrounding him even from a distance. She hurried along the corridor and slowed when she noticed part of Asher's cane on the floor. Jacey stared at the dead man with wide, horrified eyes and hurried past him without tearing her eyes from the gruesome sight. She turned and nearly collided with Asher, who held the cane dagger. Jacey let out a startled cry and jumped back with surprise. Asher grabbed her arm and pulled her along the hallway behind him.

"We've got to hurry. There's not a moment to lose."

"Asher," she gasped and pointed back to Talbert. "I don't understand. What--?"

Jacey saw the stairwell door being thrown open behind them as it struck the opposite wall with a crack that echoed throughout the hall. Asher whirled around as Jameson skidded to a halt in the corridor. Jameson raised his gun and fired at them.

"You didn't tell me you brought friends," Asher remarked while pulling Jacey along the hallway behind him and down the connecting corridor.

They ran up the stairs to the second floor. As they passed through the stairwell fire doors, Asher slid to a stop on the other side and pulled the fire alarm. The alarm blared loudly.

"That won't stop him," she said nervously and looked down the hallway. Asher grabbed the fire hose, pulled it to the door, and tied it through the bars.

"That should hold him for a few minutes," Asher announced and pulled her along the corridor. "We'll be in need of the fire department soon enough."

"Why?"

"I discovered some gasoline cans in one of the storage rooms in the basement. They were taken from my house, though I hadn't noticed they were missing until I found them here. They intend to burn the remainder of the institution and frame me."

Jacey was suddenly alarmed. "Maxwell's still in the basement," she gasped. "Monique and Coleen are around here somewhere too. I can't leave without them!"

"Considering the fright I gave them, those girls should've reached the others by now. They should be safe," he announced. "It's us I'm worried about. In order for their plan to work, I have to die."

He pulled her past the second floor nurse's station.

"Maxwell's been hurt. We have to go back for him," Jacey said nervously.

"We will, but first we have to get some distance between us and Deputy Jameson."

He hurried her into the nearby linen closet and closed the door behind them. Asher looked around the old stacks of sheets on the racks then to the linen chute. He opened the small door and looked down the slanted, metal chute. He grabbed some old blankets and tossed them down.

"What are you doing?" she asked with surprise and concern.

"Making a pile at the bottom of the chute," he replied casually.

"Why?" she demanded to know.

He turned and looked at her matter-of-fact. "So you won't hurt yourself when you hit the bottom."

Jacey's eyes widened. "I'm not going down there!"

"It's a shortcut to the basement," he remarked. "I'll be right behind you." He suddenly grinned. "It'll be fun."

She could hear someone running along the hallway. Jacey frowned, removed her high heels, and climbed into the chute. Asher supported her as she went in feet first. She looked into his eyes briefly. He smiled reassuringly and let her go. Once he released her, she slid down the metal chute. Jacey held back her scream. She landed in the laundry room on a pile of blankets. A hand appeared before her face. Jacey gasped then saw Timon standing over her. She accepted his hand. He pulled her to her feet and looked back at the chute.

"Should I ask?"

"No," she replied and looked up the chute as well.

"Expecting someone else?" he asked.

Asher didn't appear. She feared calling up to him. She spun toward Timon and tossed her shoes aside. "Get Sheriff Monroe," she ordered. "Jameson's a killer. He's after Asher on the second floor on the west wing. Get help to him."

"Where are you going?" Timon asked.

"Maxwell's been hurt," she said nervously. "I have to see if he's alright."

Timon's eyes were wide with fear as he nodded. "I'll get the sheriff."

Both ran from the basement laundry room in separate directions. Jacey scurried along the corridor and into the first storage area. It took her several minutes to figure which way she needed to go to reach the corridor where she'd left Maxwell. She reached the corridor and saw blood on the wall near the floor. Maxwell wasn't there. Jacey stood immobile a moment. She then looked toward the corridor that led to the west wing stairs. She hurried to the connecting corridor. She spun around the corner and nearly collided with Jameson. He aimed his gun at her.

"Going somewhere?" he asked with a sly smile.

Jacey stared at the gun as her heart pounded with fear. She didn't know if Maxwell was even alive, or what had become of Asher, but she had a more immediate problem to consider.

"We're going to take a little walk now," he informed her simply and motioned with the gun.

Jacey backed into the main corridor and stared at the gun aimed at her. "Why, Jameson?" she asked sadly. "Why would you do this?"

He frowned and shook his head. "You wouldn't understand. Don't think I want to do this," he said. "I never intended to hurt you, but there's too much at stake to allow loose ends."

She was forced to walk along the hallway and through several storage areas. Jacey noticed the gas cans near the wall where Asher said they were. They approached the basement morgue. Jacey made a conscious decision to stop suddenly. She turned to face him and hid her fears.

"You killed Kate Asher, didn't you?" Jacey demanded with angry, hurtful eyes. "This is all because of what happened ten years ago."

He shook his head with irritation on his face. "Don't pretend to know. You don't have any idea what happened here ten years ago or today, for that matter. The only way to stop this is to burn this place to the ground once and for all. Your cousin and her friend had to get involved. Most of this could've been avoided if they'd minded their own business."

Jacey shook her head with some confusion. "I don't understand. They didn't tell me they found anything. What do you think they know?"

"They have the evidence that Kate found," he remarked. "They took some photos from Roseanne's belongings while helping Dr. Talbert." He shook his head with annoyance. "Kate discovered the experiments Dr. Talbert had been conducting in his secret lab. She even took photos. It was necessary to get rid of her before she had a chance to tell anyone."

"Did you kill her?" Jacey asked firmly. Her fear was quickly turning to anger.

Jameson didn't respond.

Jacey slowly nodded. "I see," she announced. Jameson was the reason Asher lost everything and suffered the last decade. She suddenly wanted to see Jameson dead. "So you framed Hal Burgess. Except it didn't work as planned. Something went wrong." Jacey almost couldn't stop her mouth. She'd never been this bold before. She wasn't sure if she was being brave or stupid at this point, but she wanted answers.

"He was a little smarter than I anticipated. He used the scalpel I'd left behind to cut the straps on his straitjacket. Probably used his feet. By the time I saw the discarded straitjacket, he was already behind me and hit me with my flashlight," Jameson informed her. "I had no idea he'd set the fires to escape the institution and kill all those people."

Jacey didn't want to hear about his guilt. She was becoming increasingly angry and felt her entire body twitch. She felt as if she was about to explode. "Then when the fire broke out," Jacey snapped, "Dr. Talbert took time to destroy his files; the ones Kate was looking for in the file room. He knew they'd investigate." Her eyes were hateful and demanding. "When he should've been saving patients, he was busy covering his ass."

Jameson was again silent.

"And he also disconnected the fire alarms. Why?" she asked sternly.

She knew she was playing with fire, but she couldn't seem to stop herself. There was the very real possibility she was channeling all Asher's anger over the years. Something about herself felt oddly different at that moment. She was no longer herself.

Jameson inhaled deeply with a sad look on his face. "He needed to disconnect the alarms to use the facility for his experiments. The fire alarms were tripped every time he used the lab. He'd forgotten to turn them back on," Jameson informed her. "Don't you see, we had to destroy this place, but if it would've burned while empty, there surely would've been an investigation. Jill created a perfect way out. We needed to blame someone, and since everyone believed Asher was a killer, he was the perfect scapegoat."

"So you killed Roseanne just to frame Asher?"

He shook his head with wide eyes. "No, of course not. Rosanne resorted to blackmail. She found out what really happened that night from papers she'd taken from Kate's purse. She finally put it together the night she went with Dr. Talbert to Asher's house. That's why she had to be silenced. We never wanted to hurt anyone, but there was just no other way." He tilted his head with a look of sorrow. "I'm really sorry, Jacey. You know how I feel about you. If you only had remained my girl, you wouldn't even have been here tonight. None of this would've happened. But you had to get involved with Asher and mess around with that scientist. It's your fault I had to kill him," he said with some anger in his voice. "It's because of you that I'll have to kill those girls as well." He shook his head violently. "I'm not looking forward to that at all."

Jacey knew he was feeling trapped and would soon kill her despite his feelings for her. She stared at him and attempted to remain calm until she could think of a way out. Nothing came to mind.

He motioned toward the morgue with his gun. "Inside," he ordered. "Let's get this over with."

Jacey backed against the wall near the door. Her heart pounded harshly and she breathed rapidly. There was a shadowy movement just down the hall behind Jameson. Jacey's mouth opened slightly with a glimmer of hope, though she didn't know who it was. She looked back at Jameson and held her breath. She needed to be brave just a minute longer. Her eyes strayed to the diamond tennis bracelet around her wrist. What would Asher do? Her eyes suddenly narrowed and lifted to meet Jameson's gaze. Her look was chilling and nearly psychotic.

"Poor pathetic Jameson," she hissed while sneering. "Dr. Talbert is dead, and by now, those girls have told the others about your involvement. You won't be getting away with anything." A twisted smile crossed her face as she portrayed Asher. "They know all about you."

Maxwell appeared in the glow of the red lights with the rusted sling blade in his hands. He no longer wore his jacket, revealing the blood on the shoulder of his white shirt. She attempted to keep her attention on Jameson, but she couldn't get her mind off Maxwell's blood or the nearly psychotic look on his face. She knew she needed to be strong now more than ever. She needed to play Asher another minute longer.

Jameson laughed lowly in his throat while shaking his head. "I know what you're up too, but it won't work."

"Give it up, Jameson," she scoffed and maintained her psychotic demeanor. "Give it up, and maybe you'll make it out of here alive." She suddenly grinned and almost mocked him. "But I'm not making any promises."

By the look in his eyes, something about her struck a nerve with Jameson. He seemed unusually tense now. His arrogant smile again returned.

"Nice try," he announced. "But, if you don't mind, I'm short on time."

"No," she replied while sneering. "I'd say you're out of time."

As Maxwell coiled back, the sling blade parted the air with a distinctive sound. Jameson spun from the sound and gasped to the sight of the sling blade swinging at his head. Jameson ducked. The blade struck the stone wall and cracked the cement. Maxwell pulled back with a loud, animal like growl and swung downward at Jameson, who attempted to aim his gun. Jameson cried out and rolled. The blade sliced Jameson's side, almost impaling him with the long blade. Jameson cast himself against the wall in a sitting position and aimed the gun at Maxwell. Jacey cried out and kicked Jameson's arm. The gun flew in the air and slid into the shadows. Maxwell slung the blade as Jameson dove in the direction of the gun. The blade struck the floor roughly, causing sparks. The blade snapped in two. Maxwell tossed it aside and lunged for Jameson. Both men punched each other violently while rolling around the floor. Maxwell punched Jameson several times while straddling his waist. Jameson tossed Maxwell off him. Maxwell tumbled across the floor and clutched his shoulder in agony. He slowly moved to his knees.

Jameson removed the scalpel from his pocket and quickly stood. Jacey screamed and pulled Maxwell to his feet. They ran along the corridor and ducked into one of the darker rooms. Maxwell stopped by the sole red light in the large storage room and smashed the bulb. They ran through the darkness. He toppled several boxes behind them. Jacey could hear Jameson fall over the boxes in the darkness. They continued to run for several minutes until they reached the stairs to the west wing and the gardener's workshop just before them. Maxwell skidded to a halt and pulled her toward the stairs.

"This way. The west wing," he announced while gasping for air.

Jacey pulled on him harshly in the direction of the workshop. "No, this way!"

Maxwell ran after her. They entered the workshop and slammed the door, bolting it behind them. Maxwell breathed heavily and clutched his shoulder painfully. He looked around the workshop and grabbed a hedge clipper. Jacey grabbed his arm and pulled him toward the door.

"Don't be stupid," she shouted.

✝

*W*ithin the cluttered basement, someone in black dress shoes slipped through the dimly lit area and approached the gas cans stolen from Asher's house. Black gloved hands dropped the bloodied ax on the floor then lifted the first gas can and doused nearby mattresses with the flammable substance. A match was lit and tossed onto the mattress. The gas ignited and flames swiftly engulfed the mattress against the wall. As the flames brightened the room, Mayor Howard Norad removed his blood covered, black gloves and tossed them into the flames.

Chapter Thirty

Maxwell and Jacey ran from the workshop into the cool night air. The tied horses jumped nervously while watching them. There was a thump against the inside door of the workshop. They ran toward the horses. Jacey untied the paint and mounted without use of the stirrups, allowing the slit in her dress to tear several inches from the sudden movement. There was a loud crack from the workshop. Maxwell untied the black horse and attempted to mount with lack of experience on the nervously dancing horse. There was a crack of a gunshot. Maxwell spun and fell to the ground. The paint horse reared high in the air with a loud squeal. Jacey maintained her balance and stared at Maxwell on the ground while attempting to control the paint horse. She looked to the workshop. Jameson stood in the doorway with his gun aimed at her. Jacey kicked the horse sharply as her only escape. The horse squealed and reared high in the air then bolted forward. She'd forgotten Storm Cloud's soft touch, and it cost her dearly. She toppled off the back of the horse and hit the ground roughly. Jacey lay motionless a moment as she gasped to catch her breath. Jameson approached. She slowly rolled onto her side and attempted to stand. Jameson aimed the gun at her head. Jacey stared at him from where she knelt. Her eyes remained fixed on the gun he held.

"Goodbye, Jacey," he said simply.

Maxwell grabbed Jacey from behind on the ground with her and shielded her in his arms. Jameson's finger tightened on the trigger.

"Haven't you forgotten something?" came the all too familiar voice from behind him.

Jameson's eyes widened. Maxwell and Jacey looked up from their huddled position on the ground. Jameson spun to face Asher while aiming his gun. Asher plunged the long dagger into Jameson's throat and straight through the back of his neck. Jameson's eyes widened as blood flowed from his mouth. The gun fired in his hand, shooting Asher at close range. Asher was thrown backward and forcibly struck the side of the building. His eyes rolled back, and he slid down the wall.

"No!" Jacey screamed as she pulled out of Maxwell's arms and sprang to her feet.

Maxwell was now on his feet and staggered after her. Jacey ran to Asher's side and pulled his jacket away from the shoulder wound. The bullet had gone straight through. She looked back at Maxwell, who held his own bleeding shoulder.

"Stay with him. Keep pressure on the wound," Maxwell called out. "I'll get an ambulance." He attempted to run to the front of the institution.

Jacey applied pressure to Asher's shoulder wound. He gasped loudly and jerked awake from his unconscious state. He looked at her with some disorientation. His eyes rolled shut.

"Katie," he gasped softly while smiling and touched her face. "I thought I'd lost you."

Jacey moved closer to him and clung to his neck. "Oh, Asher," she gasped softly. "You're going to be fine. An ambulance will be here soon." She pulled away just far enough to look into his eyes and forced a smile. She knew that was a lie and that they'd never get to him in time. "It's going to be fine," she said as tears rolled down her cheeks.

His eyes once more opened. His hand stroked her hair. "I won't ever leave you, Katie."

His mouth covered hers, and he kissed her passionately. Jacey tensed with surprise then returned the kiss. Asher's arm slipped from her shoulder, and he lie motionless. Jacey's mouth opened with horror as the tears flowed.

"Asher?" she gasped.

Sirens could be heard in the distance. Jacey lifted her head with confusion. Maxwell couldn't have gotten help already. The nearest ambulance was half an hour away. The fire trucks, police cars, a taxi, and ambulance pulled onto the institution grounds. They were responding to the fire alarm Asher pulled in the west wing! Jacey sprang to her feet and threw her bloodied hands in the air. A dark figure was seen fleeing from the workshop not far from her.

"Over here," she cried out and wildly waved her arms to the approaching ambulance. "Here!"

There was a loud squeal from a horse. Jacey spun around and saw Mayor Norad climb on top of the paint horse. He spun the horse into a tight circle then sent the horse into a gallop across the back lawn. The ambulance crew rushed around the building. Monique, Coleen, Timon, and Sheriff Monroe came out through the workshop entrance. Timon and Sheriff Monroe pulled a barely standing Brian from the building. Timon released Brian and ran past the ambulance crew attending to Asher.

"There's a fire in the basement!" Timon cried out and pointed to the workshop.

Monique ran across the lawn and stared after Mayor Norad riding her horse across the estate. The disgust was evident on her face. She placed her fingers in her mouth and whistled loudly. The big paint skidded to a halt and slung its large head while Howard fought it with the reins. Monique whistled again. The horse slung its head violently, kicked out its back legs, and bolted back toward the institution despite the taunt reins. Howard fought the horse. The horse ran directly for Monique. She firmly placed her hands in front of her.

"Whoa!"

The horse skidded to a halt. She raised her hand high in the air with a cluck of her tongue. The horse snorted and reared up, pawing the air with its hooves on command. Howard toppled off the back of the horse, landing on his backside. He sprang to his feet and ran across the grounds. Monroe yelled and ran after him. The sheriff stopped halfway across the grounds and fired a warning shot. Howard didn't stop. He passed through the back gate and disappeared into the woods with Sheriff Monroe in hot pursuit. Jacey hurried alongside the stretcher, holding Asher's hand as they approached the ambulance. Another paramedic escorted Maxwell to the ambulance as well. Professor limped toward them with a look of astonishment on his face.

"What did I miss?" he asked in an airy breath.

Jacey looked at Professor. "Watch the girls," she instructed and climbed into the ambulance with Asher and Maxwell.

The doors slammed shut and the ambulance sped off. Professor walked toward the small group as the paramedic tended to Brian, who was an off-white color.

"What happened?" Professor asked with knitted brows. "What's going on?"

Monique and Coleen saw Professor. Both screamed and ran to him. They hugged him happily and talked at once. He calmed them, held onto both of them, and looked from Doc and Timon to Brian.

"What happened to you?" Professor asked Brian.

Brian looked up and shivered while clinging to the blanket around his shoulders. "I--I locked myself in a freezer."

Professor tilted his head with disbelief then looked at the bloodied body of Deputy Jameson. The firefighters pulled the hose in through the workshop and worked frantically. Professor looked back at his colleagues.

"I don't suppose anyone wants to hear about my evening, huh?" he remarked.

Monique and Coleen tugged on Professor's arms.

"We have to go to the hospital," Coleen begged.

Monique nodded. "We made a terrible mistake about Asher. Now he might die."

"That's the guy who took me to the hospital," Professor said simply. "Was that him on the stretcher?"

Both girls nodded.

"Professor, why don't you and Timon take the girls to the hospital and keep Jacey company? Angela and I will look after Brian and assist the fire department," Doc announced and nodded them away.

Professor nodded. Timon hurried after them.

Chapter Thirty-one

*J*acey, looking worse for wear in her torn dress, walked along the hospital corridor with Monique and Coleen. It was a little after midnight. A nurse stormed out of the last room on the right. Jacey paused by the doorway. The nurse looked at her and frowned.

"Are you going in there?" she asked firmly.

Jacey slowly nodded.

"Lord help you," the nurse scoffed and walked away.

The nurse was heard muttering the entire way down the hall. Jacey wondered what had happened and uncertainly entered the room first. She could hear two male voices arguing loudly. Asher and Maxwell lie in their respective beds while aiming their remotes at the sole television in the middle of the room. The channel switched back and forth. Jacey paused near the foot end of Asher's bed and stared at both men disapprovingly. She cleared her throat and folded her arms across her chest. Both men looked at her. Asher tossed the remote aside and looked at Maxwell with a broad smile.

"Television's yours. I have visitors," Asher said while reaching for the curtain and pulled it shut.

Maxwell pulled it open with a frown. "They're my visitors too," he sulked.

"Knock it off you two," Jacey snapped. "You sound like a couple of children."

Both silenced, appeared scolded, and looked at her. Monique and Coleen entered the room while looking down at the floor with sorrowful expressions.

"Monique and Coleen would like to talk to you, Asher," Jacey said gently then nodded them toward him.

Jacey walked between the two beds and pulled the curtain for privacy. Monique and Coleen approached Asher's bed.

"We're so sorry about how we treated you the last couple of days," Coleen said softly.

Monique nodded. "We were scared, and we didn't know what to do, especially after what we'd seen--"

Asher smiled warmly. "I understand that you were frightened. After all the things you'd been told about me by Deputy Jameson, you had every right not to trust me." He inhaled deeply then cringed with some discomfort to his shoulder. His smile returned. "I hope I hadn't upset you too much with what I had to do in the corridor."

They shrugged.

"I think we'll survive the trauma," Monique teased.

Jacey sat on the edge of Maxwell's bed on the other side of the curtain and smiled reassuringly. "They're keeping both of you overnight just for observation."

Maxwell chuckled softly and raised his brows. "I think our nurse is in for a long night," he announced. "Your friend is a terrible patient."

"I heard that," came Asher's voice from the other side of the curtain.

"You were meant to!" Maxwell shouted back at the curtain. Maxwell then returned his attention to Jacey. "I can't believe I was shot and stabbed in the same night." He appeared to consider. "In the same shoulder too. What are the odds?"

She smiled and shrugged. "I'd say pretty good," she remarked. "Jameson was obviously a lousy shot."

"I'm grateful to that," he replied. "Are the others coming?"

Jacey nodded. "Brian wanted to come along, so Doc and Angela are going to bring him in an hour or so. Professor is with Timon in the emergency room. He needed stitches on his arm. They'll be up just as soon as he's been seen."

Maxwell looked at her torn evening dress and stockings then met her gaze. He smiled timidly and raised his brows. "So--did you enjoy the party?"

Jacey hid her smile and shook her head while laughing softly. "No, not really, but it certainly wasn't boring. I think we should spend a quiet evening at home on our next date."

Maxwell gently tilted his head and smiled timidly. "You really want to go out with me?"

"Yes, I really do," she replied warmly and stroked his hand. "I'm looking forward to spending time with you." She leaned closer and kissed him on the lips. Jacey pulled away and gently bit her lower lip.

His smile broadened. "I'm not doing anything for the next fifty years," he said and gently stroked her lower arm without looking into her eyes.

Jacey giggled softly, kissed his cheek, and whispered in his ear. "Neither am I."

The curtain bounced as something struck it. "It's too quiet over there," Asher snapped.

Maxwell held Jacey in his arms and moaned softly. "And I thought Timon made a terrible roommate."

"Talking about me?" came Timon's voice from the foot end of the bed. He stared at them and grinned. "Oh, Asher! He has her in his bed!" Timon laughed evilly.

Professor, Monique, and Coleen peeked around the curtain as well. Jacey cleared her throat and stood while blushing. She pointed to the curtain.

"I'll be right next door."

Jacey walked toward the foot of the bed and playfully smacked Timon as she passed. She walked around the corner and saw Asher holding a stuffed teddy bear in a hospital gown. He looked up at her and smiled.

"Look what your friends got for me," Asher said with a boyish grin.

Jacey approached his bed and sat on the edge facing him. "I think they're your friends now too," she said warmly.

"I think you might be right. Our first official poker game is the day after tomorrow," he said with a tiny laugh. "I like them. They're a nice bunch."

Jacey placed her hand on his with tears in her eyes. "I was really afraid you were going to leave me," she said softly.

He squeezed her hand and mocked her with his smile. "You couldn't get rid of me even if you tried. I'm beginning to think I'm immortal or something," he teased warmly. "The doctor said the gunshot wasn't bad. He was more worried about my concussion when I hit the wall."

Jacey laughed softly. She then looked down and touched the torn dress with her left hand. "I'm afraid the dress didn't survive the evening," she said gently.

"It's unimportant," he replied. He tilted his head slightly. "I spoke with Sheriff Monroe in the emergency room. He told me Howard got away."

She nodded. "He tried to burn the evidence, not that it would've mattered."

"Not considering I received a full confession from Dr. Talbert on Howard's involvement," Asher informed her. "He gave the orders for the killings, and he intended to cover any evidence of it at all costs."

"I'd rather not discuss it anymore tonight," she said softly. "I'm just starting to feel better after all that's happened. At least you're in the clear."

Asher was silent a moment. "There's something I wanted to tell you for a long time, Jacey. It's not really important, but it's something you may want to know about me."

Jacey stared at him and held her breath. Her heart skipped a beat with nervous anticipation of something she may not want to know.

"When I met Katie, I was working for the CIA," he said gently. "All my records were kept classified when I left to protect me and those I loved. It's because of this lack of information that everyone thought I was some sort of criminal. I can't divulge this to anyone else, no matter what the town may think of me. Maxwell promised he'd never tell."

Jacey smiled with a tiny, relieved laugh. "That's the big secret?" she asked. "I knew that years ago."

Asher appeared puzzled and tilted his head. "You did?"

She nodded with some embarrassment. "I found some old papers in that box of pictures we went through. I assumed you'd tell me when you were ready."

Asher rolled his eyes and chuckled softly. "I don't suppose I have any secrets from you, do I?"

"Maybe one or two," she replied warmly. Jacey placed her free hand on top of his and played with his wedding band. "Asher?"

"Yes, darling," he said warmly.

Jacey hesitated without looking up. "Did you know you called me Katie earlier?"

She looked up and met his gaze. He stared at her a long moment. A tiny smile crossed his face.

"I was a little delirious," he said softly and stared at her hands while gently caressing them. "I should probably apologize for my behavior."

Jacey forced him to meet her gaze and shook her head. "Don't apologize," she said gently while smiling warmly. "I didn't mind. You're my best friend, Asher. Although I've never said it, you know I love you."

Asher squeezed her hand then pulled her against him and held her. Jacey clung to him and closed her eyes.

"I know," he whispered and gently rubbed her back.

✝

*A*sher entered his cabin in the dim light of the table lamp he'd left on earlier that evening. Two days had passed since the incident at the institution, and he seemed to be recovering nicely. He closed the door behind him and tossed his keys on the nearby hall table. He walked across the sitting room and collapsed in a plush chair. Asher looked at his watch then picked up the phone and dialed a number. He waited a minute then smiled.

"Good evening, Jacey," he announced cheerfully. "It's midnight. Send Dr. Alvord home now." He laughed softly. "The poker game went fine. I let them win this time." He listened then laughed again. "Yes, we had a great time starting rumors about you and Maxwell. Just behave, and give Maxwell a message from me. Tell him I have a wedding band and a shotgun, so he'd better behave." Asher laughed again. "Good night, darling."

Asher hung up the phone and sighed. He stood slowly, rubbed his shoulder, and headed for the kitchen. He filled a water container and entered the dark sunroom. He turned on the light. Howard Norad sat in the wicker chair with his feet propped on the coffee table. Asher studied the gun in the mayor's hand then turned and proceeded toward the hanging plants.

"Would you mind removing your feet from the coffee table? It makes smudges."

Howard placed his feet on the floor and stood abruptly. "Sarcastic to the very end," he snapped coldly. "Honestly, I'm not going to miss you."

Asher set the water container down and nodded knowingly with a tiny smile. "I should warn you, killing me isn't as easy as you might think."

"I'll take it under advisement," Howard replied and snorted a laugh.

✝

8:00 A.M.

*J*acey rode her horse to Asher's house the following morning and dismounted near the fence surrounding the garden. She tied her horse and hurried through the back gate. She had some exciting news and wanted him to be the first person she told.

"Asher," she announced excitedly. "Wait until I tell you about last night!"

Jacey looked around the garden but didn't see him anywhere. She turned and hurried toward the sunroom entrance. Jacey opened the door and saw all the wicker furniture was gone. She wondered what happened.

"Asher?" she called and looked around.

She was about to enter the sunroom, when she heard a sharp yell from behind her.

"No!"

Jacey spun around and saw Asher approach from the garage. He wiped his soiled hands on an old rag and smiled broadly. He had startled her, but she suspected he enjoyed those moments.

"The floor's still wet. I just shampooed the carpet this morning," he said simply. "So how did your date go with Dr. Alvord?"

Jacey sighed happily. "Oh, he's wonderful."

Asher rolled his eyes and pretended to frown though his smile slipped through. "I suppose he stayed all night."

"No, he's a gentleman," she said with a smile then giggled. "I think he's afraid of you."

Asher snorted a soft laugh. "Me? Like I could ever harm anyone." His smile broadened and he appeared pleased. "It's good to see you this happy. I only hope it turns into something permanent. I like Maxwell."

Jacey giggled. "He's not going anywhere. He told me he loves me. Isn't that great!"

Asher laughed and gathered her in his arms. "That's wonderful, darling."

Jacey then pulled away. Her expression became serious. "Sheriff Monroe stopped by this morning," she said nervously. "Howard was seen in one of the neighboring towns early last night.

He may come after you, since Dr. Talbert confessed to you about his involvement. Monroe's concerned he may try to eliminate you as a witness."

"If I see him, I'll be sure to take precautions," he said with a warm smile. "But I don't think he'd be stupid enough to come after me." He placed his arm around her shoulder and guided her along the path in his extravagant garden.

"Do you really think he won't come after you?" Jacey asked with a nervous smile. "I'd hate to think of you here all by yourself. Maybe you should come stay at my house until my parents return from their cruise."

He chuckled warmly. "Three's a crowd. I'll be fine, I promise." Asher stopped her near a recently tilled plot of land. A young, weeping willow tree was planted in the middle of the fresh soil.

"You've got a new tree," Jacey said with a warm smile.

"It'll provide some shade in later years," he announced cheerfully. "The soil is very rich here, and I've blended a *special fertilizer.*"

"Someday you'll have to let me in on your secret ingredients," Jacey announced. "You're special fertilizer really does wonders for the garden."

Asher's smile brightened as he chuckled lowly. "I think I'll keep that my secret."

The End

Other books by Holly Copella!
Reviews left on Amazon are appreciated!

"Insanely Deadly"

When the dead return to life, it's up to an admiral's daughter and a mildly insane, former war hero to save their small town.

Jetta Cross, a Navy Admiral's daughter, is tasked with keeping her father's comrade, a former war hero turned town crazy, grounded in the real world. Capt. John Hunter is still fighting the war in his head, where imaginary dead people are part of his world. When a viral outbreak brings about a zombie uprising, Hunter is left to his own devices. He must resume his role as a one-man commando unit in order to destroy the ravenous undead. With Hunter still fighting his own inner demons as well as the undead, the townspeople fear their zombie neighbors may not be the only threat. Stranded at the island's luxurious resort with a handful of workers, Jetta is forced to live up to her father's reputation and take charge of the deteriorating situation at the hotel. She must wage her own war against the infected before the government declares her hometown a total loss.

"The Battle for Andrea Maria"

A cruise ship attack turns six survivors into overnight celebrities after they take credit for the heroic act of a stowaway who died saving them.

The cruise is just what Jess needed--a bit of harmless fun far from her daily grind. But what begins as a relaxing vacation turns into a desperate fight for her life when terrorists take over the ship and start piling up bodies. Teaming up with a mysterious stowaway, Jess attempts to send out a distress call but knows they cannot wait for help to come. If she or the few remaining passengers have any hope for survival, Jess must act now. The papers dub it "The Battle for *Andrea Maria*," but to Jess it is the moment she fought side-by-side with her enigmatic Romeo, saving the ship--and losing him. She thinks the story ends there, but really, the nightmare is just beginning...

"Town Darling"

After surviving a brutal attack that claims the lives of those she loves, a young woman seeks revenge on a corrupt town.

Going back home is never easy, but for Casey, it means returning to her corrupt hometown where she barely survived a brutal attack. Accompanied by two *family friends*, she seeks justice for the night that destroyed her life. Her physical scars are nothing compared to her emotional ones, forcing the local sheriff to believe that the town darling is back for revenge. As the conspiracy for her revenge appears to be leading up to the coveted town fair, the sheriff is determined to stop her from fulfilling her vengeful scheme...but guilt over his role on that fateful night continues to haunt him. His desperate need for Casey's forgiveness could be his undoing.

"Screenplays: The Island Collection" *"Jungle Princess", "A.L.F. Resort", "Brighton Island"*

Discover how romance and fun in the sun can be downright *chilling*!

"Jungle Princess" is a romantic/thriller that leaves a teenage girl stranded on an island with two male shipmates and a creature of "unknown" origin. She soon discovers the island is home to an abandoned prison with several prisoners roaming free. What really killed over one hundred prisoners? And is it still out there--?

"A.L.F. Resort" is a romantic/thriller set on an island resort with Artificial Life Forms as the main draw. At this resort, all your fantasies come true...until a malfunction removes safety inhibitors on the A.L.F.'s. Zombies, biker gangs, and mobsters run amuck, turning fantasies into nightmares. A young reporter gets more of a story than she anticipates, but will she survive long enough to write the story?

"Brighton Island" is a romantic/thriller set on a private island. When the owner's niece brings her psychic friend to the mansion, his presence awakens the spirits' tortured souls. As the psychic attempts to solve the old murders, the niece is confronted with the possibility that she's next to join the mansion ghosts. Stranded on the island with a crazed killer, he uncle wages his own war to save them. Will his "shock and awe" tactics actually save them or get them killed?

ABOUT THE AUTHOR

Holly Copella has been writing since the age of twelve when her frustration at a book's poor plot drove her to author her own story. Over the last decade, she's written a number of screenplays, some of which she's now adapting into novels. Her fascination with zombies and other darker material lends an edge to her writing, which tends to lean toward horror. As a fan of Agatha Christie, she appreciates the craft of a good plot and the importance of creating significant characters.

Hailing from Pennsylvania, Copella lives in the Endless Mountains on a farm with her rescue horses and other animals. In addition to writing and reading fiction, she enjoys riding horses and traveling to Las Vegas and Disney World.

www.ingramcontent.com/pod-product-compliance
Lightning Source LLC
Chambersburg PA
CBHW060919180626
46817CB00004B/1322